SURRENDER

Gareth Harris Part 1

A BRITISH SPORTS ROMANCE NOVEL

AMY DAWS

Published by: Stars Hollow Publishing
ISBN: 978-1-944565-48-0

Editing: Stephanie Rose
Formatting: Champagne Book Design
Cover Design: Amy Daws

Dedicated to the fine folks at Tires, Tires, Tires.
Thanks for the unexpected inspiration and of course…
the complimentary coffee.

AUTHOR'S NOTE

There will be some football dates and mentions that will not be factually accurate in this novel. For the purpose of this story and to make it a more pleasurable reading experience, I took some liberties.

I hope you enjoy Gareth and Sloan.

They're pretty hawt.

A Firm Touch

Gareth

29 Years Old

"GARETH!" MY SISTER'S LOUD VOICE ECHOES THROUGH THE phone as soon as I answer the call. "You need to call Camden. He's absolutely going mental because he had to take a train to the stadium since Tanner and Booker left for practice without him and Dad's out scouting a new player and, oh my God, I'm going to lose it! These are grown men!"

The speaker on my mobile rattles from the shrill tone of her voice. I have to pull it away from my ear to prevent my eardrum from rupturing. I silently apologise to the hair stylist attempting to gel my hair.

It's not Vi's fault, though. Our three younger brothers are far too similar to the Three Stooges. If they weren't full-grown, professional athletes, I swear they'd be in a case study for how apes could function in society.

I take a deep breath. My reply is slow and controlled because I know that's exactly what Vi needs to hear. "Vi, just hang up on them when they get like that. I've been telling them for years that they need to move out of Dad's house. They are still too dependent on you, and you have to stop helping them solve all of their problems."

1

Vi groans. "I know, Gareth. But it's hard. They are a special brand of stupid."

I have to fight back a chuckle. "That they are, but you know they'll figure it out. They have to grow up eventually."

"I know, I know," she sighs deeply. "Thanks. This is exactly what I needed to hear."

"It's no problem," I reply with a smile.

This is a routine between me and Vi that's as old as we are. Even now as adults, she continues to break up the ridiculous battles our brothers get into down in London, and I have to talk her off the ledge from up here in Manchester. She's like a sergeant on the front line of a battlefield, and I'm the commander calling the shots from the safety of the King's palace. Control is my middle name.

"I keep reminding myself that this is exactly why I finally moved out of Dad's house," Vi replies. "To get some space from those idiots. But somehow, they still make all of their problems my problems."

"Well, that's a Harris for you," I grumble into the phone. "You going to be okay?"

"Yes, I'm better. Thank you, Gareth," she coos, her tone ten times more relaxed.

"Anytime, sis."

"Are you at your photoshoot?"

I nod. "They are trying to put makeup on me as we speak."

"Eep! Okay, I'll let you go. Call me after!"

We hang up and I glance up at the male makeup artist coming at me with a sponge. "Don't go crazy with that thing," I warn.

"Oh, don't worry, I won't." He giggles and flirtatiously adds, "You don't need it. Now close your eyes, handsome."

I close them and try to relax, but a female voice with an American accent sounds off behind me. "Hi, my name is Sloan Montgomery. You can call me Sloan. Can you tell me your name, please?"

The makeup artist stops touching my face, and my eyes open as he steps back. He drops the compact on the counter and slips out of the cosy hair and makeup area where I'm situated, leaving me alone with a brunette who's swiping furiously on an iPad.

The woman says nothing more, clearly engaged in whatever is on the digital screen, so I take a minute to look her up and down. She's tall with long, chestnut waves cascading around her shoulders. She's wearing a demure black dress, and her long, dark lashes fan her pale cheeks. I have to bite back a laugh because she still hasn't looked up from the damn screen.

I narrow my eyes and clear my throat. "Are you addressing me?"

Her brows knit together for a brief second, then smooth. Painting on a polite smile, she finally looks up and stares at my face in the mirror. Her mouth is a bit too big for the delicate features of her face. Her lips plump but natural-looking, unlike some of my teammates' wives. Her honey-coloured eyes are big and sparkling in the warm glow of the LED bulbs. She's pretty much all lips and eyes with a tiny slip of a nose.

And she does not look impressed by me.

Arching a perfectly plucked brow, she responds smoothly, "Yes, I am speaking to you."

"And you're asking me my name?" I cross my arms over my chest. "You really don't know who I am?"

Her smile remains even as she licks her lips. "I don't like to assume I know who anyone is."

This gives me pause because, from the second I arrived on set today, every single person I've come in contact with has gawked at me like a treasured artifact they want to steal from a museum exhibit. It's what comes with the title of being a seasoned footballer for a Premier League football team.

I became a starter for Manchester United at only twenty-one years old. Now, at twenty-nine, I'm practically their fucking poster boy, like it or not. This circumstance evokes a certain level of familiarity between me and nearly every single stranger I meet. People speak to me like a long-lost friend they had sleepovers with as a child. Like somehow watching me play on the pitch every week for the past eight years means they know me intimately. Throw in the fact that my brothers all play football for our dad's championship league team in London and that makes the Harris Brothers a bit of a phenomenon in England. Not to mention our father was a famous Man U footballer in the eighties. Hell, even our mum's dad played for a time in Sweden. Our family's legend precedes us. It's not something I'm arrogant about. It's just a fact.

So this American acting like she doesn't know me puts me on the defence and not because that's my position on the pitch.

"Who do you think I am?" I ask, my tone a blatant challenge.

Her smile is pinched, like she's agitated but trying to hide it. "Are we playing a guessing game right now?"

I narrow my eyes cautiously. "No, but I wouldn't mind playing Twenty Questions." I shove myself against the counter so my chair swivels to face her straight on. She's even more striking than her reflection. A green ring loops around her pupils and turns her pale brown eyes into a stunning forest-like colour.

Her inspecting gaze drops to my legs, concealed beneath a pair of jeans. They slide up my white cotton shirt before landing on my face. A flicker of regret shadows her eyes as she replies, "I'm afraid I don't have time for games, Mr. Harris."

"So you *do* know who I am," I reply knowingly.

She inhales and takes a step forward, looming over me in her black stiletto boots. "I asked for your name because I'm styling three soccer players for this ad campaign, and I wanted to be sure I have the correct one."

"We're called footballers over here, Sweets." I shoot her a cheeky wink and add, "And you just called me Mr. Harris quite confidently, so why bother asking at all?"

"Because I don't think *footballers* need their egos stroked any more than they already are," she retorts, her tone even and firm.

"And I don't like how all the athletes I work with around here don't introduce themselves. I find it rude." Her hand moves to cover her mouth like she's trying to stop herself from saying anything more.

A smile lifts my face as her cheeks flush pink. This woman is beautiful and stronger than she gives herself credit for.

My response is light-hearted—a tone I don't give out to just anyone. "By all means, Miss Montgomery, don't hold back."

"I told you to call me Sloan," she replies while rubbing her hand against her forehead.

I'm annoying her. I don't annoy many. In fact, most people are constantly kissing my arse and trying to get something out of me, so this is a fun change of pace.

"I'm sorry," she acquiesces, looking over her shoulder. "I'm a bit stressed. The photographer is rushing me because the lighting out-side is perfect, so we really need to get you dressed—"

"No, you're right. I'm sorry," I interrupt and her wide eyes snap to mine. "You're right. It is rude not to introduce myself. My name is Gareth Harris. Please call me Gareth. It's a pleasure to meet you, Sloan."

I reach out to shake her hand. With a puzzled look, she slips her delicate hand into mine, her face heating as we touch. It's clear that I've taken her completely off guard. But if there's one thing I hate, it's being lumped into the same category as all the other footballers in this area. This woman is just trying to do her job, and she probably gets a lot of shit from people like my teammates. Especially because she's stunningly beautiful.

My thumb brushes over a ring on her finger. I glance down and a surprising jolt of disappointment rushes through me when I see that it's a wedding ring.

"It's a pleasure to meet you, too," Sloan replies. Shaking off her initial shock, she looks behind her again. "We really do need to get you dressed, and I need to check a few things out with you first."

I release her hand and grip the armrests of the chair to stand, bringing me nose-to-nose with her. In her heels, she's just a couple inches shorter than me. Since I'm six-foot-one, that puts her around five-eight or so.

"I have a note in your contract that says you have fabric requirements," Sloan states, but her voice sounds far away as the smell of her sugary sweet perfume invades my nose.

My body tremors involuntarily from the unwelcome memory the scent evokes. It's an image of my mum making pancakes in our family's Manchester flat we lived in when we were kids. My youngest brother, Booker, is only a few weeks old in a bassinet beside her. Vi is holding up toys to him, completely unaware that he's not old enough to care about toys yet. The twins, Camden and Tanner, are wrestling on the floor in the dining area. And before I can snap out of it, an image of my dad walking up behind my mum and tickling her sides barrels in. Mum squeals and turns around to thump him with the spatula. The happy scene makes my stomach churn.

It was nothing like that at the end.

"Gareth?" Sloan's voice is louder, like she's been trying to get my attention.

I shake my head, the foggy memory rolling away as fast as it came in. "Yes? What is it?"

"Are you all right?" She steps closer, concern evident on her face, but the smell hits me all over again.

"I'm fine," I bark and step back, trying to regain control of my own bloody mind. "Let's just get on with it. Do you have a rack of clothes? I can usually pick out what works best for me."

She frowns at my tone. "Is it a tactile defensiveness you have?"

"Tactile what?" I sigh with annoyance because I don't want to talk about my texture issues. This is why I hate endorsement deals and anything that requires styling. People try to make all the decisions for me and I don't like being controlled. If my manager didn't keep pushing me to do them so much, I wouldn't bother.

I move past her and glance around the studio for the clothing options. "Just point me in the direction of the clothing and we'll get this over with."

"Mr. Harris." Sloan says my name with such firmness, I can't help but turn on my heel to face her. She clutches the iPad to her chest and narrows her gaze. "I'm the stylist on set today, and I'm trying to understand your needs better. Then I can execute the clothing request."

I shove my hand through my hair and grimace when I remember the hair stylist gelled it already. "It's difficult to explain," I murmur, wishing I was anywhere but here.

Sensing my discomfort, Sloan's expression instantly softens and her entire approach changes. She sets the iPad down on the chair behind her and walks toward me with a gentleness to her gaze. Her black lashes fan her creamy cheeks as she looks down my body. "Are these your clothes from home?"

I nod, my jaw tight from her close proximity. She reaches out, and I wince as she places her palm firmly on my chest. Her touch is hard and pressurised, which allows me to exhale with some relief. If it was soft and feathery, I'd probably start trembling. I hate soft touches. They leave a tingling wake of sensation that's like nails on a chalkboard. The truth is, it's made it difficult for me to enjoy any sort of intimacy with women as a result. I'm the only footballer known to mankind who doesn't shag everything that walks.

But with Sloan, it's like she knows something. Something I don't fully understand myself. Her brows lift as she strokes her hand over my pec and onto my side, continuing the strong, pressured exploration across my abs like she's a sculptor moulding clay. It's an odd act to experience with a stranger, but the way she touches me is soothing. My busy mind relaxes. My clenched jaw falls open as she walks around me, firmly dragging her hand along my ribs as she moves. She releases me to pull the neck of my shirt open.

"You removed the label," she states, her breath warm on the back of my neck.

I clear my throat. "They irritate my neck…This one is still on." I lift the hem of my shirt to reveal the silky tab sewn inside the seam.

She moves around me, her scent wafting over me as she angles her head to read. I force myself to stay in the moment and not fall back into a memory. I notice her eyes pausing on my abs before zeroing in on the label.

She looks up and half smiles. "This is a nice shirt."

I shrug halfheartedly. "It's just a shirt."

She shakes her head and murmurs, "Imported from Italy and custom orders only."

Before I have a chance to realise what she's going to do next, her head dips down as she begins fingering the back of my waistband. She pulls on my jeans and air suddenly hits my arse cheeks. A noise reverberates from the back of her throat as she gets more than a view of my bare abs this time.

Unwilling to be scared away, she fiddles with the tab on the denim. When she releases it, her flushed face returns to mine. "I think I know exactly what you need."

I can't help but smile at her wavering tone of voice. "You mean besides underwear?"

Her returning smile is genuine and maybe even a bit life-changing. "Yes, Mr. Harris. I can think of a few things you need."

I chuckle. "Then I hope I can hire you year-round because it's kind of nice having someone tell me what to do for a change."

Two Years Later

Seriously, Lady Godiva?

Sloan

I PULL INTO THE DRIVEWAY ON ROSSMILL LANE AND ROLL MY CAR window down to type in the code on the gate keypad. Before my fingers touch the buttons, the large wrought iron fence begins to open on its own. I look up to see our groundskeeper, Xavier, approaching.

I smile brightly and give a jovial wave as he makes his way past me in his white utility truck. He doesn't wave back. I lean my head out to say hello to him, check in on the family, the usual, but he doesn't stop. In fact, he looks like he's trying to avoid eye contact with me completely. *That's weird,* I think to myself with a sense of unease overcoming me. Xavier is usually so friendly. I wonder what's wrong?

Granted, he wasn't always so kind in the beginning. He and the rest of the staff all thought I was crazy. I can't say I blame them. A bright, bubbly American moves into a Manchester, England mansion with her rich British husband and asks ridiculous questions about how they like their coffee and the kind of pastries they prefer for breakfast. It's definitely not the way most wives in this neighbourhood behave, so it's understandable that I was a little off-putting at first. Not to mention the British are a bit less open. They don't dig the sharing. The connecting. The peopling.

I, on the other hand, feed off of it.

But I thought Xavier and I had gotten way past the whole British coldness. Just last week we were talking about his baby's colic and how he can be more supportive to his wife. He never avoids saying hello to me now, no matter how bad of a day he's having.

My thoughts are distracted when I spot an unfamiliar car parked in front of the house. The staff usually park on the east side of the estate, and I know this little silver Audi doesn't belong to any of them.

I park alongside it and slide out of my car to make my way inside, ignoring the chill running up my spine. My eyes are cast downward as I dig for my keys in my bag, so I don't see the person standing before me right away. I don't see them when I reach the first step. I don't see them when I reach the second step. The third. The fourth. The fifth. It isn't until the eighth step that I realise another human is watching me.

A human who just came out of my house.

A woman.

My eyes land on her feet first—platform, red-soled, Louboutin ankle boots. They are covered in crystals, and I know instantly I'm staring at a six thousand dollar pair of shoes. As a clothing and accessory stylist, it's my job to recognise expensive things. I dress some of the wealthiest soccer players in Manchester, as well as their partners. I style for executive wives, plastic surgeons' mistresses, even some London movie stars. I buy expensive clothes for people. It has been my career since moving to England three years ago, and I've embraced all that the job entails.

However, in all three of those years of working with the most affluent residents of Manchester, I have never, not once, had a desire to style people in crystal-encrusted footwear.

This is definitely not a client of mine.

My gaze passes the shoes and slides up a pair of bare, feminine legs. I wonder briefly if she's naked on my doorstep in six thousand dollar boots, but I see a hint of a leather skirt at the very top of her thighs. Just enough to cover her pussy lips. Good for her.

Her appearance doesn't get any more modest as I raise my eyes up her torso and take in her ten inch line of cleavage. Is that dark spot an areola peeking out? Wow, what a brave soldier we have here. A modern-day Lady Godiva on my doorstep!

When I steel myself to glance up at her face, I know exactly what I'm about to see before I even see it. The shocked expression of a blonde, barely twenty-something-year-old with smeared makeup and freshly fucked hair, wearing six thousand dollar shoes. Blondie here is not from these parts.

You see, I didn't grow up with a lot of money. My mom was a single parent who worked two jobs just to live paycheck-to-paycheck. I remember thinking my sisters and I were rich when she gave us each a fifty dollar bill for school clothes at the end of the summer.

Perspective is everything, though. And after working for people who come from wealth that would make the Queen of England envious, I know when someone comes from money and when they don't. Neither is better than the other. Just…different. There's a sixth sense you get about it.

Suffice it to say, Blondie did not buy herself those shoes.

"I was just—" The blonde begins to speak, but I raise my hand to cut her off mid-sentence.

"You were just leaving," I grind, wincing at the sound my clenched teeth make inside my head. I could say so much more, but this woman—girl—doesn't deserve my words. The man who bought her those boots does.

Without another look at her, I swing the front door open and walk up the grand, eighteenth century staircase to our bedroom. The whole house creeks with every step, like it's moments away from crumbling to the ground. It's the oldest in the neighbourhood. And rather than tearing it down and building something modern like most estates in this area, it's been restored to its creepy, Edwardian baroque glory.

My steps are slow and steady. My breathing is even to match them as I prepare myself for what's about to happen. If my husband, Callum Coleridge, was a gentleman, he'd have used one of the seven spare bedrooms we have. It's the decent thing to do when you decide to cheat on your wife of six years. It'd be impolite and cliché to fuck the whore in the master suite. Wealthy Brits are all about propriety, aren't they?

But lo and behold, before I even reach the doorway to our bedroom, I hear my husband's voice call out, "Did you forget something, Callie, baby?"

Callum and Callie. That would look oh-so cute on stationary. I push the master suite doors open and my eyes land on our bed—a huge, four-post, hundred-year-old monstrosity. This morning, it was perfectly made up. I took care to ensure that all four corners of the mallard duck bedspread that Callum's mother picked out were tucked with neat hospital corners despite the fact that we have people we pay to do that sort of thing.

Now those duckies are rumpled and tossed, squished together like the photos of the carnage Callum brings home when he comes back from a weekend of shooting in the country.

Freaking mallards.

My gaze shifts from the bed to my husband who's standing in the doorway of the en suite bathroom, shirtless and buttoning his expensive, tailored trousers. Trousers that I bought for him. Trousers that I had custom-fitted for him. Trousers that look fucking fantastic on him.

He looks up with a smile, but his face drops when he sees me instead of his beloved Callie Baby. He winces like he's been kicked in the balls. Did I kick him in the balls? I look down at my feet, both planted firmly on the floor in modest black stiletto boots. No sparkles on mine. That's probably what our marriage has been missing. Crystal-encrusted footwear.

"Sloan, I—" he falters.

"Yeah, it's Sloan. I met your Callie *Baby*, was it?" I hook my thumb toward the door. "I saw her downstairs. She seems fun. Did she forget her pants up here?" I look around the room, scowling over how the cream fitted sheet is popped off of one corner of the bed. "I wondered if she forgot her pants because I don't think that leather strip around her vagina classifies as a skirt. She really should consider hiring me to style her. Her footwear indicates she can afford me."

Callum clears his throat and straightens his shoulders. "I was going to talk to you about all of this." He approaches me with the same swagger he always has.

How does he have swagger right now? I literally caught him with his pants down, yet he's walking toward me like a businessman at a board meeting. I shake my head as his words sink in. Did he say, "all of this," like there is an actual *this*? Not a one-off thing?

Stepping away, I decide to continue my quest for Lady Godiva's clothes. Mostly because avoiding eye contact seems vital to my mental state. If I really stop to think about what he means by "all of this," then I'll know that what I've suspected for years is coming true. And I didn't want it to come true. I'm living in a foreign country, in a mansion owned by my mother-in-law, styling people who have the kind of wealth I didn't even know existed in real life. I'm in way over my head, and I refuse to accept another change in my life right now.

"Stop walking away from me. We need to talk," Callum barks in his demanding, bossy voice. The same voice that I've been listening to for the past six years from the mouth that only speaks and never listens.

I swallow past a painful lump in my throat and look up. "You want to talk about the cheating? Or the reason Callie Baby doesn't wear pants outdoors? Because both should be addressed at some point."

His lip curls at my sarcasm. Callum hates sarcasm. Can you believe that?

"This has been coming on for a while, Sloan."

I love that he doesn't have a term of endearment for me. In our six years of marriage, he's never once called me anything other than Sloan.

"So you're telling me that this isn't the first time you've cheated on me, your wife?" My eyes are wide and blinking, barely concealing the pit of despair in my belly.

"For the last few years, you and I haven't been—"

"Haven't been connecting much?" I narrow my gaze at him. "Yeah, I've noticed."

"Our marriage has been a sham and you know it," he scoffs. "What happened between us was an accident, and I thought I was doing the right thing. But I have needs, Sloan."

"Oh my God, you want to talk about needs?" I cry and a bubble of laughter erupts from my throat. I shouldn't be laughing. This isn't at all funny, but hearing him say all this is pushing me to the point of hysteria. "Do you want to hear what my needs are, Callum?"

He slides his hands into his pockets, and the image of him suddenly makes me sick. His waxed chest. His sandy blonde hair perfectly cut and swept off to one side like a prep school brat. His manicured fingernails. Yes, manicured. I make his appointments.

He doesn't look like a millionaire CEO right now. He looks like a chump. Like a joke. Like a poser. Like the cheating bastard he is.

My voice is loud when I continue. "My needs begin and end with our daughter!" I'm screaming now. I'm pretty sure. Mostly, there's a ringing in my ears, so I can't fully hear myself and this level of emotion is unfamiliar to me. "My needs ended when hers began."

He rolls his eyes. He actually rolls his motherfucking eyes! "She's been in remission for three years!" he barks.

"Remission doesn't mean she's all better!" I exclaim, blinking a battery of tears from my eyes. I can't believe I'm having this argument with the father of my child. The man I married when I was six months pregnant because his mother threatened to take away his trust fund if he didn't make things right. "Sophia is still a child, Callum. She's only six years old, and she had cancer for three of those years. She still has nightmares that she's back in the hospitals. Her healing doesn't just end because she got the cancer-free balloon!"

"She'll never be better in your eyes," he growls through clenched teeth. "And I'm tired of living this way. You don't give a toss about me, and you haven't since the day you found out you were pregnant with Sophia."

I shake my head, pain erupting in my core. A deep, dark pain that I've been ignoring for years because I didn't want to rock the boat. I didn't want to break up our family. I didn't want to admit that I knew we didn't love each other. That I knew Callum was cheating on me. I've known for a while it wasn't working between us, but I didn't want to disrupt the only life Sophia knows. I understand the pain of growing up without a father and of having no security in your living situation when you're too young to help. She has already suffered enough for someone who had the nerve to be born with a tumour. This isn't fair to her!

My voice is soft when I reply, "Cal, we moved here to England for you. I left my first job as a designer behind for you! We're living in your mother's mansion with staff, and a butler, and freaking mallard ducks on the bedspread all for you! If I didn't care about you, why would I have uprooted my entire life in Chicago?"

"Because you didn't want to lose Sophia," he snaps with a cold, calculating stare. "Because you knew my mother never would have let you keep her, and we have the means to make that reality possible."

My heart drops. Is he really threatening to take her away? Truly? He can't be. None of this can happen. I can't lose Sophia. Not to Cal, not to his mother, not to anyone. I can barely stand to be apart from her for one night. We've been through so much together. It was me who was at every single appointment with her. I was there when the doctor told me my six-month-old baby had a brain tumour. It was me holding her tiny head over a toilet bowl after she went through a slew of radiation. It was me who comforted her when the doctor had to run another PICC line because the nurse couldn't find a vein. I rubbed her bald head. I kissed her bruised veins. Me! Callum was just in the background while I worked with Sophia to get past her fear of touch because the memories of hospitals haunt her. This can't be happening. I can't share my daughter!

My voice feels like acid when I utter, "Maybe if we do some counselling—"

Cal's haughty laugh cuts me off. "You're not understanding me, Sloan. I'm not doing this anymore. You...I'm not staying with you. I've filed for a divorce with joint custody. If you make a fuss, I'll file for full custody." His expression is grim.

It feels like I've been punched in the stomach. My knees feel weak and the room begins to spin as I whisper, "But you barely spend time with Sophia as it is. Even right now, she's spending the night with your mother because I have to work tonight. You could have been watching her. Instead, you're here fucking Lady Godiva!"

"Lady what?" He scoffs and moves to put his shirt on while sliding his feet into his loafers. "Sophia is everything to my mother, and I'm not taking that away from her."

"From her? From her! What about me?" I scream and drop down to the floor as reality crashes all around me. "What about what you're taking away from me, Cal?"

"You're hysterical, Sloan. We'll discuss the particulars with lawyers present." He walks past me, then pauses in the doorway. Turning on his heel, he looks back at me, chin raised like a dictator looming over his people with all his power and wealth. "And don't waste your money fighting for full custody. My lawyers will bury you."

With that nail in the coffin, he leaves without another look back.

My head drops. He's right. Cal has the best lawyers money can buy and more money than I'll ever have. Even if I tried to gain full custody, I would lose. Aside from this indiscretion, he's a pinnacle of Manchester society. His company employs hundreds. The Coleridge family name—that he never allowed me to take in our marriage—is adored.

The tiny shred of control I had over my life is officially gone, all because I decided to come home and catch my husband cheating. There's nothing else I can do other than submit to being a part-time mom to the best thing in my entire existence.

It's over an hour before I move from the floor of my bedroom and drag myself into the bathroom to pee. It's weird how your body keeps working when your soul is dead. All my organs continued digesting the water I drank today and alerted me that I had to relieve myself despite my grief. Despite my despair.

I stare at myself in the mirror as I wash my hands. My long brown hair is stuck to the dried tears on my cheeks. The hollows of my eyes are dark and veiny. The whites of my eyes, red. A dribble of snot has crusted on my upper lip. I'm twenty-eight years old, but the woman looking back at me is a sixty-year-old drug addict. I can't help but be grateful that Sophia is with Cal's mother this evening. I would hate for her to see me like this.

My hands tremble as I push the strands back from my face and pull my hair into a low ponytail. Callum's ominous words pierce through every part of my soul. They pierce through the memories I have of Sophia when she was born. The pictures I have of her as a toddler with no eyebrows or lashes. The sensitive hands and skin she rarely let me touch because she was conditioned to think touch meant pain. It's been three years since her treatments, but I've just gotten her back to being a little girl again. She's no longer a sick baby afraid of anyone who comes near her. She used to cry when I'd try to hold her hand. Cancer tried hard to kill her spirit. A spirit that was beautiful, even on her darkest days. I've dedicated my life to bringing her back from all of that, and now Cal is changing everything.

This is torture.

This is why I would have stayed married to him. To avoid missing a single day of her precious, miraculous life. So many choices have been made for me up until this point. It makes sense that Cal decides when it all ends as well.

I slide my three carat diamond ring off and shakily place it by the sink. It represents a lie. It represents a cheater. A womaniser. A monster. It represents a side of myself that I can hardly look at in the mirror.

I jump when I hear my phone ringing from the bedroom. I'm ashamed to say that a sick part of me hopes it is Cal calling to say he's sorry. My thoughts are completely out of control. To think I'd take him back after everything that's happened. That I would welcome him home after how awful he made me feel. What's wrong with me?

I stride out of the bathroom and fish my cell out of the side pocket of my purse. My seamstress and business partner's bright, freckled face lights up my screen.

My voice is hoarse when I answer. "Hey, Freya."

"Hiya, Sloan!" Her Cornish accent is high-pitched and oh-so blissfully unaware. "Oh my God, my international flight has free WiFi! Can you believe it? I can watch all the *Heartland* on Netflix that I want!"

"That's nice," I reply with a forced laugh. Thankfully, Freya is so caught up in her own world, she doesn't notice the weird sound of my voice.

"I just wanted to make sure you didn't forget about Gareth Harris' suit delivery. He needs it dropped off tonight because he has family coming into town tomorrow morning. I dropped it off with your butler, and it's hanging in your coat closet."

Mindlessly, I mumble a thanks before disconnecting the call, grateful Freya was oblivious. I don't have the energy to tell her what's happened. I don't have the energy to believe it's true. To believe that, once again, my life is forever changed without deciding it for myself.

The last thing I want to do right now is see Gareth Harris. He's the one client of mine whom I actually respect. He's the one client who has never once looked down his nose at me or made me feel insignificant in the two years I've been styling him. Of all the people I've met in England since moving here, he's the one I might even dare to call a friend.

But I don't want him to see this side of me. I don't want him to see me broken, so I will put on a professional front. I have to because soon I won't be married anymore. Soon I'll have to support myself and Sophia the way my mom supported me and my sisters. I won't have access to Callum's wealth. His mother made sure of that with our prenup.

I will need to be the single, working mother I grew up watching.

No. I need to be better.

I need to feel empowered by this new life and embrace my independence. I can do this. I can get control of my life again.

You're the Boss

Gareth

A STIFFY PALACE.

That's what my idiot of a brother, Tanner, calls my home. *A stiffy palace. A sex mansion. A bone-a-thon fortress.* I could keep going because his obnoxious phrases are endless, but repeating them might actually make me as stupid as him.

Standing in my dressing room, I drop the damp towel from around my waist and reach up to pull down a navy cotton T-shirt from a hanger. The selection disrupts the perfect rainbow of colours positioned exactly an inch apart from wooden hanger to wooden hanger, all meticulously ordered and hung with care. My closet, while obnoxiously large, is organised impeccably. It pretty much has to be considering one whole side of the wardrobe is made of clear glass that overlooks my bedroom, like a giant fishbowl.

My entire house is aquarium-like with floor-to-ceiling glass windows throughout, including my bedroom. It's ironic considering I relocated to this secluded residence in rural Astbury to remove myself from the snow globe life I was living in Manchester. In my early twenties, I wanted to be immersed in the football scene. I lived in a posh downtown flat situated in the party district even though I rarely went out. My building had a butler and a chauffeur whom

21

I never used. The paparazzi camped outside of my flat on a regular basis just to get a glimpse of what I ate for bloody lunch. And if it wasn't photographers, it was fans trying to take pictures of me. I couldn't go out for a coffee without feeling eyeballs on me.

That's what being a Man U football player gets you. The city is obsessed with footy players. With two professional teams and the National Football Museum plopped right in the middle, the people around there eat, sleep, and breathe football. Everywhere you look, there's someone wearing some sort of a team shirt or a street vendor selling foam fingers and flags. And it never fails that at every city park, there are a couple of old geezers on a bench, arguing over which Manchester team has more silver in their trophy cases.

It's an odd feeling to be a part of something people are so obsessed with, but it's the gig I signed up for. It's the gig that's made me millions. And it's the sport that now holds my family together when we were once ripped apart completely.

Our father, Vaughn Harris, was a star striker for Man U back when they won the FA Cup in '83 and '85, but he quit when our mum got sick with cancer in '93. Without so much as a goodbye to the team, he broke his contract, sold the Manchester flat, and moved us all out to the empty mansion he owned just outside of London in Chigwell. There, our mum got sicker and sicker, and he got angrier and angrier. When she died, he became a shell of a man. He had the outward appearance of a human, but he was stone on the inside. He stayed that way for many years, and I was left to pick up the slack. To hold our family together.

It wasn't until Bethnal Green F.C. came courting him to manage their team that he turned things around. But instead of atoning for what he'd done to all of us for so long, he simply acted like nothing happened. He started encouraging us to play football and embrace our God-given talents. My brothers were so eager and excited, I couldn't say no to them.

So we played. We kicked a ball around and soon saw that we all had quick feet and the natural movement of footy players. It was in our blood. Dad enrolled us in the Bethnal Green Academy, so we pretty much grew up on the Tower Park pitch. Vi was there a lot, too, but never seemed interested in playing. She was on watch to make sure we all finished secondary school.

But school wasn't something any of us spent much time on. We preferred retrieving balls and running plays with the team. Football was all Dad cared about, so it was all we did.

Essentially, our dad went from being our pathetic excuse of a father to our sports manager. We never had a say in the matter. We never even had a say in what team we played for. It was expected that we play for Bethnal. We were just players in *his* game.

I grab a pair of jeans off the shelf and slide them on, making sure to tuck every bit of me inside the denim before zipping up. Looking over my shoulder, I check the time on the large clock mounted on the wall next to three big screen TVs. A bit obnoxious for one room, but this is a bachelor pad. And with a family full of footballers, there's usually more than one game I need to be watching at a time.

Sloan Montgomery is due to arrive any minute. Having a personal stylist is something my brothers tease me mercilessly about. But as the captain for Man U, I'm required to attend a lot of events. And the fact that I am so particular about my clothes means that having her help is a tremendous relief.

I've had difficulty wearing certain fabrics ever since I was a kid. Anything that feels stiff on my body—like bumpy seams or rough material—sends chills down my spine. Dad actually ordered our team football kits from a special company because of my issue.

Shopping was a nightmare, so I wore and re-wore the handful of clothes that worked for me. I'm not typically one to give a shit about gossip rags, but the papers started remarking on my appearance. So when I met Sloan at an endorsement shoot a couple of years ago and she knew exactly what was going on, it seemed like a no-brainer to hire her.

And let's face it, between my Man U salary, product endorsements, and business investments, I have more money than I know what to do with. My empty fishbowl closet was also looking rather pathetic. Having someone fill it for me was the grown-up thing to do, even if the only other person who sees much of my home is my house manager, Dorinda.

Within a week, Sloan and her assistant flooded my closet with a whole new selection of soft shirts, pristine suits, expensive jeans, and boxers that I rarely wear. Items that don't feel like wet polystyrene sliding against rubber. Sloan even took the time to remove the labels from the necklines. She pays attention to everything, so I never have to give clothes a second thought. I love that. The sense of confidence she has in my needs is a luxury I haven't had too often in my life.

We've developed a sort of friendship over the last couple of years, which says a lot because I don't really have friends. Sure I have teammates and my neighbour up the road, but I tend to keep everyone at arm's length. I don't have time for expectations. I'm also usually wary of people because, with the level of success I've achieved, it's rare for me to meet someone who isn't angling for something that's self-serving.

Besides, if I did have free time, my siblings would most certainly find a way to consume every second of it. On any given day, I get a call from at least one of them. Often, it's Booker checking in because he's awkward and needy like that. Dad calls to talk football; Camden calls to talk women; and Tanner calls with a dick joke. Most of the time, it's Vi relaying an issue that one of our fully grown, idiotic brothers is dealing with and how we're going to handle it because handling things is what I do. I've been doing it since I was barely eight years old, and it's become my lot in life.

Needless to say, I'm an extremely private person, so the fact that I connected with Sloan almost instantly when I met her wasn't something that was easily ignored. There's just something about her that's easy to be around. Perhaps it was the way she instinctually knew how to touch me without me really having to tell her. It formed a bond between us.

And the views of her inside my bedroom for the past two years have been an added bonus. Looking is all I've ever done, though, because the rock on her finger isn't something I would overlook. In fact, I annoyingly notice it every time she comes by. I also notice how she never speaks of her husband or her home life. She's a stunning little untouchable mystery.

A million different scenarios have played in my mind about what Sloan's life is like outside of my bedroom. I imagine she is unhappy in her marriage. I imagine her husband travels a lot and comes home just to fuck her. Not even asking, just taking. Constantly taking because it's what he wants. I wonder if she ever orgasms. If she ever screams with pleasure. Or if her husband ever asks her what *she* desires. What *her* opinion is. I doubt it because the one thing I've learned about Sloan is that she can be a bit of a chameleon, which I find rather frustrating.

She's been to my house numerous times for fittings and restocking my closet. Every time she arrives, she has an uncanny way of shifting her mood to what suits me. If I'm angry at my dad about something, or if we've lost a match and I'm in a foul state, she instinctually senses it and addresses me with care. Or if I've just gotten off the phone with one of my brothers, who always manage to make me laugh, she absorbs my demeanour like a sponge and projects a beaming reflection of warmth. I remember when Vi called to tell me she and her fiancé are having a girl. I was so bloody happy when Sloan showed up while I was on the phone. After I hung up, we were laughing so much, she could hardly take my measurements for the tux she was fitting me for.

I've never met anyone like her who is so adaptive. It makes me wonder if anyone ever alters to her mood. How much of herself does she suppress every day just to keep other people happy?

Who keeps Sloan happy?

Regardless, a quiet friendship developed between us over the past couple of years. I'm comfortable with her, and we're familiar enough with each other now that all of our meetings feel very natural. We know what to expect from each other, and that realisation has a certain peacefulness about it.

But I'd be lying if I didn't admit to fantasising about her firm hands on my body as they were the first time we met. She's careful not to touch me like that anymore, and I can't help but wonder if she was as affected by that day as me. I liked that side of Sloan. The unwavering confidence she has is sexy. I wonder what shade of her I'll be seeing tonight? Likely whatever shade I project.

I yank my shirt down over my head and stride barefoot out of my closet just as my gated driveway entrance buzzes. I make my way over to the small LCD screen mounted by the light switch. It shows a black SUV waiting at the gate. I tap a button and Sloan's face fills the screen. The quality of the security camera isn't great, but I can make out her facial features. She looks different than normal. Still sexy, though.

Sexily married.

"I know you're there." Her voice cuts through the speaker, making me jump. "There's a little red light on that wasn't there a minute ago. Can you let me in, please?"

My brow furrows at her unusually brisk tone, but I hide it as if she can see me through the one-way camera. Without a word, I press the admission button and make my way out of my bedroom, stopping for a second at the propped hallway mirror to check my appearance.

My dark brown hair is tousled and still damp from my shower, so I run my hands through it to smooth down the edges. My hazel eyes look tired, creases beginning to show signs that I'm not in my twenties anymore. My five o'clock shadow is overgrown and patchy, but I save shaving for the morning of a match. It's part of my ritual, and you don't mess with game day rituals.

I jog downstairs and open the double front doors, propping myself on the frame just as Sloan steps out of her car. Her strides are long, her tall body lithe and fit beneath her demure black dress. Her chestnut hair is tied back into a low ponytail, revealing the smooth contours of her pale complexion in the evening light. It's late for a house call, and I'm sure she's not happy about driving nearly an hour out to Astbury. Although, most women would be thrilled to be working in the fashion industry up close and personal with a footballer. They'd trip over their words and show off their cleavage. Anything to get noticed.

However, Sloan doesn't seem to be in the industry for the fame. She's never dressed to impress. She's never star-struck. She doesn't make a fuss.

She lifts her eyes as she climbs the stairs and my heart sinks. Her normally vibrant, honey-coloured gaze is red-rimmed and the skin beneath her nose is pink. She looks like she's been crying.

"Hey, Gareth. How are you?" Her wobbly smile is disingenuous. Forced. She looks as beautiful as she always does, but something is seriously wrong.

"Is everything all right?" I ask, concern pulsing through me as I puzzle over what could have possibly happened.

"Of course!" She smiles again, but the trembling of her chin says otherwise. "I have your suit."

I stare back at her in confusion because this is not a side of Sloan that I've ever seen. She's normally cheerful and composed, completely put together. But it's clear she's a mess right now, and it's killing me that she's acting like everything is fine.

This is the problem with having a friend whom you know very little about outside of work. It's similar to knowing your teammates. I might know which foot our star striker prefers or what kind of drink he keeps in his water bottle, but I know sod all about his home life. It's the same with Sloan. I know that she hates tea but loves teacups. And that she has a genuine laugh and a fake laugh, and the genuine one is a rare unicorn that only comes out when she is completely surprised. But none of that knowledge will help me figure out the baggage she's carried to my doorstep.

"Has someone died?" I ask, cutting to the chase because the longer she stands in front of me acting like she's fine, the less civil I become.

"No!" she exclaims, her fake smile finally dropping as her shocked eyes dart to mine. "Why would you ask that?"

"Because it's clear something is wrong, Sloan, and I'll be damned if I just stand here and don't bloody well get some answers."

"Why do you assume something is wrong?" she asks, covering herself with the garment bag as her suit of armour begins to disintegrate.

"Because it's written all over your face and you're a crap liar." I step closer to her and hear the shakiness of her breath as she inhales. It triggers a deep, burning need to fix whatever is hurting her. Desperation taints my voice. "Tell me what I can do?" *Who do I need to fucking murder?*

I know I'm coming on rather strong, but I simply can't help it. I've always reacted intensely when women cry. Perhaps it's because I only have one sister, and my brothers and I take protecting her so seriously that I nearly went to jail after choking the last fucker who broke her heart. Or maybe I am this way because of those months as a boy when I literally had to defend my mum against my dad because he couldn't cope with the fact that she was fucking dying.

The wateriness in Sloan's eyes doesn't seem to get better when she looks up at me. It seems to get worse. Her voice is hoarse when she replies, "You can just let me do my job." It's a demand and a plea all rolled into one. She could bark it or beg it and I'd submit if that's what takes the sad look off of her face.

"Whatever you say." I step back, holding the door open. "Please, come in."

28

She moves past me to head inside. Her posture straightens now that she has purpose again and I make another mental note about Sloan. She doesn't do conflict. The creamy scent of her vanilla perfume wafts over me, and I follow it like a starved dog as she makes her way toward the staircase.

"Has your exercise regime changed recently?" she asks, clearing her throat and attempting to change the focus to me. "I used the same measurements on your suit, and they weren't too tight on your legs before."

"Erm, yes. Man U got a new trainer and…" I continue jabbering about the new leg work we've been doing while trying not to trip as I notice her left hand clutching the railing.

Her ring finger is bare.

As in no wedding ring.

In all the times I've seen her, she's never not had her ring on. Not once. This has to mean something.

My eyes mindlessly drift from her delicate hand to the curves of her hips. It's amazing how the lack of a wedding ring changes how you see a woman. The black dress she's wearing is nothing special, but the thigh-high boots revealing a couple inches of thigh at the top…*Fuck me.*

Suddenly, her tears don't hurt me. They excite me. If she's crying over a failed marriage, I can think of a myriad of ways for her to truly forget about him. My stomach somersaults with visions of Sloan naked and screaming my name.

The fact that my body is reacting like this is impressive. There haven't been many women I've looked twice at over the last several years. I've grown tired of the Harris Ho groupies who blatantly rub up against me any chance they get. The neediness they emit isn't a turn-on anymore. They expect me to throw them against a wall and fuck their brains out. Go complete dominant alpha dog on them, and that's not what I'm looking for. I'm exhausted from having control over every other aspect of my life. I don't need them coming at me with thoughts of who they expect me to be.

Even if I try to force myself to engage with them, my body re-fuses to react. It's not impotence because I have no problem getting rock-hard in my dreams. And lately, they've been so bone-chillingly intense, I wake up and only need to jack myself a couple of times be-fore coming like a bloody freight train. The problem is, the women I'm seeing in my fantasies don't exist in real life.

Sloan turns to make her way into my bedroom and drops the garment bag on my bed. She unzips it and pulls out three morning suits in varying shades of blue. The femininity of her curvy body in the masculine design of my room is always a sight. My room is various shades of grey, black, and white. At the foot of my bed is a charcoal tufted lounge sofa, like something you'd see in a high-end porno. The truth is, it's never looked more appealing than it does now that Sloan is in my room, seemingly unattached for the first time since I've known her.

"I brought three options for your press conference," she says with a sigh as she spreads them out on the grey duvet. "One of these should definitely fit over your thighs or I'm going to start to think you're on 'roids."

I chuckle, relieved to hear her having a laugh. "I assure you, I'm definitely not on steroids."

"I know you're not," she replies as she turns toward me. She crosses her arms and slides her gaze up to my face with a curious sort of expression. "Tell me, Gareth, why do you have a morning press interview tomorrow? Usually you talk to the press after a match. This isn't something I've styled you for in the past."

Clearing my throat and trying to ignore the fact that Sloan fits perfectly in this space in all her womanly glory, I reply, "We're play-ing Arsenal for the first time since my brother Camden signed with them as a striker."

"So?" She jerks her chin, shoving back a few loose strands of glossy hair that are glowing in the blue rope lighting that lines the ceiling of my see-through closet. "Brothers have played against brothers in soccer before, I'm sure."

"It's called football, Sloan," I correct with a cheeky wink. She gives me a wry smile, and seeing her face slip back into her old self makes me feel like a fucking champion. This is a fight we have almost every time we see each other, and I'm pleased it's helping her feel better. "And you're correct. Brothers have played against brothers. But not the Harris Brothers."

"What's so special about the Harris Brothers?" she asks, tilting her head to the side, looking me up and down once more.

My smile wavers. "I guess it's because there are four of us and we all play."

"You all play soccer?" Her brows lift in genuine surprise.

"Yes," I reply with a laugh. I love that after two years of working together, she has never Googled me. "My three brothers all played together for Bethnal Green—the championship league club our dad manages. But Camden signed with Arsenal, so he's joined me on the Premiership, and the media are having a heyday with that."

She sighs heavily with a shake of her head. "Wow. Four boys, all professional athletes. Your mom must be exhausted."

Her offhanded comment cuts through me harsher than I would have anticipated. They say grief gets better with time. Eventually, the parts of you that broke will mend. That's not been the case for me. Maybe it is because I was with my mum when she drew her last breath. I've never been able to shake the sensation of her body going limp in my arms.

For me, grief is a lot like the ankle injury I suffered years ago. The doctors said it was a really bad sprain, but I'd get back to one hundred percent with solid physio and training. I never did get everything back that I lost, though. I'll always feel that tendon a little more. I'll always step a little differently wherever I go. Be a bit more aware of my surroundings. And if I close my eyes, I can remember the feeling of the horrid popping sensation in my bones, and the nausea pummels me like the weight of an entire football team.

My jaw ticks as I attempt to conceal the fresh stab of pain Sloan's words have caused. Clearing my throat, I reply, "My mum died when I was eight."

Sloan's face falls, and the look that casts over her features is like kicking a person when they're down. "Oh my God, Gareth. I am so sorry. I'm such a puke!" She covers her cheeks with her hands, her head shaking back and forth in horror.

"You're not a puke." The word sounds odd coming from me. "You didn't know. It's fine."

"God, you were eight?" Her mind seems to have drifted somewhere else. "You were eight and without your mother. Only your brothers and dad...I'm so sorry."

"My sister, Vi, was there. She's younger than me but an old soul. She held us all together." My words don't seem to be helping her calm down, so I add, "We had Vi and football. We didn't need much else."

Her lips are downcast. "Still. Five kids and no mom. I'm so sorry, Gareth."

"Stop saying sorry. I'm fine." My jaw clenches, fighting back feelings I normally keep locked up tightly. This is why I keep people at a distance. Surface level relationships are easier. Safer.

And I hate talking about my mum.

I hate thinking about her. I hate remembering her. When the media try to bring her up to me, I instantly shut down. My agent prefaces all of my interviews with that information, and I am desperate to change the subject entirely right now.

"How's the husband?" I ask, knowing it's a dick thing to ask. She's clearly upset, but she's managed to slice into my personal life with very little effort. It'll be easier to have the tables turned.

Her eyes flash to mine like a zap of electricity has been shot through her veins. "Why do you ask?"

She looks just as confused as I feel about this entire conversation.

Dead mothers and secret husbands. Tonight is blurring every single one of our once cosy personal boundaries.

I look down at her hand. "I noticed you're missing some hardware."

She pulls her hand up in front of her chest, chewing thoughtfully on her lower lip as she looks down at the floor. Her thumb strokes the inside of her ring finger that shows a faint tan line. "We're not together anymore. It's kind of new," she adds with a sad look on her face.

Silence falls over us. I should say something. Something respectful. Something proper. Something meaningful. Something to cheer her up. "I'm sorry to hear that." *Or something painfully generic.*

"Yeah, thanks." She gazes up at me, her eyes squinting with question. "I suppose that's the proper response, right?"

"I guess so?" I respond with a question because I'm not sure what she's getting at.

She looks around the room, searching for her answer. "I should be sorry. I should be concerned. I should be sad, right?" She looks back at me for my response.

I can only shrug. She looks sad enough to me. Although, perhaps sad isn't exactly the look I see in her red-rimmed eyes. More *lost*. "I think you should feel how you want to feel," I reply sternly.

"That's the thing, though!" she peals, her eyes wide and anxious. "I don't know how I want to feel. My marriage is over and I don't know how I should feel. I thought about it the entire drive over here, and it's making me crazy that I don't just know." She tugs nervously on a strand of hair that's fallen loose from her ponytail. "Can you tell me how to feel? Please?"

"No," I state quickly, taking a step back. If I tell her how I want her to feel, it's happy. Turned on. Liberated. I'd tell her to feel fucking euphoric to be free to do whatever she wants with whomever she wants. But telling her that would only serve me, not her. "It's your life. A life I'm just learning about. So it's certainly not my place to tell you your feelings. They should just…come naturally."

"Well, they're not." Her tone is exasperated. She looks like she's going to lose it again.

"They have to be there," I retort, stepping closer to her, loathing the lost look in her eyes. "Fuck, I'm an unfeeling prick nine times out of ten, but even I'd have some sort of reaction to not being with the person I loved anymore."

"That's the thing!" she exclaims, her voice rising in pitch. "I don't think I love him! I was just existing with him! So now that I've told you that, how do you think I should feel?"

This is the most bizarre conversation I've ever had, and that's saying a lot because my brothers have spoken to me for hours about the size of their balls. But in all the visions I've had of Sloan and her husband, I never considered her not even loving him.

Swallowing hard, I reply, "Try saying the first thing that comes to your mind. I've split with my husband and I feel…"

"Out of control!" she exclaims, her eyes wide and watery. She moves closer to me, an urgency causing her hands to shake in front of her body. "I feel like I've been out of control through the entirety of my marriage and getting divorced doesn't change a damn thing. He will still have all the power, and I'll still have zero control of my own damn life."

"That can't be true," I argue. "You won't be with him anymore. That's the ultimate freedom. And you have an incredible business you've built. You work for some of the wealthiest people in England."

"He pushed me into this job! And those people just tell me what to do!" she replies with a laugh I don't entirely trust.

"They ask for your opinion," I scoff. "You tell them what to wear."

She smiles, but it looks like it hurts. "I'm a glorified order-filler. I shop and make thoughtful selections, then they send me back to get them something else. You're my only client who wears what I tell you to wear. Why is that, Gareth?"

She steps even closer to me and grips the sides of my arms with her long, delicate fingers. I flex in response because her hands on me normally feel strong and reassured. But with the crazy look on her face, I'm not sure how to feel right now. "I don't know. I guess I just tr-trust you," I falter.

"You're the only one." She sniffles and swallows down a lump in her throat while staring at my chest. "You're the only one who listens."

She presses her forehead to my chest and her body trembles against mine. Instinctively, I wrap my arms around her. One hand cups her neck while the other wraps around the small of her back. We've never embraced like this, but she fits perfectly beneath my chin and I can tell she needs this. I squeeze her tightly in a vain attempt to take her pain away. Then I envision punching her fucking husband for turning her into this out of control, emotionally tortured mess before me. Sloan deserves so much better.

"How can I fix this for you?" I ask, wanting to kiss the top of her head but holding back because I don't know if she'd welcome the touch. "I fix things, so just name what you need."

Her head lifts, her eyes rising to my face, zeroing in on my lips. My gaze falls to her mouth in response. Her lips are pink and wet and open just enough for me to see the tip of her tongue. A shift in the air has me pulling in a deep, cleansing breath. She looks tearful like before, but there's a spark in her eyes that I've never seen. It's electric. Mesmerising. Meaningful.

I can smell her perfume and feel the warmth of her breath against my whiskered jaw, and it's doing things to me. Things I should probably put a stop to. She's clearly not in a good place, but what's happening right now isn't voluntary.

"Why are you so kind to me, Gareth?" she asks my lips. Her voice is deep and different than I've ever heard. "I don't have many friends out here, and you're one of the only ones who's *kind*."

My voice is like gravel when I reply, "I li-like you."

Her gaze roves over my features, taking in every millimetre of my expression like she's looking for a lie. It hurts to see her like this. Sloan is always so thoughtful and patient. So understanding. What kind of a sick bastard could make her doubt herself so much?

I would never make her feel this way. In fact, I would do literally anything to take away this pain she's feeling. Seeing her falling apart feels dangerous, like she could break and disappear at any second.

I lean in toward her lips. The sugary scent wafting off of her makes my mouth water. I can practically taste the sweetness of her skin and we haven't even touched yet. "Tell me what you want, Treacle."

She sucks in a quick breath and tightens her grip on my biceps. "What does Treacle mean?"

My eyes close because I didn't mean to say it out loud. It's an East London word that an old trainer for Bethnal used a lot, and for some reason it stuck. "It's a British term for sweet. Treacle is a type of sweet molasses."

Her nose wrinkles with disgust. "Why would you call me molasses?"

I press my lips to fight the chuckle that is rising in my chest. "Because you smell sweet. You've always smelled sweet since the first time I met you. Like syrup."

"Oh," she says, looking down and thinking that over. "And you like that?" she asks, looking up at me with hope.

Not at first, is the reply that pops into my head. Instead, I press my nose to her neck. The skin is soft and puckers with goosebumps as I inhale deeply. Lightly touching my lips to her neck, I murmur against her flesh, "I do now."

Sloan swallows slowly as I pull back and take in her flushed cheeks. "So it's like a term of endearment?"

"You could call it that."

Her eyes well with tears, and I fear that I've gone too far. A droplet slides down her cheek, so I reach out to cradle her delicate face in my hands. My thumb slowly slicks the moisture away. "I'm sorry if that was too much. I won't say it again. I just really want to make this pain you have go away. I have to make these tears stop."

"It's not too much," she croaks, leaning into me so our bodies are pressed against each other. I thought it was my lips on her neck that upset her, but now we're so close I can feel every breath she takes. "I've never had a term of endearment."

I've never been inspired to give one, is what I think. Instead, I reply, "You should have that and so much more, Sloan. Just tell me what you want and I will give it to you." My body is roaring to life in a way I've never experienced, and it's taking every ounce of my control to not ravage her on the spot. But that's the last thing she needs. She's come to me saying she feels out of control. I'm not about to enable that feeling.

"What do you mean?" she asks, watching my lips as she licks her tongue across her own.

"Tell me what to do. Give me an order. Whatever you want. You're not out of control right now, Sloan. You are completely in control. With me. I give it *all* to you."

A breath she had been holding escapes her lips in a garbled sort of moan, like the thought of me giving in to her is turning her on. God, I want to see her turned on. I want to see her let go so fucking badly I could roar.

She inhales and husks against my lips, "I…want a lot of things." Her eyes drift down my body, and her chest rises and falls with deep, labourious breaths.

"Considering how badly I want you right now, I'm bloody well positive you could have anything from me."

Her eyes snap to mine, and an ember burns in them that wasn't there before. "Anything?"

I swallow slowly, a heavy, important weight pressing down on me with that single word. "Anything."

Her voice is quick and brisk, like a flash of lightning. "I want to see you naked."

Fuck. Me.

It has just been confirmed that the woman I've fantasised about nineteen different ways since the second I met her wants me naked. It's not at all what I expected but more than I could have ever hoped for. I want to thrust my victorious fists in the air and hoot for joy, but I'm going to conceal my childish excitement.

She's fragile right now. Raw. This needs to be about her desires. Not mine. It's important for her to know I'm taking her seriously. And there's no way in hell I want any of this to stop.

Releasing her cheeks, I step back and yank my shirt off over my head. Before my eyes open, she's in my space, raking her fingers over my shoulders and through the short hairs on my chest. Her eyes watch the action as her nails bite into my flesh, leaving thin red lines as they go.

My grunt has her eyes back on mine. "Do you like that?" she asks nervously, trying to read my expression.

Swallowing and trying to maintain control of my impending erection, I nod slowly. I like it too much. I like it more than I've liked a woman's hands on me in ages. My tone is guttural. "I like it a lot."

My chest begins rising and falling quicker the longer she looks at me, eyeing me with renewed strength. "Can we really do this?" she asks.

"Yes," I reply automatically, needful for more. "We can do whatever you want." And I seriously mean whatever she wants.

"Unbutton your jeans," she whispers tremulously and takes a step back to watch my reaction.

Her eyes are strong and full of passion. They look confident, no longer crazed and out of control. Giving her this control is a turn-on like I've never felt before.

Reaching down, I unbutton the snap of my jeans, pulling apart the zipper seam with a simple bend of my wrist. Sloan's eyes travel down the line of hair running from my navel to my groin. She bites her lip and her head lolls back like she's trying to maintain control of herself.

Fuck me. I'm not even touching her and she's reacting this strongly. Don't fucking stop, Treacle.

"Tell me more," I croak, my voice deep and gravelly as I stare at the beautiful flesh on her neck. "Tell me everything you want me to do."

She nods, her shoulders rising with this newfound empowerment she's trying so hard to embrace. Her hands slide up her body to the back of her neck. "Rub yourself," she states. "Over your jeans."

My brows lift. God, why am I so proud of her in this moment? *She's fucking stunning, that's why.*

I press the heat of my palm over the crotch of my denim, careful not to do anything more than what she's requested. My dick is hardening from watching her watch me. She's a fucking vision.

My forearm flexes as I begin to massage my groin, my dick pressing against the seam of my jeans and growing by the second.

"Go inside your jeans. Rub your bare…cock." She hesitates on the last word and pulls her lip into her mouth, clearly unsure of herself.

"Anything," I whisper, my voice quaking because my level of arousal is a bit terrifying.

My reply gives her confidence. She licks her lips and eyes the veins running up my arm as I slide my hand into my tight jeans. I'm rock-hard now, but there's no room to play. Regardless, I'm following orders and everything feels so fucking good.

"I want to see you, Gareth," she all but moans. "Take off your jeans."

Thank fuck, I think to myself as I slide the jeans down my legs and kick them out of the way. She's asked me to take off my jeans for a million different fittings, but I usually remember to put underwear on when she comes by. Perhaps it was destiny that I forgot tonight.

I'm completely naked while she remains completely clothed. It's the most erotic thing I've ever experienced with a woman. There's a shift in the room. In the universe. A change in our axis. The power she has over me as I stand in front of her naked and vulnerable is a heady, sexy sensation. A strange desire to fall to my knees and worship her overcomes me, but I remain on my feet, slowly stroking my cock for her half-lidded eyes.

"Will you drop to your knees?" she asks, wringing her hands together in front of her.

I look at her like she's reading my fucking mind. "Will you demand it?" I want to hear the order. I crave it.

Her jaw tightens. "Drop to your knees."

The conviction in her voice is like a defibrillator to my chest, shocking the last remaining control I've lived with my entire fucking life out of my body. I've entered into some sexy as fuck fantasy world where she's the queen and I'm her servant. *And, bloody hell, it's just like my fucking dreams.* My mind has clicked off and is uninhibited. Ready to listen, to respond, to please. I'm prepared and waiting for more orders because, for once in my life, I'm not in control. I'm not the celebrity footballer. I'm not the big brother. I'm not the support system, the mediator, the protector. I don't have to solve things or play a certain role. I can just be myself without expectations. I'm… free.

The feeling is completely liberating. I don't want to challenge her. I want to make her happy. I want to keep that confidence in her voice. I want to follow her commands, praying like fuck she'll reward me with her body.

My grip tightens around my cock, and I close my eyes briefly to concentrate so I don't come like a fucking teenager.

"Eyes on me," she states.

My eyes snap to hers.

She's in another place, too. Her voice is different. The emotional sponge she once was has vanished. She's controlling the feelings in the room. The atmosphere. The pleasure. She's found me hiding in that faraway fantasy land where she's the queen and I'm hers. All hers. We have hit a point of no return, and everything around us will crumble if we don't give in to our desires.

I stare at her strength and grow harder as every muscle and vein stretches and tightens along the length of my cock. I want her so fucking badly.

She lets out a moan and says, "Stand up. Take my clothes off. Right now. Fast...Please."

I rise, eliminating the few feet between us and reach down for the bottom of her dress. There's a faint sound of fabric tearing as I yank it over her head, but I can't help myself. A frenzy has taken over. And as much as I want to glance down at her black lace bra and her tiny slip of knickers, I can't look away from her gaze.

"I want you to grab my hair and fuck me against that dresser as hard as you can. Don't hold back. Don't take it easy on me. Make me scream." Her muscles twitch beneath her skin. She's struggling so hard to maintain control, yet she's still a vision.

I'm getting pictures in my head of not following her orders and being punished. The sight is everything I never knew I wanted.

I grip her by the waist and pull her against my body, walking her backwards to the dresser. I stare at her lips and move in just as she states, "Don't kiss me. Don't you dare kiss me."

I all but growl with agitation and swirl her around so fast on her heels, she loses her balance and falls onto the dresser. She's bent over the furniture with her arse perched toward me, like a delicious buffet that I can't touch without permission.

"Rip my panties off and bury your cock inside of me. And you better have a condom, so help me God."

Her voice is a cry at the end as I grip the strip of fabric lining her crack and jerk them off of her in one strong tug. I fist her knickers in my hand and stride over to my nightstand. I drop the material into the drawer and grab a foiled packet.

Moving back to her, I tear the condom open with my teeth.

"I didn't say you could open it!" she exclaims, watching me over her shoulder and staring at my bobbing cock. "Bring it here."

I do as I'm told, and it's the hottest fucking thing I've ever done with a woman and I haven't even penetrated her yet. She silently takes the condom and pulls the rubbery object out of the wrapper.

"You gave me control, so I'm taking it." Her gaze is a powerful pool of copper, twinkling in the dim light of my room. She grabs my cock and tugs it. "I want to put this on you."

I grunt and stifle a moan as she holds a death grip on me. My pain makes her smile in awe. God, she is beautiful.

"I like your voice," she says. It sounds like the old Sloan, but she clears her throat and adds, "It's really sexy. I want to hear it when you drive into me, okay?"

"You got it, Treacle," I reply.

With a pleased smirk, she drops down on her knees and rolls the slippery condom over me. I'm so turned on, I could probably ejaculate this second. It's been way too fucking long. But I'm certain that would end badly for me, so I focus on her commands and release my mind to her desires again.

"Now, grab my ponytail and fuck me hard. Really fucking hard. So hard I forget everything." Her voice is a bit manic, but the neediness calls to me.

Her command is my wish, I think to myself. I wrap her thick chestnut hair around my fist and jerk her around so she's bent over the dresser, her arse level with my cock. It's a good thing she still has her boots on or we would not match up. I bend at the knees and position my tip between her folds. My fingertips brush her entry to prepare her, and the wetness between them makes me want to roar with pride.

"Speak, Gareth!" she demands as I press my forehead between her shoulder blades.

"You're fucking soaked, and it's making me crazy," I growl.

"More!" she cries.

"You're so soaked that all I want is to lick every drop coming from you because I've been thinking about your wet little pussy since the second I met you."

"Oh my God," she moans and splays her hands out on the dresser top. "I want you to lick me, too. I want you to do about ninety different things with your tongue. But right now, you have to fuck me. I need to be filled, Gareth. I want to feel your big dick stretch me."

I ram inside of her with all my strength, and she screams in response. Fuck me, she's tight. Why is she so tight? If I was married to her, we would be fucking every bloody day and twice on Sundays. What's the matter with her husband? Why am I thinking of another man right now?

"Gareth!" she screams, begging for more with just the sound of my name.

"You're so fucking tight. Your husband is a bloody idiot."

"Don't bring him up!" She reaches back with one hand and digs her nails into my arse.

I flinch and squeeze my eyes shut to stop myself from coming. Fuck me. Pain and pleasure is a fine line indeed. I tug her ponytail and her grip on my arse loosens. "Your tight, wet pussy likes my big cock, so brace yourself because I'm not holding back."

My arse and thighs flex as I thrust up into her and reach around with my fingers to squeeze her clit at the same time.

She screams. She screams so bloody loud, I hesitate.

"Don't you fucking stop!" She slams her palms against the mirror attached to the dresser. I find her face in the reflection and she pins me with a threat. "You stop and I'm out of here faster than you can get that condom off your dick."

"Fucking tease," I murmur, yanking back on her ponytail so her head is thrust up toward the ceiling as I pound into her so fast, I knock over all the decorative shit on the dresser. The mirror shifts as she props herself on it, trying to find purchase against the onslaught, but I don't stop. I can't stop. I'm following orders and she's

43

praising me with the sexiest fucking sounds I've ever heard from a woman. The whole scene is the freest and most aroused I've ever felt in my entire fucked-up life. This strong, sexy, confident woman said I needed to fuck her and, somehow, obeying her is just as hot as the fucking.

When I feel her pussy clench around me, she lets out a loud, ear-piercing cry. My teeth grind together as I pray to Christ she tells me to come soon because I don't think I can hold out a second longer.

"Come, Gareth. Fucking come with me!" she bellows, her voice broken and high-pitched, out of breath and panting.

Instantly, hot liquid spurts out of me and encompasses the tip of my cock as I ejaculate into the condom, still thrusting into her as I blow. The pressure of her tight pussy tremoring around me as I move is like a vibrating vice-grip of complete ecstasy.

"Holy freaking shit," she cries, her voice sounding more like her again.

I open my mouth to reply, but the buzz from my security panel stops me mid-breath.

"What the hell?" she squeaks. "Are you…Are you expecting someone?" She shoves me off of her and yanks away from me like she's been infected.

"No!" I exclaim, annoyed as she begins covering her body with her hands.

"Oh my God, you're an athlete. Of course you are!" She pulls up the strap of her bra that slipped down her shoulder and squats down in her boots to scoop up her dress.

"I said I'm not expecting anyone!"

"I don't believe you!" she barks.

"You have no reason not to!"

This brings her up short, but she's clearly not convinced.

"Except for the fact that you soccer players are the biggest sluts in Manchester. That's what everyone says."

"I haven't fucked anyone in a bloody year!" I roar but instantly feel bad for shouting in her face. I take a step back and soften my tone. "I have no idea who the fuck could be here at this time of night."

Still only wearing a condom, I rush over to the screen and tap the button to see who's in the white Mercedes. A bearded, man-bun freak stares back at me. "Christ, it's Tanner."

"Who's Tanner?" Sloan asks, clutching her dress to her chest.

"My brother," I growl through clenched teeth. "He's here to watch the match tomorrow, but he wasn't supposed to be here until the morning."

I press the admittance button without a word, and Sloan and I begin scrambling for our clothes. I pop into the loo and yank off the condom that has to contain my biggest load to date. When I stride out, Sloan approaches.

"What are you doing?" I ask, glancing down at her fully dressed state.

"I need a minute!" she snaps, moving toward the loo. "Just go down and stall!"

I shake my head and slide back into my jeans, still feeling semen seep out of my tip and into the denim. The texture is bone-chilling, but I'll probably be leaking for days after that epic fuck. I yank my shirt down over my head and make my way downstairs, barefoot, trembling, and exhilarated beyond belief.

Euphoria overcomes me as I swing open the door just as Tanner strides up the steps with bags in hand. A curvy, dark-haired woman stands beside him, frowning at something behind me in the house.

"Tanner!" My voice booms, deep and throaty, maybe even a bit hoarse from all the dirty talk I just did. I nervously smooth my hair and adjust my shirt over my groin as my eyes dart back and forth between him and the entryway behind me, unsure what the fuck Sloan is doing. I cough out an uncomfortable noise and say, "Surprised to see you tonight."

The girl frowns at Tanner. "Didn't you tell him you decided to come early?"

Tanner shrugs. "Didn't occur to me."

The girl looks like she's about to apologise for my brother's rudeness when Sloan's hand touches my arm to move me out of her way to exit. The sensation is like needles.

"It's fine. We're all done here," she states, smooth and confident, like she didn't dominate me upstairs five minutes ago. She throws an empty garment bag over her shoulder and smiles.

"Who's this?" Tanner smirks, amazement on his face.

"This is no one," I answer quickly, wanting to knock the look off his face before Sloan bolts. Her eyes look to mine with barely contained fury. "I mean, she's someone, but…Sloan is my personal shopper."

"Personal shopper?" Tanner's curious tone gets right up my nose.

"I prefer celebrity fashion stylist," Sloan corrects, her tone crisp and unforgiving as she moves past us. I stare wistfully at her retreating frame, hating that whatever just happened has ended so abruptly. "And I really need to be going. I only did this late call as a favour. Good luck at your event tomorrow, Mr. Harris."

Without a glance back, she strides toward her car. Tanner's friend frowns as she watches Sloan leave. I wonder if she notices the messy appearance of Sloan's ponytail.

"Who the fuck was that really?" Tanner asks, placing a hand on my shoulder and waggling his brows at me. "Cam and I thought you were fucking celibate!"

I roll my eyes. I pretty much was until a few minutes ago.

While standing in the kitchen with my brother and Belle—the woman he's fake dating for the next month to get out of some salacious media scandal—my phone vibrates from where it's plugged in on the counter. The two of them are busy making googly eyes at each other, so I unlock it and read the text that came in.

Sloan: That WILL NOT be happening again. Ever.

My brow furrows, disappointment clouding my buzz. Begrudgingly, I type back.

Me: You're the boss.

And a fine boss at that.

A Little Place Called
Hell on Earth

Sloan

I T'S BEEN SIX MONTHS SINCE I SLEPT WITH GARETH HARRIS. SINCE that one, shining, life-altering moment of pleasure, I have moved to a little place called Hell.

It's hot in Hell. And cold. Hot and cold. Not warm. Not simmering. Not even room temperature. Just all hot or all cold. That is how my life has been the past several months of dealing with lawyers and Cal…and Cal's mother.

Now I find myself staring across the boardroom table at them, finally ready to sign the documents for my new life as a part-time mom.

Callum's mother, Margaret, sits dutifully beside him with her tiny hands in her tiny lap. The pair of them look like strangers to me. Sure I recognise Margaret's blonde-dyed bob and her affection for beige draped fashion. And Cal sits there with the same smug look on his face, wearing a suit he probably doesn't remember I bought for him. But other than slight facial recognition, I don't know this family at all.

I was married to Cal for six years. We lived together in Chicago for three years, then Manchester for another three. I drove Sophia out to the Lake District to see Margaret every Sunday. I've never particularly cared for Margaret, though. She's posh and prim and likes to make backhanded comments about my clothing selection every time I see her. To say she's not a fan of mine is a huge understatement. But, miraculously, this divorce has made her impression of me even worse. Now she stares back at me like I'm a disgruntled member of her staff.

My how quickly things have changed.

Cal's lawyer speaks first while pouring himself a glass of water from the pitcher in front of him. "With Margaret Coleridge's terminal illness, my client is requiring a fifty-fifty custody split. One week on and one week off with every Sunday being dedicated to a visit with Margaret in the Lake District regardless of whose week it is."

I want to scoff. I want to scream. I want to cry. Cal's mother has lung cancer. A cancer she could fight but opted not to because she doesn't want to lose her hair. That's why we moved to England in the first place. Because Cal's mother is dying. Because Cal wanted to be near her for her final months. Here we sit, three years later, and the woman is still alive and still controlling all of us.

My lawyer leans over and whispers into my ear. "I know this hurts. Just remember that Sophia's inheritance is contingent on this, and it's all temporary." Translation: Once the seemingly immortal Margaret finally does kick the bucket, we can attempt to renegotiate the custody agreement.

My divorce from Cal has taken six months to finalise because I refused to agree to the true fifty-fifty split. I wanted Cal to take every other weekend like most absentee fathers, but his mother was in his ear. When she threatened to take Sophia's trust fund away, it took ten billable hours for my lawyer to get me to submit.

Money is a horrible reason to agree to these terms, but I know what it's like to work a job that isn't your true passion. Ultimately, the trust fund will give Sophia opportunities that I never had. It will give her control of her own life. Something I still don't freaking have.

Cal's lawyer takes a sip of water and continues, "Callum Coleridge will maintain residence at the Coleridge Estate on Rossmill Lane—"

My lawyer interjects, "And my client has secured a residence a few blocks over on Weygates Drive. She is renting the guest house to her business partner, who has cleared all background checks as you requested."

When Margaret's mouth pinches a fraction of an inch more, it takes everything I have not to jump across the table and claw her eyes out. What no one is saying is that I *had* to lease out the guest house because it was the only way I could afford to live in the same area as my child. Granted, Freya is a friend, not just a colleague. And the fact that my home has a guest house means it's by no means a shack.

But this is what it takes. Back when I signed the prenup with Cal, I didn't want or need his money. My mother yelled at me for not negotiating for something, and now I realise she was right. Our move to Manchester put us in a neighbourhood and a lifestyle very different from what we had in Chicago. Since I refuse to be more than a stone's throw away from Sophia, I'm doing whatever it takes to make her life as unaffected as possible.

My lawyer continues, "And you still agree that Ms. Montgomery will be first on the call list for any emergencies."

Cal's lawyer leans in to whisper in his ear. The two nod before he replies, "That is correct."

Margaret clears her throat and Cal puts a worried arm around her. "Do you need some water, Mother?"

She nods and he hurries to pour her a glass, sloshing some on the table nervously as he does.

Where was this person when Sophia was sick? Why wasn't he this devoted during our times at the hospitals? Is it the inheritance he will receive when she finally dies that makes him oh-so attentive? If I had money, would he have cared more about Sophia's well-being? Does Margaret realise how uninvolved her son was during all those dark months we spent in and out of hospitals?

I bite my tongue as the lawyer moves on even though all I want to do is cry over the thought of being apart from Sophia for seven days straight. This entire situation is inhumane. It's indecent. This is not how a family is supposed to be. We should have access to each other whenever we want. Not only on our designated days.

"Very well then," Cal's lawyer states. "I believe we're settled on all the other terms. All we need to do is sign."

My lawyer pushes the contract over to me, the yellow tabs sticking out everywhere I need to sign right below Callum's name. A glorified contract of my life, all laid out in black and white with me on the bottom, as usual.

My hand trembles as I sign away my rights as a full-time mother. I follow orders from the men in this room, wishing for a time machine so I could go back and make this all go away. But no. Those days are over. With money comes power. Until I have one, I can't have the other.

Unless of course you're Gareth Harris. He doesn't seem to desire power the way Callum does. He seems to want to give up the power. The control. He doesn't want to pick his own clothes and bark orders like so many other wealthy people.

He enjoys being controlled.

I'm forced to close my eyes in a vain attempt to stop the memory of the night I experienced with him. It was the last moment I had any true pleasure in my life. I have no idea what came over me. What we did was insane. It was irrational. It was unfathomable. It was perfection.

For the past six months, I've been avoiding Gareth and telling myself I didn't love every second of having control over such a strong man. I didn't love how my nails bit into his muscular flesh. I hated the tone of his voice when he followed my orders. Because if I allow myself to recall how turned on I was when he knelt in front of me and gave himself to me completely, my entire body would begin to tremble.

What's ten times more terrifying isn't the strange sexual experience we shared. It wasn't just about fucking one person to forget another. It was the fact that in one of the darkest moments in my life, Gareth had the ability to reach inside of my body and prop me back up on my feet. He stabilised me at a time I wanted to simply crumble to the floor.

Having that kind of connection with a person was something I'd never experienced. And to have a man put his needs behind mine was definitely a first. I'd give anything to have that sense of strength once again.

5

Hello, Stranger

Gareth

"**K**EEP YOUR CHEST HIGH, GENTLEMEN! DIP IT IN, THEN DRIVE it back. Keep perfect control through the whole range!" Our assistant trainer, Raul, shouts stretching formations at us in his thick French accent while walking around the lot of us positioned in a perfect circle on the pitch of the Trafford Training Centre. "Dip it in, then drive it back."

My teammate Hobo lets out a snicker from beside me. "I love dipping it in and driving it back." His brown eyes flash to me with a lewd smirk. "When's the last time you dipped and drived, Harris?"

"Is that a proposition, Hobo?" I ask flatly, turning my unamused face to him. "Because I have to say, my type is a bit less desperate."

A few of our teammates roar with laughter as Hobo's face crumples. Raul's voice cuts everyone off. "None of you will have the ability to dip and drive if you don't shut it and focus on the task at hand."

As we move through the formations in stony silence, my thoughts drift to the woman I'd like nothing more than to dip and drive with again and again. It's been a fucking year since the night I slept with Sloan. I would think that night was a dream if it weren't for the ripped black thong that still sits in my nightstand as evidence.

It's also been a year of unreturned calls and texts. I even forced

Tanner to use Sloan to style the men for his wedding this past summer, hoping it might get me some facetime with her. But she was in and out like a shot, doing everything she could to ensure we weren't given any time alone to talk. I also tried sending flowers to the address on her business card as some pathetic form of apology, but they were returned with a note saying her address had been changed.

I shake my head, attempting to push the thought of her to the back of my mind again. She's probably back with her husband for all I know. Clearly that night meant a great deal less to her than it did to me.

For me, it was a sexual awakening I never imagined could happen. It was a realisation that maybe the reason I haven't had many great sexual experiences with women is because they didn't happen that way. I want all that and more. But how do I even attempt to approach that sort of relationship with another woman? I'm too famous. There's no way it wouldn't get out. What happened with Sloan was spontaneous and not a word of it was leaked to the press. It just aggravates me more that I can't get a hold of her because she's the one woman in Manchester I actually trust.

I shake the niggling feeling away because I need to move on. Focus on my game. We have a match against Huddersfield, and their strikers are some of the best in the league. I need to keep my team focused and on point. We are having a great start to our season. We can't afford to lose sight of that.

I glance around the Trafford facility that employs more than three hundred people. This state-of-the-art campus cost over sixty million pounds to build. The Man U team practices in the main building, but there's another whole attachment where Academy players train. The weight and money that Man U puts behind its athletes is unprecedented.

I remember the first time I stepped onto the grass at Old Trafford. I was a twenty-one-year-old prick with more talent than I knew what to do with, but all I cared about was pissing off my father and besting him any way I could.

"Harris!" Our head coach, Maurice DuPont, shouts my name, and my head snaps over to where he's standing on the sideline with a couple of men in suits. "Get over here!"

I hop up onto my feet and jog over to where the three men are standing, covering their mouths as they talk. Frowning, I slow my approach and eye them cautiously.

"Harris, do you know who these men are?" Coach asks, staring me down like I'm in trouble.

My eyes look at the two staunch, balding men standing before me. "I'm afraid I don't, coach."

Coach narrows his eyes and crosses his arms over his chest. "These men are on the board of the FPA. They are here to tell me you've won some bloody award."

Confusion mars my face as I turn to them in question. "I've won what?"

"Gareth Harris"—the short round one steps closer to me and reaches out to take my hand—"on behalf of the Football Press Association, I'd like to formally congratulate you on being selected as England's Player of the Year."

My brow furrows in disbelief as the other man—a taller bloke with a potbelly—reaches out and shakes my hand next. "This award is given to the player who is proven to have had a superior statistical season and has demonstrated great humanitarian efforts. Your accomplishments here in Manchester with the underprivileged youth football program you organised have been impressive to say the least."

"And that stunt you and your brothers pulled in London this past summer certainly got a lot of attention," the short one adds with a laugh. "The four of you running in mankinis…Britain has never seen anything like it!"

I wince with embarrassment as I recall the ridiculous scene Tanner talked us all into. About a year ago, my brother started a nonprofit to fund clothing for homeless and low-income residents of England. He organised a celebrity 5K and job fair event, and a wealthy donor offered to double an already huge donation if the Harris Brothers ran the race in neon green mankinis.

Thank fuck we were running in July and not December.

"The people loved it!" the short man exclaims while fisting both his hands in front of him. "And it's that sort of outside-the-box thinking that the FPA celebrates!"

"My brother Tanner is the one who deserves the credit for that," I argue. "Shirt Off My Back is his charity."

The men smile ruefully at each other before the short one replies, "I'm sure he'll receive credit in time. But with his suspension last year, his stats for the season didn't measure up. And, Gareth, what you've done locally here in Manchester is no small feat."

The tall one nods in agreement. "Five years ago, when you spent all that money to bring the old Manchester training grounds back to life for a free football program, the whole city thought you were mad."

"But it's been tremendous for both the city and Manchester United. Because of that, we will be honouring you at our annual awards gala here in Manchester in a couple of months. Congratulations, son."

"Think you can rent a decent tux?" The tall man roars with laughter at his apparent attempt at a joke.

"I'm...speechless," I state, jaw dropped.

The two men smack me on the back and congratulate me once more before exiting. Coach murmurs something about not being one for sentimentality, so instead of telling me he's proud of me, he tells me to skip the rest of practice and take the day off.

I'm in a daze as I make my way off the pitch, my mind replaying everything they said. I feel somewhat guilty because starting the program was a bit self-serving to say the least. My first few years here, I was a prat. I was defensively the strongest player on the pitch, but I felt no joy over it. No accomplishment. The truth is, I spent most of my free time in London staying with the one person I had more issues with than anyone on the planet and brooding over ways I could outdo his legacy on the team.

Then I had a breakthrough moment when Vi helped me see that all I was accomplishing was actually turning into our father— the man I've resented for the better part of my life. That wakeup call spurred the action to create a youth enrichment program called Kid Kickers. I wanted football to be available to anyone, no matter how much money they had or who their parents were. After all, I knew what it was like to grow up without something to do to keep you focused, keep you moving, keep your mind clear. I only wish I could have had football sooner in my life.

I still remember the first time I started training with Dad's team, I was angry at him. Angry that he kept the sport from me for so many years. As a child, you can't afford your own kit. You can't sign yourself up for teams, camps, training. It all costs money. Football is an expensive sport, so you're at the mercy of your parents and what they earn. And if you have a vapid father like I did, opportunities pass you by for most of your life.

I wanted something more for kids. Opportunities that could improve their mindsets. So I sunk a ton of money into refurbishing The Cliff—Man U's old training grounds. There are fifty staff members who keep Kid Kickers afloat and manage the day-to-day operations of the program. All I do is provide financing, press, and occasionally help coach the trainers to ensure that the kids are getting the best skills we can teach them.

Going to an awards gala seems like capitalising on the struggles of others for my own benefit, but I don't see how I'd be able to work my way out of attending.

I'm so deep in my own head when I enter the changing room that I think I'm hallucinating when a familiar figure stands in front of one of my teammates' locker.

"Sloan?" I hear myself saying, knowing it can't possibly be her.

A frightened yelp comes from the figure as she turns and confirms my thoughts to be true. "Oh my God, Gareth. You scared me half to death."

My jaw drops in amazement at the sight of her clutching a garment bag to her chest. It's been so long since I've seen her alone. Now, here she stands in my changing room, like I conjured her here myself.

"What are you doing here?" I ask, propping my hands on my hips and fisting the sides of my red jersey. I do a cursory glance around the changing room to confirm the fact that the stars have aligned and I'm alone with Sloan in a room.

Her face blushes crimson as she hangs up the garment bag and adjusts the waistband of her yellow skirt. "I'm dropping off a uniform for Laurent. He has us alter his kits. He likes short shorts. It's very French of him." She nervously looks at the door. "The security guard said the team was at practice and that no one would be in here."

"I got off early." I can't help but look her up and down. She looks like she's lost some weight, but her curves are still present as ever. Her hair looks longer, too. Loose and full down her back. My hand itches to touch it again.

"How nice for you." Her large lips pull back into a forced smile as she begins moving the long way around the room toward the door. She's practically sliding her arse against the perimeter of the lockers to stay as far away from me as possible. "I really should be going…"

"You've been avoiding me," I state, crossing my arms over my chest and holding my ground in front of the door.

"I have not!" she peals as she continues to take baby steps around the room and fidget with her fingers. "I saw you when your brother got married this past summer."

"For a whole two minutes and you were twitching the entire time."

"I wasn't twitching!" she argues, looking defensive. "I was busy. I've been swamped with new clients. Business is really picking up."

"Sloan"—I narrow my eyes at her—"we used to see each other on a very regular basis. What happened to me being your favourite client?"

"You are my favourite client." She laughs nervously and sweeps a lock of chestnut hair out of her face. "Don't be silly."

"Are you divorced?" I ask boldly. If I have her alone, I'm taking full advantage.

She pauses mid-step and answers, "Yes."

My brows lift. "Then why are you behaving this way?"

"I don't know what you're talking about." She makes a move for the door, but I sidestep in front of her, my pecs brushing against her ample chest as I block her path.

The muffled groan she makes has flashes of our night together barrelling into my mind's eye. The spark we had is still very much there, and it's enough to keep me warm for weeks. "Sloan."

"Gareth." She states my name so firmly, my mind instantly transports to the way she was when she was commanding me to strip.

A small smile teases my lips. "Yes?"

Her honey-coloured eyes look up at me with a renewed sense of determination. "Step aside so I can leave."

I tilt my head and shoot her a cheeky grin. "Is that a command?"

Her jaw drops with indignation. "Do you want me to make you freaking kneel?"

I smile at the faint sign of bemusement in her expression. It's so sexy. I don't know why I'm proud of her when she's like this, but I bloody well am. The strength in the depths of her eyes is mesmerising.

"Promises, promises," I murmur, chuckling softly.

The corner of her mouth quirks up, then she frowns, clearly frustrated that she's enjoying herself. "We shouldn't be doing this."

"Doing what?" I ask, reaching out and clasping her elbow in my hand. My fingers brush the soft skin in the crook of her arm, and her eyes dart down to watch the movement. "I miss you, Sloan. We used to be friends."

Her eyes are practically hooded when she licks her lips and replies, "We were never friends."

I smirk. "We were friendly."

She smirks back. "Too friendly I seem to recall."

I lose the humour on my face and pin her with a sincere look. I do miss her. I miss her face and the effect she has on me. She makes me feel lighter, even if she's twitching nervously. "Well, I don't have many friends, but I counted you as one."

My words have her composure dropping. In a bold move, I reach out and tuck an errant strand of hair behind her ear. Her lids flutter closed, those impossibly long lashes fanning her cheeks perfectly as I lean in and murmur into her ear, "It's good to see you again, Treacle."

Her eyes snap open. "That! That is why I've been avoiding you."

"Because of a silly nickname?"

"It's not silly." She looks offended.

"Then what is it?"

Her eyes go starry for a second as she glances down at my lips. "It's...nice. It's nice, and I'm divorced, and I have baggage, and I'm sooo not ready to jump into a relationship."

"Who said anything about a relationship?" I ask, completely serious. I can't remember the last time I had a girlfriend. There were a few women I saw on a regular basis, but no true relationships. No one I'd ever considered bringing home to meet my family. Perish that bloody thought. They'd eat a girl alive.

Sloan's face turns red, and she covers her cheeks with her hands. "I just assumed. God, this is mortifying. See! I'm so horribly out of practice, I just thought—"

"You think too much, Tre," I state, cutting her off before she tumbles into a tangent. She's so flustered and unsure of herself, I want to kneel down and beg her to take control again. I want her to find that power she had with me last year and embrace her inner goddess. The image has my dick stirring in my shorts. But above all, I don't want her to avoid me anymore.

"I really need to be going, Gareth."

Her face looks resigned, so I step back with a lightness to my expression that is a rarity when I'm around anyone else. "Very well. But we really should do this again sometime."

"What?" She barks out a laugh, moving past me and wafting her glorious scent all over me. "I don't even know what we're doing! We're meeting in a locker room. Is that what you're talking about?"

My eyebrows waggle. "It's a fantasy for some."

She punishes my cheekiness by whacking the back of her hand on my chest. Hard. "I'm going back to work before I humiliate myself even further. I'll see you around, Mr. Harris."

I smile and rub the aching spot she left behind. *That's the Treacle I remember.*

Single Mom or Mum?

Sloan

"**M**ummy, I want to play football," Sophia sings, her head peeking out from the top of her purple and teal quilt.

"It's *Mommy*, sweetie. Call me Maaahhhmmmy," I correct, knowing I'm a jerk but hating that she gets more British every day.

"Maaahmmmy, can I play football?" Sophia's brown gaze looks up at me with wide-eyed innocence.

Sighing heavily, I reply, "Do you mean soccer?"

"It's the one where they kick the ball around on the grass and they wear really cool socks."

I groan slightly. "Soph, that's a boy's sport."

"No, it's not! There are girls from my school that play."

Smiling, I slip under the covers on her bed, turning on my side to face her. She turns to face me as well. We're nose-to-nose in her tiny single bed. Brown eyes on brown eyes. Brown hair mixing in with brown hair. My little mini-me. I bring my hand up and brush the tips of her dark lashes. She flutters her eyes closed as I stroke her lids, marvelling at how her lashes are longer than mine, which is saying something because mine have been mistaken as fake. I trace her perfectly imperfect eyebrows in need of a tweeze if they were on anyone other than the cutest little seven-year-old I've ever seen.

Once upon a time, she didn't have eyebrows. She didn't have lashes. She didn't have hair. I run my hand through her long strands, thick and lush. Full of renewed life.

She lived.

My baby lived through something no child should ever have to endure. The Big C is an awful thing to happen to anyone. But when it happens to a six-month-old, it's spirit-crushing. Regardless, this bright, shining star survived and we've been cancer-free for four years. Now I'm laser focused on hitting that magical five-year remission milestone when I'll finally be able to breathe again.

Four years down, one to go.

Thankfully, she rarely speaks of her time in the hospitals anymore. Her thoughts are now in the present and future…of her life here in England.

Hence football.

Hence Mummy.

Hence me having a British daughter and needing to get over it one of these days.

"Please, *Mom*, can I play football?"

I drop a soft kiss on her head. "Soph, let's give it one more year. I've seen a couple soccer games, and they can get pretty physical. I think you're too young to be worrying about sports quite yet anyway."

Her furry little eyebrows pinch together in the most adorably serious way. It takes great effort to bite back my smile.

"I'm not too little. I'm big. There are kids littler than me playing already."

Shaking my head slowly, I reply, "Not this year, sweetie. Maybe next year." *When you've hit the five-year mark.*

She huffs out an angry grunt and rolls away from me, scowling at the wall. I kiss the back of her head and slip out of the bed. Flicking off the overhead light, I whisper, "Good night, Sopapilla."

She sniffs haughtily. "Good night, Mummy Gumdrops," she

mumbles into the pillow.

Maaahhhmmmy, I think to myself and step out of her bedroom to close the door. Exhaling heavily, I make my way downstairs and turn right toward the kitchen, craving a cup of something a hell of a lot stronger than British tea.

"Hiya," Freya chirps from behind the sewing machine she has set up on the long oak table in the dining area that we've repurposed into a sewing room.

"Hey." I lean over the table to glance down into the coffee mug beside her. "Whatcha drinking?"

"Tea," she responds with a smirk. "And by tea I mean chardonnay of the chilled variety." Her round, freckled cheeks pull back into a wide smile. "Want me to get you a cup?"

"Please." I smile graciously and take the seat across from her by my own machine. I glance down at the red Gucci shift dress she's taking in for one of the Man U players' wives and wish I could be working on it instead of her.

Freya makes her way into the galley style kitchen, her round hips swaying as she walks. She's a pleasantly plump redhead with freckles everywhere as far as the eyes can see. We met when I ran an ad online looking to hire a seamstress to work for me as my client base grew beyond my means. My background is in clothing and textile design, so I know my way around a sewing machine, but I couldn't do the alterations and the merchandising. And Freya is a whiz with a seam ripper.

She's been a lifesaver for me the past year as both a friend and a colleague. Her constant good mood and fun zest for life have made my weeks without Sophia a smidge more bearable. Who knows the mess I'd be without her.

Freya places a matching kitten coffee mug of wine in front of me. "Mmm, good tea." I giggle and take a fortifying sip.

Freya sits back down and nods oh-so seriously. "It's herbal."

I shake my head. "The best ones always are."

We both snicker for a moment, but her face drops as she says, "Sunday tomorrow."

I take a deep breath. "Sunday tomorrow."

"Think you might not cry this time?"

I look straight at Freya, praying for strength that I know isn't coming. The mere mention of the day when Sophia happily leaves me to spend seven days with Callum continually brings tears to my eyes. "No," I croak, disgusted with myself.

I often wonder what kind of mother I would have been to a child who didn't have cancer. To a normal, healthy child. Would I care if he or she was gone every other week? Would I mind not knowing what they eat or how they're feeling? If their dad is checking to make sure they don't run a fever? If they're taking their vitamins like they should? Or is it only because Sophia was sick that I lose my mind for the entire week she's away?

"Oh, Sloan," Freya says with a sigh. "The Zumba class I suggested didn't help? Those instructors are so cheerful."

I shake my head. "No, nothing has helped."

Since the divorce, I've tried eleven different kinds of exercise classes to get my mind off the time Sophia is away. I've tried yoga. I've tried meditating. I've tried paint and sip classes, thinking maybe what was missing was alcohol. My doctor even gave me antidepressants, but I couldn't stick with them. They made me feel like a zombie, and I don't want to be one of those medicated divorcées who can't get through a day without popping a pill.

"Blimey, it's been months of this arrangement. I thought it would be easier by now."

"Me too," I murmur, sipping from my mug. The only silver lining is that, despite Callum's poor parenting skills in the past years, Sophia seems to always enjoy her time with him.

"This probably isn't the best time to tell you this, but maybe focusing on work is what you need. There's a new potential client who's requesting a meeting with you on Monday."

My ears perk up because new clients mean big, new commissions. "That's awesome! But why does your face look like that?"

"Well, he called in on a referral from Gareth Harris." She presses her foot on the pedal of her machine, and the noise of the motor prevents me from responding with an excuse that normally falls out of my mouth so easily.

Freya knows I've been avoiding Gareth for many months. Although, last week when I saw him for the first time, it wasn't nearly as awful as I thought it'd be. I worked myself up into such a state after the night we slept together. It was unprofessional, unladylike, dirty, filthy, kinky, and a million different things. I told myself that what happened between us was because he felt sorry for me. I was crying after all.

I expected Gareth to look at me with pity from the weird night we had together. Instead, he stood in that locker room and smiled that cocky smile. Raised those serious brows. He *flirted* with me.

He didn't seem disgusted by me. He certainly didn't look like he was uncomfortable. I'd been avoiding him because I was certain I had to. But after last week, I'm more embarrassed by the avoidance than I am by the actual sex act we performed.

And I'd be lying if I didn't admit to thinking about him more this past week as a result. Replaying some of the scene in my mind. Recalling the feeling of his firm muscles beneath my hands.

Freya finally stops the machine and watches me curiously. I sit up straight and pray that the heat in my cheeks isn't noticeable. "Where does this client live?"

"Astbury."

I roll my eyes. "What are they, neighbours?"

"Next property over," she replies. "But, good Lord, the estates in Astbury are enormous. It's not like he'll see you through the bloody windows," Freya tuts.

She has lost all patience for the bait-and-switch act we've been doing with Gareth. Probably because she has to take all our appointments with him and I won't give her any inkling as to why.

"Are you refusing to go? Is that what you're telling me?"

"I can't do consultations anyway, Sloan!" she replies. "I don't have style, I have skill. You are the lucky lot who has them both."

Piercing her with a determined look, I ask, "What time does the new client want me out there?"

"It's a couple actually," she corrects. "A male and female footy duo."

"They both play?" I ask, surprised because I never work with female athletes. Mostly because they don't make enough to hire me. "How adorable. A married soccer couple."

"They aren't married," Freya corrects. "But I double-checked, and the email says the consultation is for both of them."

"Okay," I acquiesce. "I suppose I should go prep."

"I have a suit you need to drop off to Gareth, too, while you're at it."

My face falls. "No, Freya. No way." There's no way I can go back to his house. I can't drive onto that property and act like nothing happened.

"You're driving all the way out there!" she argues.

"I don't care!"

Her shoulders drop. "Sloan, he is our nicest customer. We kit him out with an entire wardrobe change every season and he needs fitted suits practically every other month. Don't piss off Gareth. If we lose him, we'll have to start styling more of the beetches!"

Despite the argument on the tip of my tongue, I snicker at the way she says bitches. She's referring to the lovely women in Cal's circle who have wealthy husbands, no jobs, and no sense of humour.

She pins me with a serious glower. "You know I hate styling the beetches. They don't appreciate my curves."

"I don't think it's your curves they have a problem with," I interject. "I think it's your constant need to talk about *Heartland*."

"It's a wonderful, heartfelt family drama with horses!" she

bellows, her voice cracking with emotion. "You know this because you and Sophia watch it with me, and now Sophia wants to be a trick pony rider. And screw you. I saw you tearing up when Amy Fleming got married."

"Well"—I raise my chin to argue—"she came down the aisle on a damn horse with her dad and grandfather. It was freaking beautiful."

"You're bloody well right it was!" she booms. "And screw those beetches for not embracing a wholesome Canadian program."

We both burst out laughing before pausing to sip our chardonnays.

"You know you have to do this. I was giving you time because I knew you were going through a lot with the divorce, but other than your every other week of depression, things have been settled around here for a while now." She pauses and gives me a soft smile. "It's time to get on with your life and, at the very least, do your job."

"I know," I groan and stand up from my chair, feeling too nervous to stay sitting at the table with her. It's one thing to run into him without time to think. It's quite another to have hours to obsess over actually seeing him again. "I'll go…prep for Monday I suppose."

"That's the spirit!" She reaches out and grabs my arm as I pass by. "You're still not wanting to tell me in great detail exactly why you've been avoiding Gareth Harris for the past year, right?"

"Right."

"Just checking." She winks.

"Love you," I call over my shoulder.

"Mean it," she finishes.

7

Harris Sunday Dinner

Gareth

"**H**APPY BIRTHDAY TO YOUUUUUU!"

Scowling at Tanner's high-pitched yodeling, I turn and whack him in the stomach to get him to shut up.

"Ouch, ye tit!" he bellows loudly just as everyone in the room stops singing.

"Tit!" peals the newly one-year-old voice with all the enthusiasm of a happy little girl on her birthday.

All heads swerve to our niece, Adrienne—affectionately nicknamed Rocky. She's a blue-eyed, blonde stunner in a fluffy pink dress, perched in her pale pink painted highchair adorned with a rainbow of colourful ribbons. The pink cake in front of her is glowing with a single birthday candle.

"Fuck," Tanner groans, rubbing his stomach where I thumped him.

"Fuck!" Rocky peals again with a giggle and nearly the entire room inhales sharply.

"Tanner!" Vi exclaims, shooting him a murderous look.

His eyes go wide. "It's Gareth's fault. The wanker elbowed me in the guts!"

"Wanker!" Rocky sings.

69

"That's it. I'm moving to a different country," Vi grinds through clenched, smiling teeth as she bends over to speak to Rocky in a sugary sweet voice. "We're going to move far away from your naughty uncles who don't seem to know how to filter themselves in front of their niece. We're going to move to a place where my stupid brothers can't find us, aren't we, my little sweetheart?"

"Stoopid!" Rocky mimics.

I swear I hear Vi begin to weep.

Vi's fiancé, Hayden, shoots us all a scowl.

Tanner shoots him a pouting scowl back. "I'm just as upset as you are. I've been trying to get Rocky to say Unky Tan for months, but she won't do it. Give the princess an expletive and she repeats it like a losing footballer on the pitch!"

I elbow a moping Tanner and give Hayden a subtle nod in apology. We all go back to encouraging Rocky to blow out her candle, and I can't help but roll my eyes at what we must look like from behind. Quite a sight. A bunch of adults huddled around a Gaviscon-coloured highchair in the dining room of our dad's house just east of London.

On the left side of Rocky's highchair are Vi and Hayden—the proud parents celebrating their daughter's first birthday today. Vi's giant mutt of a Saint Bernard, Bruce, is eye level with our beloved Rocky, slobber dripping from his jowls in the hopes of her dropping a tasty morsel.

Then there's Camden and his bride, Indie. They shocked all of us with a secret elopement to Scotland last month. Indie is the new official team doctor for our dad's football club, so their schedules are always conflicting. However, when they discovered that Arsenal and Bethnal's schedules matched up for one rare off weekend, they ended up doing a quick getaway to tie the knot without all the fuss of a formal wedding. Since Camden and Tanner are twins, Tan was a pouting baby about the whole secret wedding none of us were invited to. But I knew it had everything to do with Indie not having any family who would have attended the wedding. Camden would do anything to save her from that pain.

Beside Indie is her best friend, Belle—a foetal surgeon just as brilliant as she is—who is happily married to our idiot of a brother, Tanner, despite the odds. How our twin brothers both found doctors to actually marry them, I'll never quite understand.

On my other side is the youngest of our family, Booker. He has his arms wrapped cosily around his childhood best friend, Poppy. His skilled goalkeeping hands are freely rubbing her small, five-month pregnant belly. They aren't engaged quite yet, but with the way they've been getting on, I'm sure it's only a matter of time.

Dad is standing on the opposite side of Rocky, smiling bigger than I've ever seen him smile in my entire life. Having a grand-daughter has changed him, and I honestly don't know what to think of him these days.

Our family has been changing in general. In a matter of only three years, my sister and three brothers have all done a complete one-eighty. All any of us used to care about were Sunday dinners at Dad's, football schedules, football formations, football scores, and football recruits. Now, it's all about babies, birthdays, engagements, and weddings. I'm the oldest of the lot, yet here I sit, fixating on the same bloody woman from last year who won't even speak to me.

I thought I was nearly over her until I saw her last week. She was flirting with me in the changing room. I know it. All this time, I thought she regretted what happened, but that little spark she had in her eyes the night we fucked was there again. Even as she smacked me at the end, I saw that fire in her eyes.

I crave that sort of fire in my life.

"Gareth!" Hayden's voice cuts into my thoughts. "Do you want vanilla or chocolate?"

Shaking myself out of my deep thoughts, I take the chocolate cake out of his hand and sit down on the stool at the end of the large kitchen counter. Looking down, I break off a bite and attempt to conceal my wandering thoughts before any of my nosey family catches on.

Vi dishes out a piece of vanilla to Booker, who sidles up next to me. "You all right, Gareth?" His dark eyes pin me with worry. "You seem tense."

I shrug my shoulders dismissively. "I'm fine."

"You're not fine," Vi interjects and hands a piece of vanilla to Tanner, who's hoisted himself up on the counter next to Vi. "You're in a mood, and I can't help but wonder if it's because you've missed a lot of Sunday dinners this year."

"It hasn't been by choice," I argue over a forkful. It's fucking delicious. God, I love when Vi bakes. "My schedule has been mad."

Vi eyes me dubiously. "Look around the room, Gareth. You're not the only footballer here with a heavy travel schedule, yet the rest of this lot manage to make it home just fine. We've been doing Sunday dinners at Dad's for years now. It's important. And this year is no different than last year."

Except it is, I think to myself as I glance around at all the happy couples surrounding me.

Tanner takes a bite and nudges Vi's shoulder. "I think it's a girl problem."

Everyone's heads snap to me, but Dad interrupts the moment. "I think our little Rocky Doll needs her nappy changed." He lifts her out of the highchair and strides out of the kitchen with purpose. I have to force myself not to roll my eyes because he rarely changed Booker's nappies after Mum died.

A dark memory hits me like a ton of bricks. Dad is sitting at the dining room table in our house in London, and I am coming into the kitchen to get Mum a drink.

Gareth

8 Years Old

"*What are you doing?*" *Dad snaps at me from his place at the table. He's been sitting there for hours. No book. No telly. No food or drink. Just staring at his fisted hands in front of him.*

My eyes narrow. I look over at Vi, who's struggling to change Booker's nappy on the floor. She shakes her head at me in fear. But I'm not afraid, so I reply, "Mum is thirsty."

I fill a glass and turn to find him standing behind me.

"*I'll take it to her.*" *He reaches out for the glass, his sweaty fingers gripping mine wrapped around the cup.*

"*No!*" *I shout, yanking it back toward my chest.*

"*I said I'll take it to her!*" *he booms and reaches for the glass again. I refuse him again and attempt to push him away just as the glass of water crashes to the floor.*

"*Look what you did!*" *I cry and bend down to pick up the shards before Booker crawls over and cuts himself. I look up at our father, who just stares down at the mess. His face is blank, like a cartoon character without any feelings. He bends down to help, but I shove him back. "Go away. I'm taking the water to Mummy. If you do it, you'll only fight, and she's really bad today!"*

He sucks in a big gulp of air and, without another word, he leaves.

I stand up and look at Vi. "Are you okay?"

She nods, her tiny four-year-old eyes wet with tears.

"*Take Booker upstairs while I clean this up.*"

Vi was only four and struggling to pin down a one-year-old, and I was taking care of our dying mother. Now Dad's changing nappies and hosting Sunday dinners like we've always been one big happy family. Sometimes it's difficult to remember what it was like before Mum died. Other times, it feels like only yesterday.

Vi turns to Tanner. "Why do you say Gareth has a girl problem, Tan?"

"Just a feeling," Tanner answers smugly. I glare at both of them while they discuss me like I'm not right fucking here. "That and I think he was shagging his personal shopper when Belle and I went to Manchester last year to watch Cam and Gareth play each other."

Vi gasps. "What do you mean? You walked in on them?"

"Well, no, not really." He looks crestfallen. "But the two of them strolled out of his house looking like cats that got the cream. Right, Belle?"

Belle laughs awkwardly beside him and murmurs, "I wouldn't say that." Her eyes shoot to Indie from across the room like they're having a secret conversation.

Tanner continues, "And last summer, Gareth was adamant about us getting the suits for my wedding from his shopper girl even though I told him I didn't give a toss what we wore."

"Nice, Tan!" Belle interjects, jabbing him with her elbow.

"Shush. I'm making a point here, wife." Undeterred, Tanner swerves his eyes to me, addressing me straight on now. "I think you were trying to find an excuse to be near her, and you were quite disappointed when she rushed in and out like a shot." Tanner strokes his beard and stares at me with a challenging twinkle in his eyes.

I stare blankly back at him. "I didn't give a toss how long she was there. I just knew that if the suits were left to you alone, we'd all probably show up in Union Jack tuxedos."

Tanner pauses thoughtfully, as if he likes the idea. After a second, he shakes his head with a scoff. "Bollocks, Gareth. I think you like her. I think you maybe even looove her." Belle smacks Tanner upside his ridiculous man-bunned head, and he scowls with indignation.

Vi looks at me with wide, hopeful eyes. "Is there any truth to what he's saying, Gareth? Do you fancy your personal shopper?"

"She's a fashion stylist, and she does a lot bloody more than just fucking shop." I huff out a laugh, completely uncomfortable with their line of questioning and how my entire family seems to be pressing in closer to me for answers.

My head snaps when I feel Camden's hot breath on my neck. "It's been ages since I've seen you with a woman, bro."

I shove him away. "So what? I'm too busy to manage a woman anyway. I have Kid Kickers, team captain responsibilities, all of your bloody dramas that are a bloody full-time job. It's enough. Just because you lot are all off getting married and starting families doesn't mean I have to."

"Of course it doesn't!" Vi responds, resting her hands on her hips in that motherly way she has about her. "But none of that means you can't fancy her. So, do you?"

Shrugging and really hating the fact that it's impossible to keep a secret in this family, I reply woodenly, "I might have…thought something could…happen between us, but it won't. End of." I need to get them off my arse before they fucking show up in Manchester and try to help.

"Not end of," Camden interjects, still standing way too fucking close to me. "When's the last time you talked to her?"

I look up at the ceiling, trying to recall what we said when we parted last week. "It had been months before I ran into her by accident last week."

"Months?" Tanner bellows. "She still shops for you, right?"

"Yes, but she sends her assistant now."

"She's fucking avoiding you!" He hoots with laughter, like her rejection brings him great joy.

"But he's gorgeous," Indie utters, her voice meek amongst the boisterous sounds of the Harris family.

Tanner and Booker burst out laughing as Camden's jaw drops

with horror. He swerves accusing eyes at Indie, who's standing be-hind us, nervously adjusting her cheetah-print glasses. Her eyes go wide as she snaps to attention like she didn't realise she said that out loud. Even Vi and Belle are failing to hide their snickers.

Indie begins jabbering out an excuse. "In that rougher, mascu-line sort of way. I much prefer the pretty boy features of my hus-band, of course." She reaches up to stroke her palm over Camden's coiffed blonde hair, and he swats her wrist away in mock disgust.

"Pretty boy?" His face is deathly serious. "I'll show you fucking pretty." He bends over, throws Indie over his shoulder, and marches toward the back door that leads to the garden. "Specs and I will be back in fifteen to twenty minutes!"

"Way to go, broseph!" Tanner cheers. "You're my fucking hero!"

"Language!" Vi shouts, rubbing her temples in small circles.

Tanner's face turns red. "Rocky's upstairs with Dad!"

"Well, you should be making it a habit!" she snaps back.

"Jesus fucking Christ," I groan and cover my face with my hands. "Our family is beyond dysfunctional. What's worse than dysfunctional?"

"Mmm," Belle says, raising a finger and finishing a bite of cake at the opposite end of the counter. "I think the word you're looking for is psychotic." She licks her lips, her face completely pleasant.

"That's the one," I reply with a finger wag. "You guys are all psychotic."

"Well, we're related, so you're part of this bloody nuthouse." Tanner tosses a peanut into his mouth and strokes his beard with a proud smirk on his face.

"But seriously," Vi states, bringing us back to the task at hand. "That is so weird she hasn't been speaking to you. Why would she do that?"

"She's ghosting him." Poppy sing-songs her statement from her seat next to Booker at the counter. All heads turn toward her. She looks surprised to have all of our attention.

"What the fuck is ghosting?" I ask, only mildly curious.

"Erm," she starts, nervously toying with her short blonde hair. "It's when someone stops all communication with a person in hopes that person will get the hint and give up."

"We're Harrises!" Tanners barks, straightening his posture. "We don't get ghosted because we don't give up. Right, Gareth?"

I roll my eyes. "I guess after a while I pretty much did give up."

"So you ghosted her," Poppy adds knowingly.

Shoving my cake plate away, I reply, "I tried to talk to her at first, but she wanted nothing to do with me. I just…Fuck me, I don't know. I just didn't do anything more."

"But you guys had a connection?" she asks.

I nod reluctantly. God, this is bizarre. It's usually me giving advice to everyone else. I hate being the focus, but I'm mortifyingly curious about Poppy's thoughts.

"It sounds more like jitter ghosting to me then."

I inwardly deflate. I'm almost scared to ask. "What the hell is jitter ghosting?"

Poppy leans forward, her green eyes alight with excitement. "It's when you feel strongly for the other person, but you're paralysed with the fear of rejection, so you say nothing at all. It usually applies to people who are too much of a coward to say what they're really thinking." Her eyes glance around the room nervously as we all stare, hanging on her every word. "At least that's what I hear the kids say at school."

"Bloody hell, my baby mama is brilliant!" Booker states, planting a sloppy kiss on Poppy's cheek. Then he leans in and whispers, "Sunshine, did I jitter ghost you?"

"A bit," she replies with a tiny shrug, then places her hands on her stomach. "But it's all right now, Lamb Chop. We're all the better for it."

Their disgusting pet names for each other are enough to divert all of our attention away. In the background, I hear Tanner concocting a game plan for me to see Sloan. I think I even hear him mention a Harris Shakedown, but my mind is elsewhere.

When I saw Sloan last week, she was worried about a commitment, which wasn't close to where my mind was going. I don't have time for a girlfriend. I'm far too busy with the team and my family drama that's an everyday occurrence. I also have no interest in sharing my deepest, darkest secrets with someone. In fact, the latter usually has women storming away from me in a huff.

But my reaction after we fucked was extremely traditional. Flowers, texts, phone calls. That's a lot to blast at a newly divorced woman. She'd just gotten out of a bad marriage. The last thing she needed was traditional bullshit. What was I thinking?

Perhaps if I approach her with something decidedly untraditional, she'll be more keen to agree. And the thought of untraditional and Sloan sounds better than Vi's delicious cake.

Friends With Benefits

Sloan

IT'S AN UNSEASONABLY WARM NOVEMBER DAY AS I DRIVE OUT TO Astbury with my windows down to visit Hobart Walter—a German midfielder for Man U—and his girlfriend, Brandi Smith—a striker for Manchester City. Two rival teams and two rival sexes.

I take in a big breath of fresh country air hoping it will calm my nerves as I drive down the gravel road that passes by the entrance to Gareth's property. I gaze wistfully down the lane and wonder if he's home. Then I shake my head with annoyance. I need to be focused today. I needed to be focused this past year. That is why I couldn't just waltz back into Gareth's home after what happened. That's why I never took his calls. I was busy having a midlife crisis at barely thirty years old. I had to prepare for life as a single mother. Real world problems to deal with. I didn't have time to obsess over the one-night stand I had with a client the night I found out my husband was leaving me.

Good God, I'm pathetic.

The Walter Estate has a similar security gate as Gareth's. After being admitted, I pull up to an old home that reminds me of the one I lived in with Callum. Steeling myself to be professional, I grab my satchel that contains my portfolio and some magazines and stride up the gravel lane to the front door.

A tall, lean man with a thick European accent steps out of the giant double doors and strides toward me just as I reach the top step. "Ah, Ms. Montgomery! Thanks for coming all the way out here!" He extends a hand out to me and I take it, widening my stance as he nearly shakes my arm out of its socket. "The name's Hobart. Call me Hobo. Everyone else does."

Smiling politely, I reply, "Nice to meet you, Hobo. Can I ask why they call you that?"

He ruffles a hand through his mop of curly brown hair. "Well, my footy career has been a bit of a mess. I've had more transfers than Joey Barton, not for the same reasons, mind you. I've just lived a bit of a gypsy life in football. People took to calling me Hobo because it seemed I was destined to be homeless for a while there. But Man U has managed to keep me a whole year, so here's hoping!"

I laugh politely at the sheepish look on his face. "Well, I'm happy you're a bit more settled now. And please, call me Sloan."

"Will do," he says with a genuine grin. "It's so nice to meet you. Gareth speaks very highly of you."

Goosebumps spread over my body at the mention of Gareth's name. The fact that Gareth has spoken highly of me, even after I blew him off like I did, invokes a nearly toe-curling sensation all over me.

Hobo doesn't seem to notice my reaction as he leans in and whispers, "I wanted to quietly mention that the little woman isn't happy about this meeting, so can we discuss fees later?"

My quizzical brow is torn from him as a tall blonde steps up behind him and leans against the doorframe with a hand propped on her hip. I can't help but ogle a bit as she stands there in all her powerful and intimidating glory. She's dressed in a pair of shimmering black soccer shorts and a black sports bra with a white Nike swoosh across the chest. Her shoulders rise and fall quickly, indicating she just completed a rigorous workout. I can't help but turn green with envy over the outlining of a perfect six-pack that becomes visible every time she exhales.

"This is my lady, Brandi Smith." Hobo introduces us. "Brandi, this is Sloan Montgomery."

"You don't need to be here," she bites in a crisp Welsh accent while shaking my hand. "Hobo thinks this is a good idea, but I think it's ridiculous."

"Schatz," Hobo says in a warning tone. "It's not ridiculous. This is how you play the game."

"I do play the game." She turns her icy blue eyes on him. "It's called football."

He scoffs with annoyance. "My Schatz is maddening."

"It's not my fault that you earn more in one week than I do in an entire year." She turns away from Hobo, crossing her arms over her chest to brood in silence.

Exhaling heavily, Hobo looks back at me. "I've asked you out here because, in order to get endorsements, you have to play the part. You have to show sponsors that you have the look. I'm attending an upcoming awards gala where there will be lots of press, a red carpet, the works. This stunner will be on my arm, and she needs to look phenomenal. She is sexy and strong. There's no reason she shouldn't be on billboards all over the world."

She rolls her eyes, but I see a tender look exchanged between the two of them that makes it obvious this is about a lot more than landing an endorsement deal.

"He's kind of right," I add, turning their attention back to me. "I've styled a lot of athletes, and it didn't take me long to learn that the game is just one part of your job."

Hobo smiles triumphantly. "Super. Where do we begin?"

After about an hour and a half of looking through Brandi and Hobo's clothes and showing them some catalogues, I get a sense of a lot more than their style. Style-wise, Hobo tends to gravitate toward mismatched eccentric fashion. Very European. Brandi likes comfort and athletic lines. A racerback gown that displays her legs is an obvious choice because, holy shit, her muscular thighs could probably crack a walnut between them.

Their relationship, on the other hand, is pretty much adorable. Hobo is the funny one. Brandi is the one who rolls her eyes and elbows him in the ribs. They play off each other. One only amusing when the other is annoyed. It's delightful. And when he told me that his sweetheart word for her—Schatz—literally means "treasure," I may have swooned a bit. Until of course it made me think of what Gareth called me the night we were together.

Treacle, meaning "sweet."

Remembering that brings a small smile to my face, and it's not only the compliment behind the word. It's the affectionate way he said it. Even in the locker room, when he uttered that term of endearment from his deep, husky voice, my toes curled inside my boots.

My palms are sweaty from my errant thoughts as we make our way downstairs. I think the world is playing a hilarious joke on me when at the foot of the stairs, I see none other than the man who's consuming my thoughts.

Gareth.

And not just any Gareth.

A shirtless Gareth.

A shirtless, sweaty Gareth.

The plastic of his water bottle cracks noisily as he guzzles the remaining drops and crushes it in his meaty paw.

"Hullo, neighbour!" Hobo booms, hopping off the railing he just slid down and smacking Gareth on the shoulder.

"Hiya, Hobo. Brandi." Gareth's deep voice reverberates in the entryway and makes a lot more than my ears vibrate. He slides his eyes to me and gives me a simple raise of his brows. "Sloan."

Good God. I have to inhale deeply to keep myself from falling down the steps because of the way his gaze drops down my body. I'm dressed in a crew knit sweater dress. It's a modest cut but form-fitted. From the looks of it, Gareth likes what he sees.

"Hey, um, Gareth," I croak like a moron as he dabs the sweat on his brow with his balled-up white T-shirt. Kind of gross. Kind of hot. Argh! Did he really need to run shirtless in November? It's freaking England for crying out loud.

"We just finished," Brandi states, hopping down the final step and accepting a friendly kiss on the cheek from Gareth. "I see you helped yourself to a water."

He shrugs. "The back door was open."

Moving toward me, he leans in to brush his lips against my cheek. It's a seemingly platonic gesture, but like an idiot, I turn my head the wrong way at the last second and we nearly smack noses. The act has me stumbling in my heels, so my hands fly out to catch myself on his chest.

His naked chest.

His naked, sweaty chest.

I force an apologetic smile I don't altogether feel. Gareth and I don't kiss hello. We've never kissed hello. We didn't even kiss the night we had sex! He's being what the British call *cheeky*, and I'm the one who's looking like a fool because of it.

Thankfully, the three of them begin talking soccer, so I can concentrate on breathing normally. This is why I've been avoiding Gareth. Because sex changes things. Because now I can't look at him like a normal guy. Now he looks...different.

I steal another glance at him, trying to figure out what it is about him that's so sexy. Other than the whole chiselled abs thing because, seriously, how are those even real?

He's not classically handsome by any means. He's not even

adorable like Hobo. And he's definitely the complete opposite of Callum's privileged prep school boy appearance. Looking at Gareth's features individually, he's extremely flawed. He has a bump on the ridge of his nose; his teeth are slightly imperfect; and the scruff on his jaw is a patchy mess. Honestly, he's what I'd call rogue.

But then there's the dark smattering of hair on his chest. And the deep lines of his hips that disappear into his joggers. And the way he carries himself is something I can't help but notice. It's confident without being cocky. Couple that with his thick dark hair and he's like a delicious, tall, dark, and handsome bad boy dessert that's the perfect blend of crunchy and creamy. A real-life glistening gladiator.

"So, has Sloan helped you guys out?" he asks, directing his smouldering hazel eyes at me.

"Definitely!" Hobo replies jovially.

"She has some cool ideas," Brandi states a bit more muted.

"That she does," Gareth concedes and smiles knowingly at me. *Have his lashes always been that long?*

"I have a suit for you," I bark out, suddenly desperate to give it to him now and not have to go back to his house. The sparks. The tension. The attraction. It's all still there, and if we go back to his house and he smiles at me like that with those naughty eyes, I know what will happen.

"Brilliant," he replies and begins moving down the hall toward the back of the house. "Bring it by when you're done here."

"You can just take it now," I say to his retreating frame. "It's just in my car…Where are you going?"

"I'm on a run." He hooks his thumb toward the sliding glass door. "Hobo and I have a hiking trail between our properties."

"It's nicer than jogging out on the roads where the nosey buggers all try to take pictures," Hobo adds. "Although, they don't give a shit about me. It's Mr. Award Winner that they care about these days."

"Award winner?" I ask, swerving curious eyes at Gareth.

He pauses in the hallway and grips his neck with a sheepish grimace. "It's nothing. I'll see you soon, Sloan."

Anxiety squeezes my insides. He looks way too good for me to be alone with. "Maybe I can just leave the suit here and you can pick it up later?"

"I guarantee I'll beat you home and have time for a shower." He winks and takes off like a shot out the back door.

My gaze stares wistfully at his back muscles, sliding and shifting beneath his skin as he hustles down the deck staircase and runs toward the rolling hills.

Why did he have to mention a shower? What am I supposed to do with that information? Was that an invitation or something? Oh my God, I'm so out of practice.

And so screwed.

A throat clearing beside me has my head snapping back to Hobo and Brandi. "So, do you have any other questions?"

It's about thirty minutes later when I pull onto Gareth's property. I may have parked on the gravel road and done some deep breathing exercises I learned in yoga. Not that it helped. Regardless, my palms needed time to dry off before I could grip the wheel safely.

It's been a while since I've been back to Gareth's home, and I can't help but gawk longingly at it as I drive down the gravel lane. I've always marvelled over how modern it is. Most homes around here are old period estates like Hobo's or Callum's.

Gareth's estate is a beautiful piece of art. Clearly some architect's passion project nestled perfectly in the lush, green countryside. A perfect snow globe in the oasis of nature. The inside is as stunning as the outside. It's richly styled with lots of comfortable furniture.

Fun, funky accent pieces. And just enough unique tchotchkes to make it feel like it's not simply ripped out of a catalogue.

I asked Gareth once if he built it himself and remember feeling a smidge disappointed when he said he didn't. But he said as soon as he laid eyes on the property, he had to have it. He said it was important for his home to be completely different from where he grew up.

I wanted to ask what he meant by that, but I didn't get the impression he wanted to share. I'm always acutely aware of when to push for more information and when to stop asking. My mom used to joke that I was an empath because I can sense a person's mood and adapt myself until they feel comfortable. It's not a skill I've ever honed. It's just what comes naturally. I enjoy keeping the peace. Peace is good. Peace is calm. Everyone loves peace. Myself included.

It also means that I tend to avoid conflict, which is why it seemed easier to avoid Gareth for so long. But with how our last couple of interactions have been, I'm hopeful we can resume the peaceful existence we once had.

Gareth is standing on the front step of his house, waiting for me as I park. He's dressed in a dark green sweater, his strong hands jammed into the pockets of his faded jeans. His scuffed leather Oxfords tie in perfectly. I bought everything on his body right now, and something about that makes my chest purr with pride.

That and I love Gareth's style.

Yes, I realise I'm the one who selects all his clothes. But I have meetings with all of my clients to figure out their style before I purchase a single item for them. Gareth gravitates toward classic, masculine, and understated luxury. You wouldn't know he's wearing thousand dollar shoes unless you knew high-end clothing. There's a beauty to that because he can go for a walk in a park or sit down in his agent's office and always fit right in.

Callum only wore a few of the things I purchased for him. He always mixed and matched my things with his own selections. It annoyed me because he liked to think his style was superior to mine.

The first night we met, he smirked down his nose at my Target dress.

When we moved to Manchester, he started asking me why I couldn't dress like so-and-so's wife. If it wasn't for Sophia, I wouldn't have lasted a month with him.

"You came." Gareth's deep voice vibrates in a place between my thighs as I nearly trip while climbing the stairs toward him.

"You pretty much forced me," I reply, tossing his suit over my shoulder and trying to stop the blush that rushes through me as our eyes connect.

"Hardly," he replies with an unamused look. "You look well, Sloan."

"Um, thanks." I tug at my sleeve, wondering why this feels like a freaking date all the sudden. "Here's your suit."

I hold it out to him. His eyes narrow conspiratorially for a brief moment before he smiles. "Why don't you come in?"

I look up at the sky and pray for strength. "I really don't think that's a good idea, Gareth."

He chuckles half-heartedly. "Why? Do you think something's going to happen? You can't trust yourself around me? Is that it?"

The challenging twinkle in his eyes has me squinting my gaze at him. "I can trust myself just fine." *It's my libido I'm not so sure about.*

"Come on, Sloan. I've missed you," he goads, reaching out and taking the garment bag from my hand. "Get your arse in here and let's catch up."

Exhaling heavily, I follow him through the foyer. My eyes immediately land on the large staircase that leads up to his room. Flashes of that night pummel me like a ton of bricks.

"Can I get you something to drink?" he asks, snapping my attention to him standing beside me. "Water? Coffee? I don't have any alcohol here."

Frowning, I reply, "I'm working anyway." Even though a stiff drink might help make this interaction a smidge more bearable.

"Right." He grips the back of his neck and looks over his

shoulder. Gesturing to the long, dark wood dining table located under a modern Edison bulb fixture, he says, "Let's sit."

He pulls out a tufted seat at the head of the table for me to slide into. Then he takes the spot adjacent to me.

"So, how are things?" I ask, desperate to fill the heavy silence. "How are you liking your clothes this season? Any texture issues? I know you hated that one Burberry cashmere sweater I thought might work for you—"

"Sloan"—Gareth's voice stops me mid-thought—"I didn't invite you in to talk about clothes."

My eyes drop to the table. "I knew this was a mistake," I murmur.

"You knew what was a mistake?" His voice is so smooth, I have to take a deep breath to keep myself sane.

"Me coming out here," I reply, pinching the bridge of my nose. "I shouldn't be here."

Gareth shifts to the edge of his seat, his masculine scent hitting me like a wrecking ball as images of him naked fight their way to the front of my mind. "Sloan, you can't just act like that night between us didn't happen."

"I most certainly can!" I argue, sitting back in my seat and feeling a nervous flush wash over me. I've been trying so hard not to ruminate over the memories of that night. With some success, I might add. "What happened between us was so long ago, Gareth. Honestly, why are you still thinking about it?" Surely he's had at least a dozen other women since then.

"Because I can't *stop* thinking about it." His eyes are dead serious. They strike right through me, saying words I never could have imagined him saying. "I'm not a bullshitter, Sloan. I don't play games. I don't chase women. But if I go a year and still can't stop thinking about a person, I'm bloody well going to do something about it."

"Like force your friends into a consult," I retort, wondering if poor Hobo and Brandi even wanted a consult with me.

"I didn't force anybody," he replies. "Hobo asked me for advice about Brandi, and I know you have connections in the industry. You seemed like the natural place to start."

Silence casts over us, so I begin picking at the cuticle on my nail to avoid Gareth's gaze. That furrowed browline of his is going to be the death of me. "I don't know what to say."

"Are you saying you never think about that night we had together?" His voice is like warm honey dripping into my mouth.

My shoulders lift. "Of course I think about it," I snap.

He exhales through his nose. "And are they positive thoughts?"

I look up and he's concealing a smile that makes the creases around his eyes look divine. "No…Sometimes…Maybe."

He shakes his head, clearly annoyed. "Well, I've never felt anything like that in my entire life."

I touch my lips to ensure the words didn't come from my own mouth because he's voicing my thoughts exactly. But it doesn't change the fact that what we did was wrong. He is a client!

The humour in his expression dies when he asks the next question. "Look, have you been trying to ghost me? Are you trying to cut me out of your life so I leave you alone?"

"No," I reply, anxiety pricking all five of my senses. "Gareth, I want to keep working with you."

"You just don't want to fuck me again."

My nerves boil over. My eyes cast downward as I suck in a large breath of air. That word out of his mouth is like an instant zap inside my panties. The way his teeth grab hold of his lower lip to utter the sound of the letter *F* is spine-tingling. I know he said all sorts of naughty things that night we had together, but it's been so long now, and I was in an alternate universe then. I've compartmentalised that night into a dream. A fantasy. This is reality, yet all I want to do is ask him to say that word over, and over, and over.

"Don't say that word again, please," I groan, running my hands through my hair and pressing my thighs together as I try to ignore the fact that his lower lip is slightly thicker than his upper lip.

"What word?" he asks, seemingly sincere.

"The…naughty word."

Careful, Sloan, your mom jeans are showing.

"Naughty word?" This makes him chuckle.

How can he be laughing right now? My body is racked with tortured awareness of how close we are sitting beside each other. His knee has brushed against mine under the table three times in the past five minutes, and all I can think about is how badly I want it to happen again. I cover my face with my hands to avoid looking at him.

He leans in and whispers, "You mean the word fuck?" The soft click of the *K* causes me to peek through the crack between my fingers. His eyes are intense on me as he adds, "Sloan, all I've been thinking about for months is how badly I want to fuck you again." His lips dampen as he slides his tongue across them. "Fucking you was the highlight of my year, Treacle."

"Gareth!" I groan his name in frustration, dropping my hands and jerking back from his honest words. "This is so insane…and inappropriate!" And wonderful, and sexy, and frustrating.

"Why?" he asks, looking incredulous. "Because you don't like it? Or because you're not over your ex?"

"I'm definitely not thinking about my ex," I reply with an immature eye-roll and fight off the shuddering thought of still being tied to Cal.

"If it's because I'm your client, I don't give a toss. It's clothes, Sloan. What we have is far more important than fashion."

"It's not about the clothes," I defend.

He narrows his eyes. "Do you regret that night we shared?"

"No," I answer reflexively, then want to cover my mouth with mortification.

"Then what's the problem?"

"I don't know!" I reply quickly, knowing I can't tell him the truth. That I avoided all his attempts at contact because I was in the throes of a custody battle for my daughter whom he doesn't know exists.

"You're giving me a mess of mixed signals." He slices his hands through his dark hair, mussing it up so beautifully, I itch to touch it. "You're saying you don't regret it, but you're over there twitching. What's going on in that head of yours?"

"I'm freaking mortified!" I bellow.

His face falls. "Whatever for?"

I blink rapidly. "What for? You want the list?"

"Top five at least," he volleys back.

"Well, I'm ashamed of how I treated you," I answer honestly. If he wants to hear the list, I'll give it to him. "I yelled at you, and clawed you, and threatened you."

"So, does that mean you didn't like it?" he asks.

"No, I loved it! I loved it so much I'm humiliated." God, what's wrong with me that I liked making him kneel in front of me? I know this lifestyle exists, but I'm a mother and business owner. I'm a people pleaser! This isn't me.

"If you loved it, what is there to be ashamed of? I wanted you to do it. I…loved it, too." He hesitates when he says the last part, seemingly a bit uneasy as well. He's been so calm and collected thus far. Seeing him falter is comforting on some weird level. "Look, Sloan. We are two consenting adults. What's the harm in any of this?"

"I don't understand why you liked it." I look at him in question, wanting to know why a strong, sexy, hugely famous athlete would let a woman take control over him.

Having the attention turned on him brings him pause. He shifts uncomfortably before steeling himself to reply, "I maintain control in so many aspects of my life. I liked giving it up to you."

I nearly snort. "Do you do this with all your women?"

"Women?" he repeats, rubbing the back of his neck in irritation.

"You say it like there are loads. First of all, there aren't. Second of all, I've never done anything like that with any other woman. Only you."

Only you.

I repeat his words in my head and they feel good. Comforting. A small smile pulls at the corners of my mouth. I can't help it. There's something incredibly empowering about this information. *Only me.*

Gareth is smirking now. He's smirking, and he's so dang handsome it's difficult to focus. "Did you like being in control?" he asks, his body language coaxing me to open up.

I nod woodenly. Nervously. Cautiously.

"Then why don't we do it again?"

"Right now?" I bark, horribly unladylike.

The low chuckle that vibrates in his chest is thigh-clenching. "Not necessarily. I just mean, perhaps we can make this a thing between us."

"I have so much going on, Gareth. I seriously don't think I'm ready for this."

"Ready for what?" he asks.

"A relationship with Manchester's most popular soccer player for starters!" I run my hands through my hair, trying hard to stop the trembling that's happening in my body.

"Footballer," he murmurs under his breath and leans across the table to clasp my hands. "And I already told you last week, I'm not suggesting a relationship, Sloan."

My spine straightens. "What exactly are you asking for then?"

"You just got out of a crap marriage. I'm not interested in being committed." His hands freeze on mine as he looks down at our embrace and searches for the right word. "So let's just call this *freedom.*"

He rolls my hand in his and runs his finger down a line on my palm. My skin is so pale and soft against his battered, weathered grip, but his touch is warm and comforting. And it's doing things to me. Naughty things and enticing things.

I release a shaky breath and whisper, "What kind of freedom?"

He half smiles at me, a look of hope brightening his dark eyes. "The kind where we both get to explore these newfound feelings... together."

"What kind of feelings are you referring to exactly?" I ask, my pulse thumping so hard he can probably feel it in my finger.

"The kind where you have all the control like you did with me that night...over...and over...and over." He pulls one of my hands to his mouth and presses his thick, pouty lips to the tip of my index finger.

My voice quakes. "That was a crazy night."

"A crazy night I want to repeat with you." The sincerity in his gaze is pure. "Can you see yourself doing that on a regular basis?"

"That's really what you want?"

"Very much," he husks, a vulnerability clouding his eyes and drawing me in like a moth to a flame.

"So this would just be a casual, friends with benefits thing?" I ask, wanting to ensure I have all the facts.

"Friendly friends," he replies. "Nothing more. Nothing less."

I clear my throat. My tight, constricted, reactive throat. "But you'd still be my client?"

"Of course," he replies flippantly. "None of that will change."

I swallow slowly. "But I have responsibilities, Gareth. Things I can't be away from."

"So do I," he argues. "It's football season. I'm busy with training, matches, media. You know my schedule is mental. I'm not asking for seven days a week, Sloan."

"What are you asking for exactly?"

He shrugs. "Whenever we're both free." He makes it sound so simple.

It's not simple for me, though. I'm a mother. I have a child. A child whom I only get to see every other week.

It's then that the most obvious realisation strikes me. Why didn't I think of that before? Gareth can brighten my weeks of darkness.

My days when all I do is obsess over Sophia and what Cal is or isn't doing with her. Instead of slipping into a state of depression, I can spend some of my free time with Gareth. It's like Zumba, but I get to make up all the moves!

My face heats from the notion that I may be saying yes to this craziness. "Where would we do this…freedom?"

His eyes narrow as he retreats into thought. "I train in Carrington Tuesday through Friday, so I could come to your place after—"

"No!" I nearly scream, picturing Freya on the couch squealing over *Heartland* while Gareth asks me to spank him. *Oh my God, would he let me spank him?*

"My place then?" he asks, eyeing me speculatively. "I just assumed since I live an hour from Manchester, you'd prefer something more central."

"Your place is perfect." I force a smile and glance around his home, curious about all the rooms I haven't seen yet. It's far from Manchester. It's far from reality. It's ideal. "But we're going to need rules or something," I rush out. "I need to know what kind of expectations you have. How far we'll go." My face heats from the naughty thoughts making their way out of the dark crevices of my mind. I'm picturing dungeons, and sex hotels, and weird clubs. I'm certainly not equipped for that kind of lifestyle.

"You don't think we can just figure it out as we go?" he asks with a pleasant smile. "I don't really have any expectations here, Sloan."

"Okay, but I'd like to do some research. I'm not very experienced, Gareth. I mean, for God's sake, I haven't even kissed a man in…" I pause, cringing over the fact that I can't remember the last time Cal kissed me. "A long, long time."

"You don't need to do research to remember how to kiss, Sloan." He leans across the table and hits me with all his rugged scent and charm. "I can refresh your memory right now."

I lick my lips and stare down at his perfect pout of a mouth.

God, it would be incredible to kiss him. To seize his lips with mine and know exactly what he tastes like.

The thought makes my blood run cold. This isn't about a connection. This is about sex. I missed out on casual sex in my twenties by getting married and having a baby. This is my chance to make up for it. I don't want to screw it all up by getting feelings involved.

The idea of kissing Gareth feels very personal. Very real. Very relationship-like. I don't need a relationship. All I need is a distraction to survive my weeks without Sophia.

"No kissing," I blurt out. It worked the first time we hooked up. Surely it will work again.

His eyes narrow. "None?"

"Not on the mouth." I blush.

"Why?" He looks agitated.

"Because it's too intimate," I explain, knowing the complications that kissing would cause. "I have a million other things on my mind, so I can't have feelings getting in the way."

He looks back and forth between my eyes like he's searching for something, then shakes his head and sits back in his chair. "You know what? That's fine. I want you to make all the decisions, so whatever you say is fine with me."

This makes me smile. "Then it's settled."

"It's settled."

After a significant pause, I stand to leave and Gareth follows me to the door. He nearly leans in to kiss my cheek goodbye, but thinks better of it and pulls back. "Can I kiss your cheek?"

Rolling my eyes, I reply, "Are we starting this now?"

He braces his hand on the doorframe, propping himself like a fucking model doing a cover shoot. "I don't see why not."

I straighten my spine and give him a simple nod. "Yes, you can kiss my cheek."

He leans in and his chuckling breath is warm on my skin. His lips brush against my jaw and linger for a beat as he inhales the area behind my ear. "The ball is in your court now, Treacle."

I take a moment to marvel over that fact.

Control.

Complete and utter control.

It feels pretty damn good for a change.

Text Contract

Gareth

AT TEN O'CLOCK, MY PHONE VIBRATES ON MY NIGHTSTAND, indicating a text message has come in. I mute the television and reach over, swiping my thumb across the screen. I can't hide my smirk when I see Sloan's name.

Sloan: Are you expecting me to be a dominatrix?

Gareth: No.

Sloan: Because I don't want to be like that.

Gareth: Have you been researching online?

Sloan: Yes, and I'm not cut out for this. I just got done watching some really disturbing porn, and I've come to the conclusion that you should find someone else.

Gareth: I don't want anyone else and I don't want what you're watching. I just want you.

Sloan: …

Sloan: …

Sloan: So you don't have expectations of me being one of those women in a corset with a bullwhip, wrapping your dick in a leather chastity belt?

Gareth: I'd prefer not.

Gareth: I just want you to be free. You're trying to label what

we're doing, and that's not what this is about.

Sloan: Well, I'm trying to figure out what you want.

Gareth: I want what you want.

Sloan: I DON'T KNOW WHAT I WANT.

Gareth: Yes, you do. Think back to that night we were together. What did you like about it?

Sloan: …

Sloan: …

Sloan: I liked seeing you touch yourself.

Gareth: I liked having you watch me touch myself.

Sloan: Why?

Gareth: Because I liked pleasing you. Pleasing you pleased me. It's a full circle act, you see. Did you like having the control?

Sloan: Yes.

Gareth: Why?

Sloan: Because I've never had control before. It made me feel strong. I don't feel strong often.

Gareth: See? You're getting this.

Sloan: Why did you like it?

Gareth: …

Gareth: …

Gareth: Because it allowed me to not be the person everyone depends on. It let me forget all the rubbish in my head and just feel. So much of my life has been tied to my past and my future. Having you in charge helped me stay in the present.

Sloan: What happened in your past?

Gareth: See, that's a question someone would ask if they were in a relationship.

Sloan: OMG, you're right! Don't tell me!

Gareth: Don't worry. I won't.

Sloan: So you really have no expectations?

Gareth: None, except that I want you.

Sloan: …

Sloan: …

Sloan: Gareth, why do you want me?

Gareth: …

Gareth: …

Gareth: I want the side of you that you don't show to anyone else. You've shown it to me once and I can't get it out of my head.

Sloan: …

Sloan: …

Sloan: If I agree to this, no one can know.

Gareth: Okay…

Sloan: I mean it. I don't want to end up in the papers or have people know that I'm sleeping with a client. I have a reputation to uphold. Can I trust you to keep our relationship completely private?

Gareth: Sloan, you know me. Don't lump me in with all the other footballers you work with. Trust me when I tell you that what happens between you and me stays between you and me.

Sloan: Will you be home at 5:00 tomorrow?

Gareth: Absolutely.

Sloan: Okay, I'll see you then.

Gareth: I look forward to it.

I set my phone back on my nightstand and flick the TV off, far more interested in thoughts about Sloan than football recaps. I lie back, hands behind my head, staring at the ceiling and realising that she is the first woman I've been excited to spend time with in years. And that's a crazy thought.

It's not that I have a problem feeling attracted to women. The truth is, I think the female body is a stunning fucking sight, and I could get hard just thinking about Sloan naked beneath me. But the pressure to connect with women on a personal level has never been something that I've wanted. I've always envisioned myself as the terminal bachelor, fulfilled by my siblings and their families more than ever wanting something of my own. I don't see myself having kids. Someone who looks to me every day for comfort, for help, for guidance…That's a lot of bloody pressure.

The second someone begins sharing personal shit with me is the second they realise how much I'm constantly holding back. Hell, I barely talk to my siblings about personal shit. I help them with their problems, but I don't need their help with mine.

So I'm grateful that I've found someone whom I can consider a friend and dive into this arrangement with clear boundaries and expectations. There's something about Sloan that makes me certain she won't fall for me. She has a wall around her heart, and that's something that will work very well in our situation.

Feelings can't be part of this arrangement.

Sloan on my doorstep in a beige trench coat evokes fantasies beyond my wildest dreams. Her sheepish smile desperately makes me want to kiss her, but I know that is an important limit for her, so I will respect it. The fact that she's here at all is a victory in and of itself.

"So I have an idea," she says, entering my home and dropping her small bag on the floor in the foyer. She bends over to rummage inside of it, then stands with a small fabric tape measure in her hand. "I'm going to fit you for a suit."

"You're going to what?"

"But first, do you mind that I brought some wine?" she asks, her eyes wild and her tone slightly out of breath as she stuffs the tape measure in her pocket.

"Erm, no. I won't have any, but I don't care if you do," I reply regretfully. I should have been prepared for this and bought some for her.

"Good," she replies and bends over again to dig in her bag. She holds a bottle of white out for me to take.

"What else have you got in that bag?" My eyes are wide and wondering.

"Never mind that," she states firmly. "Open this for me."

I pull my lips into my mouth to suppress my grin at her bossy tone. "Yes, madam."

"Oh my God, don't call me madam," she balks, following me into the kitchen just past the formal dining room where we decided to embark on this crazy new sexual arrangement.

"Well, what should I call you?" I ask, glancing over my shoulder and eyeing her stiletto heels appreciatively. God, I want to know what she's wearing under that coat so badly, I'm not sure I can focus on adult conversation.

"I like Treacle." Her voice is soft and contemplative as I set the bottle on the large island counter.

I make quick work of opening the wine and grab a stemless wineglass out of the cupboard. "Treacle it is." I smile as I pour some of the golden liquid into the glass and hand it over to her. Our fingers brush when she takes it from me, and her sharp intake of breath doesn't go unnoticed. She's extra sensitive tonight. This should be fun.

"So this concept of ours is simple," she states, drinking her wine and staring off into the distance as she speaks. "I tell you what to do and you do as you're told."

"Sounds about right." I hold back an amused chuckle.

"This isn't true BDSM. This is just…escapism. Or what you called it. Freedom."

"Absolutely."

"That means every time I come out here to visit, we will be liberated from our real lives. We will leave our personal lives at the door and only focus on the sex."

"Sounds good to me," I reply, my eyes falling down to her pointy black stiletto pumps. What if she's naked under there? Fuck me, it is going to be really hard to give her all the power.

"And I'm in charge." Sloan's words sound like they are trying to convince herself more than me.

"That's exactly what I want," I reply, eyeing her speculatively. "Is that still what you want? You seem nervous."

"Yes!" she exclaims, her eyes wide and urgent. "I mean, it's what I want. I got myself all pumped up on the drive out here. This is going to be fun, like role-playing. But instead of being a character, I'm the director!"

I chuckle at her enthusiasm. Seeing the spark in her eyes is reward enough for giving in to her desires and making mine completely secondary. This is a total transformation from the woman I've grown to know the past few years. She's embracing something for herself for once and the anticipation of seeing her really sink into it might just kill me.

"Let's get on with it then, turncoat."

She frowns at my comment. "Did you just make a joke?"

I frown back. "I make jokes."

"When do you make jokes?"

"Okay, I'm not a standup comedian, but I'm not Mr. Serious."

"No, you're Mr. Submissive." She smirks, then bites her lip.

"If you start to call me that, Sloan, I swear…"

"I want you to fuck me," she barks, setting her glass down on the counter and widening her stance with determination. She's a striking vision of power and command, like a real-life Wonder Woman.

My body's reaction is immediate. "Anywhere in particular, Treacle?"

She smiles. She likes when I call her that and I so want to please her. "In your closet."

I bite my lip and, fuck me, I think I'm already getting a little bit hard. "Your command is my wish."

"Shut up before I spank you." She giggles and cringes at her words, like she's trying them on for size and is not quite sure if they fit yet. It's pretty much perfect.

I shoot around the island and toss her over my shoulder. "Promises, promises."

She gives my arse a hearty smack as I take her upstairs and relish in the fact that this entire messed up arrangement is already ten times better than I imagined.

Sloan

Oh my God, I'm getting horny just thinking about his glass enclosed closet, never mind the fact that his ass is rock-hard under the tight jeans he's wearing. I've been fantasising about the closet in Gareth's bedroom since the first time I saw it. It's a damn shame to waste it on a man. I could make the area sparkle.

Gareth doesn't stop to flick any lights on in his room. He just continues to carry me up into his elevated closet that overlooks his giant bed. I hope to make good use of that piece of furniture eventually.

He sets me down on my feet. We're both breathing heavily, but I don't think it's from the exertion of him carrying me up the stairs. The blue rope lighting has set the scene immediately, and my fingers itch to touch him. He's dressed in another one of his classic white T-shirts that shows every bulge of his muscles, and a tiny smattering of chest hair peeks out the V neckline. I want to do so many things to him, I'm not sure where to start.

"I'm nervous," I admit, losing some of my earlier bravado.

"Don't be," he replies, bringing his warm hand up to cup my cheek. His hazel eyes are dark and his brow is serious as he stares into my eyes. "You know how to do this, Sloan. You've done it before. Just think about what inspired you last time."

I close my eyes and flashes of my entire life play on the backs of my lids. So many choices have been made for me. From the moment I peed on that stick, to the realisation that Sophia wasn't a healthy baby, to the day Cal told me we were moving to England. The divorce. The shared custody. Cal's mother. None of my current circumstances have been initiated by me, aside from the Sophia part, which isn't a circumstance. She is the saving grace of my entire life. I want to be strong for her. I want to rediscover my inner strength and prove to myself that I'm more than someone who simply reacts to life's curveballs. I'm in control of the pitch.

"Kneel, please," I state, my voice sounding like a stranger.

Gareth fails to conceal his pleased smirk and drops down on his knees. The long columns of his thighs are extraordinarily thick beneath the tight stretch of his jeans. Soccer legs. Sexy soccer legs that I get to do things with.

My hands tremble as I finger the double-breasted buttons on my coat. Gareth's eyes follow my movements as I slide the plastic buttons through the slips. When I open it to reveal my impulse purchase of La Perla lingerie, his expression makes the expense one hundred percent worth it.

Gareth's Adam's apple moves slowly down his throat as his jaw ticks with pained restraint. The desire in his eyes is making me unsteady in my heels, like a gravitational pull sucking me in.

Breaking my focus, I pull out my tape measure before shimmying the jacket off my shoulders. It drops to the floor with an audible thud. He takes in the violet sheer embroidered set and looks up at me in wonder, his face saying so much more than his words ever could.

Having Sophia ruined sex for me and Cal. He was in the delivery room when she was born, and I could tell he was disturbed by some of the things he saw. And not in the cute, "Oh, he's a guy and he's so squeamish" sort of way. It was more the, "I'm judging everything I'm seeing very harshly" sort of way. Several months later, that notion was confirmed when we were at a party in Chicago and he made a joke that my vagina was like a crime scene after childbirth. It was mortifying and it hurt me deeply. He took a beautiful moment and turned it into a crude punchline. It hurt our sex life even more. I struggled to feel desirable, so sex became few and far between until we eventually just stopped. Then Sophia got sick and life became about something so much bigger than lack of sex and body issues.

But knowing that I'm not married to Gareth—that this is casual and temporary and not about feelings—is liberating. I don't care if I feel different down there. We haven't slept together in a *year* and he still wants me. Maybe time healed whatever changed down there before.

I reach out and squeeze the thick muscles that line Gareth's shoulders. "You like a firm touch, right?" I ask, wanting to ensure his comfort as much as my own as I massage him.

He clears his throat. When he speaks, it seems difficult for him. "Yes."

"Do you like pain?" I ask, images of last night's porn binge fresh in my mind.

His shoulders shrug beneath my palms. "I think I might, but I don't really know."

I nod thoughtfully. "I'm not sure I'm ready for that anyway. Right now, I'm only interested in the control aspect. Is that okay?"

"Treacle"—he utters my nickname with such reverence it makes my knees weak—"it's not about what I want. It's about what you want to give me."

I inhale deeply. "I want to make you a suit."

He frowns. Clearly my train of thought is a lot different from his, and I understand his confusion. For me, my time at a sewing machine is when I'm at my most Zen state of mind. The thought of making something for a man as beautiful as Gareth is like sewing foreplay or something.

"I can sew, Gareth," I state, walking around his kneeling form to stand behind him. "I can sew really well. And while I have only ever bought you designer clothes, I have this fantasy of you wearing something I make with my own hands." I hold one end of the rolled up tape measure and let the rest fall to the floor. "So I need to measure you."

Gareth's chuckle is a gift. "This is like nothing I expected."

Frowning nervously, I ask, "Is that all right?"

"It's more than all right." He turns his head to look over his shoulder at me, and the wicked promise in his eyes gives me the strength I need to continue.

I bend over to grab the bottom of his T-shirt and tell him to lift his arms. He obeys and I toss the shirt to the side, feeling euphoric from the stronger male scent that's emitting from him. A touch of soap, deodorant, and the heat of his own fragrance. I return to the front of him to enjoy the view of his naked chest. A freaking Tarzan build like I've never seen, barefoot in a pair of tight jeans and on his knees for me.

I measure his neck. His chest. His torso length and midsection. His arm length and biceps. Recording each number to memory. With every measurement, I pull the tape extra tight around his muscles and watch the skin pucker beneath it. His deep groan indicates he's enjoying this quiet exchange.

"Stand," I state, draping the tape measure around my neck and stepping back to watch his movement.

When he stretches to full height, the erection constrained beneath his jeans is shocking. I know he is large. That night we had together, I figured that out rather abruptly. But seeing it with the mindset to really take it in makes my body hum with need.

Inspired, I step into his space and palm his groin. His arms reach out to hold me, but I tsk in admonishment. Grabbing both of his wrists, I pull them away from me and squeeze them together behind his back.

"Clasp your hands together," I whisper in his ear.

He obeys as my lace-covered breasts brush against his chest.

I drop to my knees and measure his inseam. My fingers tease around the bulge in his jeans, and I'm so grateful this is my life tonight. He breaks the hold of his hands behind his back when my nose brushes along his length.

"Nope," I say, pulling his fingers out of my hair despite how good they feel because this control feels even better. "You're not a very good listener, Gareth."

His smirk is sinful. "You're not making it easy, Tre."

I stand up so we're face-to-face again and slide the tape measure off my neck. I walk behind him and wrap the long strand around his fisted hands, trussing them into a really unglamorous knot.

He turns to face me so I can admire my work. His pecs are large and protrude with the restraint. His muscles flex and tense. Best of all, his hooded eyes completely lock on me and wait for what I'm going to do next.

I cross my arms over my chest and bite down on the tip of my finger.

Gareth growls.

He actually growls like a caged, feral animal. It's so freaking savage and sexy at the same time. It's such an enlighteningly uninhibited reaction, and it makes me feel brave. I can't help but giggle and move in toward him. I drop down to a squat and stand slowly, sliding my lace-covered breasts over his denim clad erection. The sharp intake of air that he sucks in when I press him hard over his jeans is icing on this oh-so exciting new cake.

He grows even more beneath the heaviness of my palm. When his head falls back with a groan, I reach up with my free hand and yank his jaw down to me. His eyes are hooded on me as he bites his lip.

"Kiss my neck," I state. He greedily dips his head and runs his tongue from my collarbone to my jaw, sucking the edge of my chin in a dirty, unsophisticated sort of way. It makes me lose my mind a bit. "Kiss my pussy. Kiss it the way you wanted to kiss it our first night together."

He pulls back and is deathly serious when he says, "I might need my hands for that."

I eye him speculatively for a moment. "Okay."

As soon as his hands are free, he drops to his knees and pulls my right leg over his shoulder. His tongue thrusts into me overtop of my panties, shoving the gritty texture of the damp fabric into the place that aches to be filled. I forget about all of my previous insecurities. I forget about my past. All I can focus on is the raging climb throbbing in my loins.

Gareth adjusts his angle, splaying his tongue out flat on my clit and begins nuzzling with his face between my thighs. It's shocking, and intense, and deliciously erotic. My voice surprises me when he hits the bundle of nerves perfectly and I scream out, "Oh my God! Holy shit, don't stop doing that!"

My command begins a frenzy. He grabs the strip of my panties and pulls them to the side, and his tongue swipes across the bare flesh. The touch of his mouth devouring my centre is like being colour blind your entire life and finally seeing fiery red for the first time. My screams grow impossibly louder when he grabs my ass and pulls me so hard against his face, I'm not sure how he's even breathing.

"No, no, nooo!" I shriek as my entire body bears down and ruptures in a riot of tremulous, painful relief. My inner thighs quake as my leg begins to give out. Gareth pulls back to catch me in his arms as I crumple to the floor. He lays me down on the plush carpeted floor and thrusts two of his fingers into me, massaging my still-spasming centre while worshipfully kissing my hip bones. I don't think I can take any more. My body seems to be trying to push him out, but my hips continue to greedily pump against his meaty fingers. The wet noises in the quiet closet are so sensual, I begin climbing the hill again. Another orgasm jumping on top of the last.

"Holy shit!" I cry when he hooks his finger into my G-spot. "Gareth!" I scream and grab the hair on his head, pulling it hard in a crazed, sexual moment of unrestraint. "Fuuuck!" My voice is lost to a hoarse, garbled cry as I squeeze my thighs together and climax again, fisting his silky strands in my fingers like they are a life rope keeping me from being sucked into the sea.

This orgasm is more than mind-blowing. It's unbelievable. It's unbelievable that a man can wreck me like a crashing ship by using only his mouth and fingers.

I lose complete track of time as I lie on the lush carpet in Gareth's see-through closet. I'm spent, I'm satiated, and I'm trying to work out in my head if the orgasm is because of Gareth or because of the control I had over him the moments leading up to it. Whatever it was, I want more. A lot more. I'm not sure how I'm ever going to want it to stop.

Suddenly, the heat of Gareth moves away from my body. I sit up to see him sitting back on his haunches. He's shirtless and panting, his face glistening with what I can only assume is me. But it's not just the dirty, hot look of him that brings me up short. It's the astonishment on his face that makes me feel uneasy.

I pull my knees to my chest. "What is it?" I ask, shoving strands of hair away from my face. "What's wrong? Why are you looking at me like that?"

"My mind is fucking shattered," he croaks and exhales heavily, his abs even more defined as his body contracts. I look down at his erection swelling through his jeans. It looks painful. "I could have come just watching you."

Wait, what? "Are you serious?"

"Completely." He laughs and runs a hand through his tousled hair. His slumped posture is unnerving. "Sloan, I've never been so turned on with a woman in my entire life."

"Okaaay," I reply slowly, not sure what he's getting at here.

"I'm telling you this because it's a good thing. I've struggled to connect with women sexually for a long time. No one has turned me on like you…No one."

I can't help it. I laugh. I laugh really freaking hard. How little old me—Sloan Montgomery from Chicago who's had a small handful of sexual partners her entire life—can have sexual control over Manchester's star soccer player is beyond any comprehension.

"It's not that funny." The irritated expression on Gareth's face has me pulling in my lips to stifle my amusement.

"I'm sorry," I concede, shimmying toward him in my ridiculous lingerie. "I can't help but laugh because this whole situation is crazy."

"Crazy stupid or crazy incredible?"

"Incredible!" I reply, pressing my hands flat on the floor and leaning toward him. "Gareth, I just orgasmed twice and have yet to have sex with you. Not to mention you are an athlete who's quite possibly England's sexiest man alive and you just let me *control* you for my pleasure. Do you have any idea how I feel right now?"

"No…Tell me." His eyes are wide and waiting. Maybe even a little fearful.

"I feel like I'm on top of the world! I feel like I can move mountains. Like I can do anything! I feel like I can start creating my own designs again. Hell, I want to start a charity. I want to cure cancer. I want to fucking live!"

"What were you doing before?" he asks.

"Existing." I exhale heavily and blink away the tears threatening behind my lids. "I'll never forget this night."

Gareth eyes me thoughtfully, his stormy hazel eyes looking pensive and confused. Without explanation, he rises to his feet and runs his hands through his hair several times, his mind clearly in another place.

"Where are you going?" I ask as he heads toward the door of the closet.

"To get some water." He pauses and grips the doorframe, the veins running down his arms tense and protruding. Without making eye contact, he replies, "I'll grab you some, too."

Frowning at his weird change of demeanour, I watch his shirtless form retreat. *What the hell just happened?*

Gareth

I press my forehead against the cool stainless steel of the refrigerator as I fill a glass of ice water for Sloan. My cock feels like a titanium rod in my jeans and my walk down the stairs didn't do anything to calm my nerves.

What's the matter with me that I left a mostly naked woman like Sloan in my closet?

Fuck me.

We've seen each other countless times. I know how beautiful she is. I know what her body feels like under my fingers. But this time, she was a different person. She was strong. Confident. Happy. She wasn't letting someone else think for her as she stood before me looking like a damned queen ready to take what she wants from her country.

Now my dick really hurts. It feels like all the blood in my body is rushing to the appendage between my legs. All I want is to sink myself so deep inside of her, we lose ourselves for the next hour. But I can't lose myself. If this arrangement gets too deep, too fast, I'm afraid of what it could mean. I feel too connected to her, too in sync.

Even her bloody scent is haunting me in a way I can't fathom.

I need some time to breathe. To step away and get ahold of myself.

She gets control of my body. She gets control of my mind. But my heart and soul are mine. I refuse to turn into my father and give myself to a woman entirely at the cost of everything that's important to me. That is exactly why I have to send Sloan home before we have sex tonight. It will probably kill me. In fact, I'm sure of it. But I need to ensure that we are both in the right frame of mind before we continue so this remains casual.

I slowly make my way up the stairs, ice clinking in the glass with every step I take. It feels like I'm walking to my death. I have to do this carefully, or I could scare her away altogether. The last thing I want to do is freak her out and make her feel like what she did tonight was wrong.

Entering my room, I see Sloan is still in my closet, rummaging through my clothes. She pulls down a grey T-shirt and puts it on over her head, threading her narrow arms through the sleeves. The hem reaches mid-thigh. I didn't think it was possible for her to look sexier in more clothes, but I guess I was wrong.

She pads out of the closet and finds me watching her from the doorway. Her smile is rueful as she fists her coat in front of her. "I didn't really think about the fact that I should have brought other clothes with me." She slides up onto my bed, tucking her feet under her as she pulls a pillow on her lap. "Putting on the trench coat seems weird now."

"Walk around naked if you'd like," I reply with a smirk, joining her on the bed. I hand her the water and prop myself on a pillow against the glass wall of the closet headboard.

"Maybe I should demand that of you." She waggles her eyebrows at me, and my amused expression fades. She takes a drink and drags her tongue across her moist lips. "You seem…different. Is everything all right?"

"Yes," I reply calmly, my muscles tensing from her perceptiveness. "Why do you ask?"

"Because your mood has changed from how it was in there." She points to the closet. "I thought this was what you wanted."

I close my eyes and feel like ten times the dick. "It is what I want."

"Then what's the problem?" she asks, running her finger down the condensation on the side of the glass. "Is it my body?"

I blanch, completely taken off guard. "Are you kidding?"

She grips the glass tightly in her hand and looks up at me. "I mean, I'm twenty-nine years old. I'm no spring chicken."

She's serious. She's actually, preposterously serious. I need to knock this idea right on its arse before she spins out of control.

"Sloan, there's not a thing wrong with a single inch of your body. You are so fucking sexy, I thought I was going to blow it in my jeans tonight when I opened the door and saw you in that trench coat." I fork my hand through my hair and exhale slowly, anger coursing through my veins because she didn't get insecure alone. Someone didn't tell her how fucking perfectly beautiful she is every day, and that someone needs his arse kicked. "And if I wanted a girl, I'd go out and get one. But I don't. I want a woman. I want you."

The corners of her mouth lift into a meek smile. "Well, then what is it because something's clearly wrong?"

I purse my lips, knowing I'm going to regret this but that it's ultimately for the best. "There's nothing wrong, but I think we should stop for tonight."

"Stop what? Stop this?" She points between our two bodies. "I thought this was supposed to be about sex. We haven't even had sex yet and you're kicking me out?"

"I'm not kicking you out," I reply, my jaw clenched. "Tonight wasn't just about sex. It was about seeing if you could handle all of this."

"I thought I did pretty well!"

"You did," I reply, running a hand through my hair and squeezing the back of my neck. "I just think it's important for us both to take a breather and make sure our heads are on straight."

The skin wrinkles between her brows as she shifts closer to me. "My head feels perfectly straight. I thought you said you liked when I took control."

"I did...I do." I point down to my offensive package still semi-hard beneath my jeans. "But I think some space after our first experiment is what's best for both of us."

"Gareth." She growls my name magnificently and stands up, setting the water down on the nightstand and looking down at me with fire in her eyes. "You're the one who gave me all the control, so why are you trying to take it from me right now?"

"I'm not taking it from you. I'm ensuring that you're serious about this *arrangement*." I emphasise the last word because I don't want either of us to get this twisted up with feelings.

"My soaked panties indicate I'm pretty fucking serious." She twirls on her heel and paces the room, making cute little fists with her hands. "This is bullshit."

I shake my head and stand up, facing-off with her from the opposite side of the bed. She's fucking striking. Her jaw tight with anger, her neck turning crimson with her emotions. It's really hard to want her as bad as I do.

Steeling myself, I reply, "Tonight was about you taking pleasure for yourself, and that's what you did. That's ultimate control."

She crosses her arms over her chest, and I have to tell my eyes not to look at her breasts when the action pushes them upward. "This is so stupid!"

"It's what I think is best," I grind out, the words as painful to say as they are to hear. She stares back at me with barely contained fury, and a sick part of me wants to laugh. She's cute when she's mad. "Don't be angry, Sloan. We're in a marathon, not a sprint."

An audible growl rips from her throat as she tears off my T-shirt

114

SURRENDER

and fumbles to yank on her coat, affording me the glorious sight of her body one last time. It's an image that will help me later.

"For someone who wanted a woman to take charge, you sure seem to be calling a lot of shots."

She stomps around the bed toward the door in long, hacked off strides. I have to conceal my smile because, bloody hell, she's dazzling. I trail after her down the stairs. It's involuntary. She's like a fucking magnetic force that pulls me in.

"I'll call you later," I say as she bends over and picks up the bag she dropped on the floor by the front door.

"No, you won't!" she exclaims and twirls on her heel to face me. "I'll call you if I can still stand you after this."

A laugh breaks its way from my chest. "You're awfully hostile for someone who just had two orgasms. I'm the one with blue balls here."

She looks down at my dick and the fire in her eyes has it stirring again. "Don't you dare jerk off!" she states, her golden eyes flashing up to me with sudden renewed determination. "That bulge in your pants is mine, not yours. If I decide I can handle your mood swings, I'll be the one to take care of it."

My stomach somersaults. In a heartbeat, Sloan has all the control again. I swallow slowly and reply, "Very well, Treacle."

She narrows her eyes and growls a deep rumble as she turns and storms out of my house. I lean against the doorframe, shirtless, barefoot, and hard as stone all over again as I watch her beautiful figure get smaller and smaller.

Gareth, you're a fucking idiot.

115

Bird Bath Killer

Sloan

"**G**OOD MORNING!" FREYA SHOUTS TO ME OVER THE NOISE OF the sewing machine as she strides in through the back door of the house. Her face falls to what I'm working on. "What is that?"

I lift my foot from the pedal and take a sip of my coffee. "A suit."

Her face screws up. "I can see that. Why are you sewing it?"

"Because I feel like it," I reply through clenched teeth and pull the fabric out and cut the thread with my scissors.

She looks down at what I'm wearing. "Why are you still wearing your coat?" I frown up at her and sniff as she adds, "Why do you look like you've not slept?"

"Because I haven't," I mumble, shoving the fabric under the needle and pressing the pedal to full speed again. "And I'm not wearing much underneath this."

I've been up all night making this suit, carefully cutting out the custom pattern I drew to be exact to Gareth's measurements. Regretfully, I've just barely finished the pants. I'm out of practice. I shouldn't have let my sewing skills rot these last few years in Manchester.

Yet another way I've let men control my freaking life.

My machine suddenly stops. With wide, confused eyes, I look

116

over and see that Freya has pulled the power cord from the wall. "What are you doing?" I bark, rage bubbling up inside of me.

"Explain why you look like a hungover Jackie Kennedy, then I'll give you power back." She props her hands on her hips and taps her foot expectantly.

"Because Gareth Harris is infuriating!" I growl loudly. "He wanted me to have all the power, but just when I started to get my footing, he ripped the rug out from under me."

Freya's green eyes are wide with excitement as she drops down on the chair beside me, plug still in hand. "Are you shagging Gareth Harris? Oh, God, please say yes because it would be the perfect sort of real-life fantasy my therapist says I need to engage in!"

"I didn't even get a chance to shag him last night!" I peal, my voice nearly an octave higher than normal.

She glances down at the sexy bra peeking out from under the trench coat. "You showed up in that and nothing happened?"

I narrow my eyes and point my scissors at her. "Oh, something happened."

She plasters on a fake smile and slowly clasps my hand in hers and lowers the scissors. "Let's not use sharp instruments for vocabulary emphasis when you've had no sleep, shall we?"

Her sing-songy tone does nothing to calm my rage that's been bubbling all night. "We messed around and then he told me to go home and think! What is that about?"

Her brows crumple. "Maybe he is worried it's too soon since your divorce?"

"That shouldn't be his concern. It should be mine!"

Freya exhales slowly. "Sloan, love, Gareth Harris isn't a man about town. He's not pictured in the papers with women, ever. He doesn't even take women to red carpet events. He's advertised as England's sexiest loner! If he's entering into some sort of relationship with you, he's probably just being extra cautious."

"That's an overly nice way of putting it," I snap. "You know what

I think he's being? A cock-tease!"

She snickers but quickly sobers when I don't crack a grin. "So, how did you leave it?"

"The ball is in my court again. I'd already taken the ball and bounced it in a fucking trench coat. Now I have to put myself out there all over again." I prop my elbows on the table and massage small circles on my temples.

"Well, that's far better than rejection, love." Freya rubs my shoulder encouragingly.

"It doesn't feel like it," I murmur.

Freya looks at the cut out patterned pieces of navy stretch cotton strewn about the table. Knowing Gareth's texture issues, I am confident this fabric is one he'll love. The very mild stretch also means that it can be fitted to his body to look more expensive than it is.

"Who is the suit for?" Freya asks.

I roll my eyes. "Who do you think?"

She lifts her brows. "Making a custom suit for a bloke must mean you like him."

"I'd like to have sex with him! The suit is a…commitment of some sort I suppose."

"Well, you've done the hard work of designing and cutting everything. Why don't you go brush your teeth and get some sleep? A hot shower would do you good as well. I'll take it from here."

My face softens. "Do we have the time?"

"We most certainly do. Today we were going to start prepping pieces for that awards gala so many of our clients are attending. Last I checked, we had a dozen people to style for that night. But we have some time. Go take a sickie, Sloan. I got this!"

"You're amazing, you know that?"

"I do, indeed!" Freya beams. "Besides, this angry, hostile, scissor-slinging Sloan is a vast improvement from the moping mess you usually are when Sophia is gone."

My heart lurches at the mention of my daughter. Then I marvel over the fact that I went an entire twenty-four hours without crying and worrying about what Sophia is doing or how she is feeling. I can't remember the last time I did that. "Well, I suppose I wouldn't mind brushing my teeth."

"Yeah, you don't want to get your stink on this nice fabric." She smiles and helps me out of my chair. "Off you go. Take a nice bath and close your eyes. I have a feeling things will look a whole lot better when you wake."

A few hours later, I've slept, showered, and groomed myself. Dressed in a neat pair of houndstooth shorts with black tights and a white blouse, I feel human again. A phone call from Sophia telling me she's home from school cheers me up even more.

But, unsurprisingly, my thoughts drift back to Gareth as I head downstairs and lay eyes on the suit I designed that's now hanging on a clothing rack in the foyer. My hands run over the seams, the stitching, the lapels, the navy button closures. Freya's been busy. She even finished off the blue-and-white-checked pocket square. The two-piece suit has been pressed and sprayed with my signature vanilla essential oil that we spritz on the inside of all the clothes we send out to clients.

I lean in and inhale, imagining Gareth's thick muscles inside the fabric, soaking up the scent of me. The stirring between my legs is all the sign I need to know that I'll be delivering this to him today.

"Does it meet your superior standards?" Freya's voice chirps from behind me.

I turn and give her a full, genuine smile. "Exceeds them, as usual." I eliminate the space between us and pull her into a hug. Getting choked up over a suit is silly, but it's such a representation of the life raft Freya has become in my life. "You are a true friend, Freya."

"You're bloody well right I am." When I pull back, she hits me with a serious look. "You know this earns me some dirty details, right?"

I laugh and hug her again. "In due time, Freya. In due time."

After a thousand more thank yous, I find myself in my car and on my way to Astbury. Freya gave me a calculated stare when I tucked Sophia's booster seat into the concealed tailgate of my vehicle but let me escape without any questions.

I can't explain exactly why it's so important for me to keep Sophia a secret from Gareth. I suppose it's since this is just a sex thing, I don't see a need to share our life stories. Telling him I'm a mother also might change the way he sees me, and I don't want that.

Today I'm going to be a sex goddess. Today I'm going to stroll into Gareth's home and command his attention. I'm going to be the strong woman I know I'm capable of being, and I'm going to quit letting him tell me how this is all going to happen.

I pull up to his gate just as the sun begins to set. It's so much brighter in the country than it is in Manchester. Maybe after Cal's mother passes on, I'll feel more freedom in where I live and I can move out to a place like this. Mind you, a much cheaper version.

I press the button on the security panel, and my heart jumps when a woman's voice peals through the line. "Hello? Who is it?"

The flirty words I had prepared for Gareth get stuck in my throat, clearly unsuitable for whomever is on the other end of the line. In all the times I've been out here, a woman has never answered Gareth's intercom. It's always been him. Every freaking time. Whomever this is must be very familiar with Gareth if she's answering his line.

Is this why he kicked me out of his house last night? Was someone due to come home? A girlfriend? Freya said he's never seen with women, but that doesn't mean he couldn't have some secret girlfriend he hides from the public eye.

I look down the lane that leads to exactly where I want to be. The place where I imagined stripping naked and losing myself for an hour or more. Clearly, someone has already beat me there.

"Hello, is anyone there?" The woman's voice chimes into my car once more and my hands tense on the steering wheel.

"Yes, I'm here," I reply as anger replaces shock. I lean out my window and shout into the speaker, "And I have a message for Gareth Harris. You tell him that I'm not taking a number and that he should find someone else to mess with!"

"What?" the lady asks, but I don't hear what else she says. I slam my foot on the gas pedal to reverse and a loud thump startles me from behind.

My hands tighten as I press my forehead against the wheel with a groan. I think I know what I hit, and I dare to say it didn't survive the collision.

I slide out of my car and wobble on the gravel in my heels to see what I've pummelled. A stupid stone bird bath that was once a quaint, ornate, little thing now rests in a heap of eight pieces on the side of the road.

"Son of a bitch!" I exclaim and move to look at the damage to my car. A lovely bird bath-sized dent is imprinted on the corner of the bumper. "Freaking hell!" I cry and kick some rocks because this is just my luck. Why wouldn't I damage my car in a blind jealous rage over a man I've barely started a relationship with yet? This makes perfect sense.

Gravel crunches from a distance. My gaze swerves down the driveway in response to find Gareth jogging right toward me. My traitorous eyes do a double take. His pecs are ridiculously bouncing under his T-shirt with each gallop he takes. He has a lot of nerve.

"Christ, Sloan, are you okay?" Gareth's face is full of worry as he presses some numbers into the keypad on his gate. As soon as it's open enough, he slips through and runs across the road to where I'm standing.

"I'm fine," I reply in a warning tone and move past him toward my car door. "I'll pay to replace your bird bath, but you should think about putting it somewhere besides directly behind your driveway. That's unsafe."

"It's not my bird bath," he argues. "It was here when I bought the place."

"You still should have thought to put it somewhere that makes more sense!" I snap, opening my door and wrapping my fingers around the frame where the window is open. "I mean, what kind of birds are going to bathe themselves next to a road?"

"It's a private drive," Gareth barks, crossing his arms over his chest. "It only leads to mine and Hobo's driveways."

"Well, you clearly have guests!" I flick my hands toward the house where his lady is probably gawking out the window at us as we speak.

"Most people drive forward out of my driveway. You know… because they actually enter my property." He hits me with a fixed narrow stare that I don't altogether appreciate.

"Oh, believe me, I know! I had a nice chat with your current houseguest. She sounds oh-so lovely on your little speaker. She probably has a future in telephone porn if she wants one."

"What are you talking about?" he asks, his body tense like he's on the verge of springing at me.

I slam my door shut, crossing my arms over my chest and leaning toward him. "The woman who answered when I called just now. Please, don't let me delay you from servicing her."

"Servicing her?" His forced laugh causes a thick vein to pop out on his neck. "You think someone I'm fucking would be answering my security gate?"

"I don't know your life!" I turn to reopen my door, but in one swift move, Gareth storms up behind me, grasps my arm, twirls me to face him, and slams my door closed.

"Running away again, Sloan?" he seethes, pressing in so close to me, I have to arch my back to keep my face from touching his. "This is exactly why I told you to leave last night. You don't have the strength to be level-headed with this arrangement. Things get a little uncomfortable and you run away like you did a year ago."

"I'm not running!" I exclaim, shoving against his chest. "Do you think I drove out to Astbury to admire the English countryside?"

"Then why are you leaving?" he asks, his nostrils flared as he hunches down an inch so we're nose-to-nose.

"Because, casual or not, I don't want to be one of many!" I nearly howl, so I clench my teeth together to maintain some control. I'm completely overreacting, but I can't help it. All I can think about is Cal and his Lady Godiva, and it's making me regret putting myself out there again. "This is the worst kind of déjà fucking vu for me, and I'm not signing up for it again."

"Sloan"—he grabs my arms so I stop struggling to get my door open—"the voice you heard was not someone I'm sleeping with. It was my house manager, Dorinda. She's here until a security guard arrives to check my cameras because there was a break-in at Hobo's house this morning."

"Oh my God." My breath catches in my throat as my hand reaches up to cover my mouth. "Are him and Brandi okay?"

"Yes," he replies with an exhale, his eyes blinking slowly as he changes his focus. "Hobo and I were both at practice, and Brandi was with her mum in London."

I awkwardly cross my arms over my chest, wishing I could shrink down to the size of a pebble. "What happened?"

Gareth shrugs. "A couple of blokes got through his security gate and stole a bunch of stuff. Trashed the property. Could have been worse if they were home."

"How awful." My voice is small, and I can barely look Gareth in the eyes as I turn to gain some space from him. I'm such a freak for assuming the person who answered was someone he is intimate with. This is mortifying. "Please extend my apologies to Dorinda."

Gareth looks at me, releasing a heavy sigh. "You actually met her before. I'm surprised you didn't recognise her voice."

I lean against the hood of my car, staring down at my feet in shame. "You want me to dominate you and you're over there assuming logical things? None of this is logical."

I steal a glance at his reaction, and the intensity in his gaze nearly takes my breath away. He moves over to me and places his hands on either side of me, caging me in like the wild animal I am right now. "I don't want you to dominate me, Sloan. I just want to surrender to you."

"Why?" I ask, wondering if I'll ever feel secure about this crazy notion.

"Because, on some bizarre level I don't fully understand, I need it. And I think you need it, too." He inhales a shaky breath and brings his hands to my waist, squeezing his palms around me to hold me captive. "Asking you to leave last night was fucking brutal, but I had to create a degree of separation between us to ensure that our lines stay clear and never blur. This is truly just about sex after all, and things got incredibly intense last night. Similar to how they did our first time together. I just felt like if you could leave and still come back, then we could do this together properly. Am I right?"

"I'm here aren't I?" I retort, trying hard to ignore how much I love the warmth of his hands on my sides. This is intense, but everything with Gareth is intense. He's an intense sort of guy. I don't like him doubting me, though.

Gareth's eyes crinkle with a poorly concealed smirk. "Technically, you're in the middle of the street with a broken bumper."

I scoff and ignore the way his body vibrates with silent laughter. I ignore the way he watches me as I look away. But I can't seem to ignore the question on the tip of my tongue. "Gareth, I have to ask again…Why me?"

His eyes close as if he's weighing his answer in his head before giving it to me. When he opens them, the dark smoulder in the hazel depths is knee-trembling. "Treacle, I want to surrender to you because I sense that it's been a long time since you've been with someone who put your needs first." He brings his hands to my face and runs his thumbs along the hollows of my cheeks. "I've watched you come into my house for years, style me, fill my closet, do your job. But it wasn't until that night we slept together that I felt like I saw the real you."

"I was a mess that night."

"You were a mess until you weren't…Until you took control. Until you asked me to kneel. Then you were the most beautiful fucking woman I've ever seen in my life. That was a turn-on for me, like something I'd never felt before. So this isn't an entirely selfless request I'm putting out there."

My body quivers in response to his words. His voice is like a sexy caress over a quiet part of my soul that I've been hiding for years. I reach up and grab his face in my hands, taking in every one of his features. Suddenly, a strong, overpowering sense of ownership nearly chokes me. He is mine to use, to please, to care for. To give and take from. I want him this way. I want to embrace whatever this is we're doing and dive in head first.

My voice is strong when I reply, "Okay, then. Let's do this, Gareth Harris. I'm all in."

He licks his lips, a pleased smirk teasing the corners of his mouth. He reaches down and lifts me up onto the hood of my car, tucking himself perfectly between my legs so we're nose-to-nose. He dips his mouth close to mine, but I pull back with a sharp intake of breath. "Not the lips," I remind him.

His jaw ticks once before he drops his mouth down to my neck and kisses me there, nibbling at my flesh with tantalising bites. He moves to the other side of my neck as his hands slide up my ribs and squeeze my breasts through the soft chiffon.

I hook my ankles behind his back and pull him in snugly so his dick presses into the heat of me. His large, firm body feels so good, I forget everything I was worried about. "Take me inside," I command.

He pulls back and looks at me so seriously, I think he's going to say something bad. "Okay. And just for your information, I'll be giving you the code to my gate." His deep voice vibrates against my skin as he leans in and peppers my jaw with feather-light kisses. "Because while you and I are doing whatever it is we're doing, I promise you that I won't even look at another woman."

My heart thunders in my chest from the uneasy feeling I get over his promise. His devotion. The look in his eyes. The sincerity of his touch. I believe him. I believe him more than the day Cal said, "I do," to me. It's crazy how a sex-only relationship can still be so committed.

Needing to lighten the mood, I grasp his face in my hands and reply, "That's good to know because I do not want to see that bird bath killer I just turned into a minute ago ever again."

He doesn't laugh like I thought he would. He stares down at my mouth and with a deathly serious tone, he replies, "That's a bloody shame because I kind of liked her."

I whack him on the chest, a gesture I'm actually growing quite fond of. He chuckles as he helps me down off the car and opens the driver's side door for me. "I think it's time to get your car out of the road, don't you?"

His wink elicits a smile of my own. "Would you like a ride?"

"Yes, Sloan Montgomery. A real ride this time."

Gareth

I hurry into the kitchen to tell Dorinda and her son, Robert—who prepares my meals for the week—that they can head home for the day. I have about an hour before the security guard I hired will arrive, and I intend to make good use of that time. Dorinda gives me a curious sort of look as she collects her purse and makes her way out the kitchen side door where their car is parked.

Dorinda has been with me since I bought the house, so she knows I don't bring women out here. In fact, I don't bring anyone out here. Sloan sort of just slipped in on a technicality I guess.

When I first moved to Astbury, I had hopes that my family would visit a lot. I spent a load of money on an interior designer to make it a place where people would want to come and stay. Essentially, the exact opposite of what we grew up in.

I still remember when our father moved us all out of the Manchester flat. It was tight quarters with four kids plus newborn Booker, but it was cosy and happy. It was a place I was excited to go home to.

Then Mum got sick and Dad suddenly uprooted all of us to live permanently in the enormous Chigwell house he had purchased in East London. They hadn't owned the property long, so Mum never got a chance to furnish it before she became bedridden.

After she died, Dad got rid of as much of her memory as he could, including everything from the Manchester flat. The Chigwell house was so barren and cold, I remember the boys loved playing with their cars in the foyer because their voices echoed off the walls and marble flooring.

We all still congregate in that house for Sunday dinners despite the fact that we don't have many great memories. The truth is, the only good ones I have of that home are when we sat around the kitchen counter, using tomato sauce bottles as players to go over football formations with Dad. Those were the only times he ever spoke to us with any sort of care.

Needless to say, my kitchen counter doesn't have stools. But furnishing this house was all for naught because Dad has never stepped foot back into the city of Manchester since Mum died, let alone Astbury. And my siblings rarely visit. Probably because I never invite them.

The longer I live here, the less I want them to visit. Like a proper masochist, I find myself going back to London and staying in the home I swear to hate. A therapist would have a field day with me. It's only recently that I realised the life I've built for myself here in Manchester seems to be more and more pointless.

I leave the kitchen and find Sloan wandering in the sunken living area to the right of the curved staircase. She's running her hands over a mirrored credenza in front of a huge glass window on the west wall. The sun casts down on her long, chestnut locks as she watches Dorinda's car drive away.

I clear my throat, drawing her attention to me. "Well, you're here now. What do you want to do with me?"

Sloan's eyes rove over my body, and the smile that plays on her lips is almost wicked. What has been running through that head of hers while I was talking to Dorinda? Gone is the insecure, hostile woman from outside. The woman standing before me, sliding the short black scarf around her neck back and forth, is a bloody siren calling in ships from the sea. It's enchanting. On the surface, she's peaches and cream with a sweet, pleasing sort of nature. But there's a fire beneath the surface of her that cannot be denied.

"For starters, I have a gift for you, Harris." She nods her chin over to a sconce on the sitting room wall where there's a garment bag hanging. "I was up most of the night making that for you. It seems when I'm pissed off, I'm kind of productive."

She giggles to herself as I stride over and unzip the bag to see a deep navy suit inside. I run my hands down the fabric, relishing in the signature softness of everything Sloan buys for me. My voice is awestruck when I croak, "You made this?"

I look over and she shrugs. "Freya did most of the sewing but, yes, I designed it."

I pull out the shoulder on one side to get a better look. "I had no idea you were capable of this kind of work."

"There's a lot you don't know about me, Gareth."

I turn to look at her big brown eyes blinking rapidly like she's not sure herself of who she is. Well, I hope whatever we're about to embark on helps her with that because I know she's a hell of a lot more than she lets on.

"Do you want me to try it on?" I ask, hoping this will be our foreplay because, for me, it sounds about as hot as a student, professor scenario.

Her nose wrinkles with embarrassment. "You can do it on your own later. For now, I'd like a tour." She turns on her heel and crosses her arms over her chest like she's an estate agent at a business meeting. "And you can do it with your shirt off."

"Oh, can I?" I blurt out, smirking like a prat and marvelling over her swift change of demeanour.

"That's what I said." She licks her lips in a vain attempt to hide the naughty grin threatening her serious façade.

"Whatever you say, Treacle." I pull my T-shirt off and drop it on the floor by my feet. Sloan's eyes are like a slow burn spreading over every hair on my chest, causing my stomach to flex in anticipation.

She clears her throat. "Well, what are you waiting for?"

Attempting not to laugh at the hilarity of this situation, I do my best to give her a tour without getting an erection. It's not without great effort, though, considering she's eyeing me, not just like a piece of meat, but *her* piece of meat. It's a huge fucking turn-on.

I gesture to the doorway on the opposite side of the living room, which leads down a glass-lined hallway into a media room with a projection screen and theatre-style seating. Sloan nods appreciatively and asks some questions about the kind of movies I like to watch.

I correct her with the word "films," and our familiar American versus English banter makes me smile.

We progress down the hallway into the training room that's kitted out as nice as a commercial gym. I have a lot of the same equipment we have at the Trafford Training Centre because, even on off days, I'm always training. Staying fit is part of my job the same way a CEO has to check his emails every day.

Past the gym is where I can tell Sloan's eyes really light up. "You have a pool!" she squeals, waltzing past me and greedily checking out the indoor pool room. The sunlight beaming in through the glass skylights reflect colourful sparkles on her face as she grins back at me. "How often do you use this?"

"Never," I reply honestly.

Her jaw drops. "What? I would be in this every day!"

I shrug. "It's not big enough to swim laps in, so I don't really see the point if I can't use it for exercise."

"What about for fun, Gareth?" She arches a challenging eyebrow at me.

I can only reply truthfully. "I don't have very much of that I'm afraid."

Her gaze narrows as she walks toward me, her heels clicking softly on the concrete. She drags her pointer finger across my bare chest and says, "Let's see about changing that, shall we?"

I rush through the rest of the tour, my job of preventing an erection becoming painfully more difficult the longer I feel her eyes on me. The more we move around the house, the more confident she gets. It's like some kind of odd foreplay for her to watch me show off my home.

I take care to leave my bedroom for last and feel a triumphant sense of relief as we finally reach the doorway. "I think you've been in here before."

Her smile is playful. "A time or two."

She splays her hand flat on my chest and pushes me backwards into the room, walking with me all the way to the tufted sofa at the foot of the bed. With firm hands on my shoulders, she pushes me to a sitting position.

"I had a lot of time to think last night when you kicked me out of your house."

"I didn't kick you—"

"Shhh." She presses her finger to her lips and lowers her chin. "I'm talking. You're listening." She eyes me thoughtfully, then closes the space between us so her chest is in my face as she climbs onto my lap. With her legs on either side, she straddles me, her hands holding onto my neck for balance as she makes herself more comfortable.

It's intimate. It's confident. It's exactly what I want from her.

My hands itch to run up her back, but I keep them fisted beside me instead. This is about letting go of control. This is about listening to her wants. Not my own. And having her on top of me has me craving that sort of mind-numbing release I had with her last year.

She flicks her long, wavy locks over one shoulder and I have to bite back a moan as the delicious scent of her perfume invades my senses.

"So I thought about how much sex is about trust." Her golden eyes dance on my chest as she moves her hands forward and begins raking her fingertips over my pecs in firm, massaging strokes. "Especially the kind of sex we're going to be having where we're not actually in a relationship with each other."

"I'm listening," I husk and close my eyes as she squeezes my shoulders and rolls her hips on my lap.

"To build trust, I think it might help to have your eyes covered the entire time we have sex."

My eyes widen instantly and I begin to argue. "Sloan—"

She presses her hand over my mouth, bringing her face up close so I can see the green loop around her pupils again. "I'm in charge, Gareth. You want it and I'm taking it. You need to trust me to guide this ship because I'm ready to try this for real. Last night was an amuse-bouche. This is going to be the main course."

I swallow slowly, the erection growing in my jeans becoming painful against the zipper as she greedily grinds down on me. She begins rocking and swirling her hips, alternating between the two. Her arse pops up behind her like she's fucking double-jointed.

"Fuck me, Sloan." I press my forehead to her chest. I'm quite positive I won't live through this experience but, bloody hell, it'll be worth the ride.

"That's exactly what I'm going to do," she says, slowly undoing a couple of buttons on her blouse right in front of my face.

I pull back to watch her unfasten three more before she slips her hand inside the material, revealing a white lace bra and a whole lot of lush skin. She drags her finger down the swell of her left breast and hooks the cup of her bra with her index finger. A hint of her pink nipple peeks out, and I know instantly that I will do whatever the fuck she wants me to do.

"You tested me last night. Now I'm testing you today." She pulls off the thin, black scarf from around her neck and holds it out in front of me. "Just let yourself go to only follow my commands. I promise you, it will be worth it."

Darkness consumes me as she wraps the fabric around my eyes and takes away the arousing sight of her. As a texture sensitive person, it's a disarming feeling to have my sight taken away from me. Seeing what's coming helps me prepare for things that may cause a negative reaction from me. But I trust Sloan more than most when it comes to my body. She's known how to touch me from the second we met. And the light in her eyes that seared into me just before she blindfolded me turns me on more than the flesh on her body. If this is what she needs, I'm going to give it to her. One hundred percent.

Her lips brush against my earlobe as she pulls the knot tight. "Trust me, Gareth. Those moments when you want to stop, when you want to think, when you want to control…Just push yourself past those feelings. Force yourself to be in the now with me. No past.

No future. Just my voice."

I can feel my Adam's apple bob in my throat from the sultry tone and I want it. Now. I want my jeans off. I want her clothes off. I want to be inside of her. I want everything she's denying me.

More than anything, I want to be free. From my mind. From my thoughts. From my past and my future. I want this.

"Let's do this, Treacle."

Sloan

My panties are soaked as I slide off of Gareth's lap and stare at his gladiator body, shirtless and blindfolded in front of me. His scruffy jaw. His chest rising and falling in suspense as the sound of my clothes dropping to the floor narrates the scene.

It's erotic as hell. To have a man so strong, so masculine, so intense and mysterious just sit here and wait for my next move is the most sensual experience of my life.

"What are you doing there, Tre?" he asks, his voice more timid than before. The anticipation is clearly weighing heavily on him.

"I'm getting naked." I bite my lip so I remain serious because this is serious. He's trusting me to be confident, and I'm trusting myself to be woman enough for this. That's why I had to do this blindfold thing. I said it's for trust and it partially is. Mostly, it's because I feel like I need a barrier between us. A shield to hide the crazy nerves roaring in my limbs.

I don't want to be nervous. I want to be brave. I want to dive into this arrangement head first and live for once in my damn life. I can do this.

Once fully naked, I glance at my reflection in the glass wall of his closet. My heart falters. I barely recognise the woman staring back at me. She's naked and curvy, and her hair is tousled in a sexy, effortless sort of way I could never recreate on purpose. She has a wild, excited look in her eyes that I haven't seen in a long, long time.

The idea is insane because I work in fashion. Mirrors and appearance are the cornerstones of what I do. I take great care to present myself on a level that my clients will be comfortable with. I look the part of a stylish stylist.

But at some point, I stopped *looking* at my reflection. I was focused on the clothes, and the hair, and the makeup, but I didn't actually see the person staring back. Maybe it's because I didn't like who I saw.

But I like who's staring back at me now. I like her a lot.

"Sloan?" Gareth's voice snaps me out of my reverie.

My reply is instant. "Stand up." My jaw is taut, legs wide, eyes assessing his every muscle.

His furrowed brow lifts curiously as he uses his thick forearms to push himself to a standing position. Now that I'm completely naked and barefoot in front of him, he seems like a giant. I'm five-nine, but I push six foot in heels, so Gareth is normally only an inch or two taller than me. As we are now, my eyes barely meet his jaw.

It doesn't slow me down. "I'm going to touch you, Gareth. A lot," I state, stepping so close to him that I can feel the heat of his skin on my nipples. "Will that be okay?"

The wrinkle in his brow indicates that he's nervous. "S—sure."

"You have to trust me, Gareth," I reply, pressing a firm hand on the thick bulge in his jeans. "If you put all your trust in me, you don't have to worry about your texture sensitivity. I'll tell you how to feel."

His throat moves with a slow swallow as he nods. "Okay."

"Good," I husk and blow cool air against his chest.

A deep noise rumbles from his throat as goosebumps flare up over his pecs, his nipples becoming impossibly firmer.

"Take your jeans off."

He does as he's told. When he stands to his full height again—shoulders wide, legs thick, muscles tense and waiting—it feels like I'm standing at the helm of a ship during a perfect storm. A storm where anything could happen. Death, life, crash, or the most exhilarating ride of my life.

Without hesitation, I move to press my bare flesh against his. Smooth against scratchy. Soft against firm.

"Fuck me," he murmurs when his bare cock rubs against my lower belly.

I press my lips to the mound of his pec. "I intend to," I reply, dipping my head and swirling my tongue around his nipple.

"Christ," Gareth falters. His hands wrap around my body in response, one in my hair and the other cupping my ass cheek.

I bite down on the nubby flesh and he hisses loudly. "You're not supposed to be touching, Gareth."

His hands drop, and I glance down to see them fisted at his sides in frustration. If I could see his eyes, I am sure they'd be shooting daggers.

"This is making me crazy, Sloan."

"Good."

"I want to feel you."

"I'm letting you."

"With my hands."

"Well, where's the fun in that?" I slide my hand down his forearm and twine my fingers with his, pulling them up so they are between us. "Besides, this is about my control. Not yours. Stop trying to rock the boat."

The tense muscle in his jaw relaxes. "That's your second boat pun. I'm going to start to confuse you with my brother Camden if you're not careful."

"Does this remind you of your brother?" I ask, placing his hands on my breasts.

His smartass remark is completely forgotten when he realises what he's touching.

If there's one part of my body I can say that I'm proud of, it's my breasts. Motherhood didn't ruin them like it does for so many women. Mine remain the same teardrop, handful they were before. No more. No less.

Gareth's rough palms massage the two masses of flesh like a caveman testing the strength of a rock. I stare down at his hands on me, grateful for the blindfold because it allows me the freedom to watch unabashedly. His skin is so tan and virile compared to the pale complexion of my chest.

I stifle a moan as he gently rolls my nipples between his fingers. The pressure causes a warmth to shoot through the core of my body, and I have to grip his elbows for balance.

"It's like I'm reading Braille," Gareth says, his jaw slack as he continues blindly assessing every inch. "You know I've yet to see these in the flesh, right?"

"I'm aware," I croak, my need becoming too much for me to handle. "I need you to sit down."

His low chuckle is like fresh oxygen as he reaches backwards for the sofa and lowers his naked body onto it. Without a word, I walk over to his nightstand where I recall him grabbing a condom from the last time. I am pleased to see he still has several left. When I grab one, my eyes catch sight of a tiny piece of familiar black fabric. I grasp the bundle and spread it out to see it's the ripped panties from our first night together. He kept them all this time? I don't know if I should be touched or creeped out.

"Sloan, where are you?"

"I'm right here," I reply, shaking off my thoughts and returning to where he waits for me.

I rest one knee on the sofa beside him and press my front against his side, allowing some delicious skin-on-skin action as I comb my hands through his thick hair. He practically purrs when I tug his head back and run my tongue along his throat.

"Do you like that?" I ask, nibbling on his earlobe and tightening my grip in his hair.

"Yes," he pants.

"Do you want more?"

"God, yes."

I bring my other knee up so I'm kneeling next to him, my ass arched up as I splay one hand on his thigh and one on his shoulder. I kiss my way down his chest, his abs, careful to avoid his dick when I press open-mouthed kisses on each of his muscled thighs.

Removing my hand from his thigh, I grip his length in a sudden, strong embrace.

"Oh fuck." He bites his lip and shifts uncomfortably in the seat as I test the firmness of his length, blowing cool air on the thick vein that runs along the underside of his cock.

"Do you want me to fuck you, Gareth?"

"Treacle, I've wanted you to fuck me for the past year."

"Say that word again."

"Which one?"

"You know which one."

He swallows slowly, steeling himself to sound stable. "Fuck."

"Yes," I husk.

"Fuck," he repeats.

"Yes," I husk again and my tongue swipes the vein on his shaft.

He nearly jolts off the sofa. "Fuck!"

I wrap my lips around him and suck him back as far as I can handle.

"Oh fuck, fuck, fuck, Sloan," he groans, his hands sliding into my hair.

"Pull my hair," I pant, then drop back down on him.

He takes care to shape my hair into a ponytail so he's pulling all the locks with the same pressure. Matching my motions on his dick, he pulls back and releases with every bob of my head, riding me instead of steering me. Dampness seeps out between my legs and my desire to have more takes over.

Unceremoniously, I release him from my mouth and feel around the sofa for the condom I abandoned earlier. I'm grateful Gareth can't see my trembling fingers as I rip open the condom and slide it over his throbbing, soaked erection.

"Fuck, Treacle." Gareth's voice is rough with desire as I position myself astride him and press his tip between my folds.

I pause there, taking in the full sight of him. Hands out to his sides, palms up, body tense and waiting. Waiting for whatever I'm willing to give him. He's so incredibly sexy. Most men wouldn't accept this kind of role reversal. They'd feel emasculated. Callum certainly would have.

But Gareth isn't like most men. He's hard and soft. Strong and flexible. He's huge and muscled but willing to be completely at my mercy.

"Take off the blindfold," I demand.

He hesitates for a moment before pulling the fabric down so it hangs around his neck.

Now's the time Gareth could look at my body. My breasts, my pussy. The apex where his condom-covered dick sits, waiting for enclosure. There is mountains of flesh he could gawk at, but his eyes are locked on mine. His hazel eyes—framed by long, dark lashes and a serious brow—are trained on my face, witnessing everything I'm feeling.

Without a word, I sink down onto him, shifting my legs out as wide as possible to take him as deep as he can go. Both of our jaws drop in silent cries and our foreheads press together as our bodies adjust to the pressure. I haven't had sex with anyone since Gareth over a year ago, and my body is reminding me of that painful fact.

But there's always a beauty with this kind of pain and burning ache that's like scratching an itch to the point of orgasm. It doesn't take long for my hips to begin grinding against the tightness of him inside of me, digging into that delicious pain.

"Touch me, Gareth." My lips drag up his forehead as I throw my head back and shift even deeper on top of him. "I want to feel your hands all over me."

"With pleasure," he growls and begins a smooth coast up my legs and over my ass. Then his hands continue a strong slide up my spine, pausing to grip my hair in a tight squeeze.

"Yes," I moan. "Pull it."

He obeys and takes the opportunity to press his lips to my neck, inhaling deeply as he does. "You smell so fucking good," he husks, suckling at the pulse thundering in my throat. "And you taste even better."

"More," I croon and swirl my hips on his lap. "I need to hear your voice, Gareth. Tell me everything you're thinking."

"I can't wait to feel you come on my cock," he replies instantly, his other hand digging into the meat of my ass cheek, riding the rocking motion of my pelvis. "When I felt you come on my fingers last night, it took everything I had not to come all over myself."

"I would have been so mad."

"Why?" he asks, clearly teeing me up to talk dirty back to him.

"Because I want to feel you come," I reply, grabbing his hair firmly and yanking his face from my neck so he looks into my eyes. I stare him down as I use his shoulder for leverage to begin bouncing on his lap. "I told you this cock is mine and I meant it."

His eyes hood at the increased friction. "Fucking hell," he moans, his own hips thrusting up to meet every drop of pressure I'm giving him.

"Faster, Gareth. Fuck me. Fuck me hard."

A frenzy takes hold of both of us. Next thing I know, I'm screaming for him to flip us over. He lays me across the length of the sofa, and I prop one foot on the arched back as he positions himself between my legs. He grabs my other leg and begins thrusting into me so hard, I have to hold my breath to stop myself from erupting instantly. No man I've ever slept with could keep a pace like this, but

Gareth seems to be doing it without breaking a sweat.

So this is why women lust after athletes. The strength. The muscles. The stamina.

I score my nails up his back, relishing the feeling of his muscles flexing with every pump of his hips, and he grunts from the pain of my hold. What began as a warm, controlled fire in the hearth has exploded into a raging house fire that will desecrate every cognizant thought in my mind.

I can't speak. Noises are coming out of me, but I'm not willing them to do so. And despite how much I crave Gareth's dirty mouth, I don't have the energy or the mindset to utter a single demand.

I don't know who's in control anymore. All I know is when we finally fall over that cliff together—when that fire hose smothers the raging inferno—all that's left is smoke, sweat, and heavy breathing. A cloud of delirious ecstasy.

Gareth pulls out and lifts his heavy weight off of me, sitting up between my legs and pulling off the condom right in front of me. I watch the veins in his forearms as he ties a knot and drops the rubber on the floor. In one swift move, he rolls us so I'm on top of him. His softening penis presses against my belly as my head and hair splay across his damp chest.

His fingers find my hair as I stare at the wall, recovering from the shock of such a powerful orgasm. I would have thought the slickened feeling of sweaty flesh on sweaty flesh would bother Gareth, but he doesn't seem tense. He seems relaxed, the rise and fall of his chest slowing as he catches his breath.

Gareth's voice is hoarse and muffled in my ears when he croaks, "If that was the main course, I do hope you'll be offering seconds." His fingers brush my scalp as he mindlessly plays with my hair.

With a smirk, I muster all the strength I have to lift my head and rest my chin on his chest. "I think I'm definitely up for seconds."

Sex and Football

Gareth

SOME SAY SEX AND FOOTBALL DO NOT MIX. CONSIDERING I JUST played the game of my life today, I say, sign me up for thirds, please.

Our boot studs clack against the concrete of the stadium tunnel as we make our way off the pitch at Chelsea Football Club. Matches at Stamford Bridge in South West London are always intense. The Blues fans are notoriously known as glory hunters and Chelsea has had an incredible season. So the fact that I stopped a shot from their star striker, Vince Sinclair, with only twenty seconds remaining means I'm not getting any smiles from these fans.

The atmosphere in the tunnels after games is always night and day different than it is before games. Before a match, it's like a family reunion. Lots of matey pats on the back and memories tossed back and forth between old teammates. Often times, there's some youth group or fans being escorted out by the host team. The energy is buzzing with intensity and excitement.

After a match, it's another matter entirely. We're forced to make our way off the pitch, side by side through a single hallway. The losing team is pissed off because they lost. The winning team is euphoric because they won. Everyone is at completely different

141

emotional levels with testosterone-driven adrenaline bubbling beneath the surface. This means trash-talking and fights happen quite regularly in the tunnels. Tonight the air is thick with the tension of someone itching to throw a punch.

I'm just itching to see Sloan again.

We saw each other a couple more times after our blindfold experiment that was a smashing success on all levels, but now I haven't seen her for an entire week. She said she was going to be travelling for work and wouldn't be due back until next Monday. I thought it might kill me, but her sexy texts and one epic phone sex session have kept me functioning.

This letting go of control is actually working for me. She makes the rules. She sets the times. She goes home every night. I'm literally at her mercy and I've never been more sexually satisfied. Hearing her confident voice through the phone line, seeing her eyes light up with strength…It's the ultimate aphrodisiac. She's a total tease when she wants to be, and she seems to really get off on edging my cock, which turns me on even more. I'm relishing in the pleasure it brings her and having orgasms I didn't even know existed.

It is the perfect arrangement.

And thank fuck she's back in two days because I feel like a starved carnivore that hasn't had meat for days. I'll stay in London through Sunday night dinner at Dad's. Then Monday morning, I'll be on the first train home to prepare for a night of debauchery with Sloan—my fucking gorgeous Treacle.

Vince Sinclair suddenly jogs past me in the tunnel and aggressively bumps shoulders with Hobo, who's a few steps in front of me.

"Oh, I beg your pardon for being totally fucking visible!" Hobo exclaims and pushes forward at Vince's retreating frame.

I reach out and yank Hobo's shoulders back, forcing him to fall in line beside me. Vince turns on his heel, walking backwards and smiling the same shitty smile he always has on the pitch. He's known for being a cocky sod. Fans either love him or hate him.

His dark eyes slide in my direction, losing all humour and pinning me with a murderous glare. I stare back with indifference. I'm too old to get sucked into the bullshit with newbies. Fights only happen between players who are insecure about their place on the pitch. Vince's contract was nearly sold last year, so he's what I call a flailing guppy in football, trying to make a splash back into the sea.

Vince's teammates push him to keep walking. Thankfully, he begrudgingly concedes. I exhale and try to shake the anxiety riddling my nerves. Vince is a prat, but it doesn't change the fact that he nearly got one past me tonight. He's fast and two-footed and difficult to predict. My tackle on him at the end could have very easily turned into a penalty kick for Chelsea, which would have fucked us royally.

But the call wasn't made despite Vince's dramatics on the ground or his obnoxious arguing with the ref. That means we were able to hold our victory over Chelsea one-nil.

Hobo gives my shoulder a shove. "Jaysus, I hate that guy. I was glad you took him down, but you gave us all heart attacks when you did it in the box like that."

I shoot him a moody scowl. "I knew what I was doing." The truth is, Vince is a hell of a lot faster than me. I'm finding a lot of strikers are nearly getting past me these days. I'm thirty-two years old. In the world of football, that's grandpa status. The last couple of years, I've had to adjust my defence to keep up.

We turn down the hallway toward our changing room where a mass of cameramen, photographers, and media personnel are standing outside the door. I intend to pass by without a word, but a female journalist who looks shockingly like Sloan catches my eye.

"Gareth! What do you have to say about rumours that you and all of your brothers will be selected to play for England in the World Cup this summer?"

My steps falter as the woman arches a perfectly plucked brow at me. Several of my teammates pause and gawk at the question my agent has been calling his wet dream coming true. The headline potential of four brothers playing for England in the World Cup would be the endorsement deal of a lifetime, but the actuality of it happening is less likely than me going back to play for my father.

I stop in front of the woman and all the other cameras press in around us, one even bumping me in the shoulder. "Where do you hear these rumours?"

The brunette smiles a flirty smile and shrugs. "Around."

I nod knowingly, my eyes narrowed. "There's a lot of season left to be played before World Cup selections are made." I know this better than anyone. I was a qualifier for the World Cup team four years ago, but I sprained my ankle at the tail end of the season. It was a minor injury in the scope of my career, but it ruined my chance to play for England.

"Well, your brother Camden's hat-trick for Arsenal tonight pretty much sealed his spot on the team."

My brows lift. Now I'm itching to get to my locker to see for myself. Normally, the very first thing I do after a match is walk off the pitch and check my mobile to see how my brothers played. Vi texts us updates of each other's matches, and reading her stream of commentary during all of our games is one of my favourite things about football. I've been telling her for years to do a podcast, but she laughs it off.

I shoot a broad smile at the reporter. "The only thing I know to be a fact and not a rumour is that Camden would have never scored three on me."

The other reporters roar with laughter. Then the woman smiles and nods a silent thank you as the others begin shouting follow-up questions. With a wink, I turn away from the crowd and find Hobo standing at the changing room door waiting for me.

"You are a cocky sod, you know that?" he jeers.

I shrug. "It's a family trait."

After finishing the post-match press conference where I was grilled about the upcoming award I'll be receiving, I hurry out to the player parking garage to find Vi waiting in her vehicle. She smiles brightly as I hold up one finger and jog over to the waiting fans on the other side of the barrier. I hurry through about twenty autographs before I give everyone a smile and wave my goodbyes.

I head to Vi's car and toss my bag into the backseat of her SUV. "I like the new car," I say, folding myself into the front passenger seat and draping my jacket over my lap. "I see you decided not to go with a proper people carrier."

She rolls her eyes. "Hayden wanted one. He said he liked the movie screen in it. I told him I'm a football sister, not a football mummy. Rocky is only one. We have a while before I need room for kits."

I smile and eye her appearance skeptically. Her blonde hair is in a high ponytail. She's dressed in a Manchester United T-shirt with HARRIS in big block letters on the back, and I know she has an Arsenal jersey and enough Bethnal Green kits to wear every day of the week. My sister is fooling herself if she thinks she's not a footy mummy already.

"Whatever you say, sis." I glance out the window at the press waiting outside like vultures. I gave them a full thirty minute interview and answered all their incessant questions, yet they still wait outside for more. "Are we going to your place? I don't want to go to a restaurant. The crowds will be awful."

Vi nods. "I have soup in the slow cooker."

"Perfect."

"Are you staying at Dad's tonight?"

I nod. "Unless you've suddenly added an addition onto your flat?"

She smiles. "I'm afraid not."

Vi turns to head northeast on the road that runs along the River Thames. Since it's a Saturday night, the traffic is buzzing. Busy Londoners ready for a night on the town. The bus doesn't go back to Manchester until tomorrow morning because our team was invited to the opening of some new club in London. It's good press, so most of the guys headed straight there.

"You're not going out with the team tonight?"

I look at her flatly. "Pass."

She giggles. "You're such a moody sod. Antisocial to the max these days. Your family used to be the exception, but it seems we're also becoming part of the rule."

"What the bloody hell does that mean?"

"You never used to miss Sunday dinners, Gareth. And you used to have no problem being Camden or Tanner's wingman at a club when they needed you. Granted, you were never the manwhore the boys were. I mean, I certainly never had to apply the Bacon Sandwich Rule to some girl for you, but you were known to partake in a proper night out."

I groan in disgust from her mentioning the rule. Camden and Tanner have a complex over having shared a womb, so that apparently meant they had to fight over food and women as well. When we were kids, Vi set the rule that if one of them licked the food, then the other couldn't take it. As the boys grew older and became more obnoxious, they realised the Bacon Sandwich Rule could also apply to women. The wankers.

"I think even you can admit that things are different in our family this year," I state, glancing out the window as we pass the Vauxhall Bridge. "Cam and Tan are both married. Booker's going to be a father. You're supposed to be getting married one of these days."

She glances over at me. "Does it bother you that everyone's paired up now?"

"No," I scoff defensively. "But it hardly calls for going clubbing with my brothers and invoking the Bacon Sandwich Rule."

"I guess that's a good point." Vi shifts awkwardly in her seat. "I just hate how isolated you are up in Manchester. I don't know what you get up to all week long. You seem like you're becoming more and more introverted every time I see you."

"Vi, I'm not some moody teenager. I'm a man, and I'm just fine on my own," I defend, fighting back a smirk about how not alone I was last week when Sloan had me tied up with her tape measure or blindfolded with her scarf. Definitely not a thought I should be having while sitting in a confined car with my bloody sister.

I can feel Vi's curious eyes on me. "What's happening with you and that stylist?"

"Nothing," I bark out much too quickly. I clear my throat and attempt to calm the fuck down. "Nothing. We're friends. Colleagues you could say. That's all."

"Friends," she mimics, clearly not believing me. "Friends who fuck is more like it."

"Vi!" I chastise, swerving my accusing eyes in her direction. "You yell at us for swearing, yet you're over there speaking like a sailor."

She giggles as she stares down the road. "I can tell something's different about you."

"How?"

"I can see it in your game."

"Bollocks," I scoff, fisting my jacket in my sweaty palms. I don't want Vi to figure this out. What Sloan and I are doing is casual. So casual I can't even kiss her on the lips. If Vi finds out we're sleeping together, she'll get ridiculous ideas in her head about my future.

"I've watched you play your whole life, Gareth. That tackle you made at the end there...It had a finesse to it. A confidence I haven't seen in you the last few years."

"It's called the act of a desperate man. I'm old, Vi."

"You're not old. You're seasoned."

"In football terms, that means the care home is on standby."

"Stop," she scolds, swatting my shoulder. "I'm just happy you're not alone."

"I am alone!" I nearly roar, annoyed that she's already getting grandiose ideas in her head with basically no tangible information. When Vi gets like this, the only course of action is deflection. "You're the one putting off your wedding with Hayden."

Her jaw drops. "I'll marry him eventually!"

"When? After you have a couple more kids and have to buy a bigger place, as well as a people carrier?"

She frowns and shrinks in her seat, chewing her lip nervously. I instantly feel guilty for winding her up because I'm sensing it isn't a simple issue. "What's the problem there, Vi?"

"Nothing!" She forces a bright, toothy smile. "We just need to get through this World Cup business first."

"Not you, too," I groan, running a hand through my hair.

"It's all anyone has been talking about this week! If they select all four of my brothers, it will be the most amazing thing that's ever happened to our family."

"You mean after the birth of Rocky."

"Yes, after Rocky." She rolls her eyes. "Rocky wants you guys in the World Cup as well. She's your number two fan, after me."

"Obviously." I can't help but laugh. Rocky is Vi's miniature in appearance already. In time, she'll be shouting expletives at the refs like her mummy.

"So the World Cup is more important than you getting married?"

Vi growls like a little dog. "Why does it matter? Hayden and I are happy. We don't need a piece of paper to tell us that."

"I think it matters to Hayden," I reply, watching her curiously. She's hiding something. I can tell by the way she's gripping the wheel and refusing to look at me. "What's going on? Why the odd face?"

"My face isn't odd!" she peals, her voice higher pitched than usual.

"Yes it is. Spill it. You know I'll get it out of you eventually anyway."

"You're going to laugh at me." She groans and stops at a red light, glancing over at me with a serious look on her face. "You have to promise not to laugh."

I roll my eyes. "I promise."

She pulls her lip into her mouth and mumbles something I can't fully understand.

"What did you say?"

"I said I don't want to stop being a Harris, all right?"

My jaw drops as I stare at my sister. I don't know why I'm shocked. Vi always says she is the glue that holds our family together while I am the rock that keeps us upright. And no one is a bigger cheerleader for our family than her. But I've seen the way she looks at Hayden. I've seen their love firsthand. They had a rough go at one point, and I thought I was going to have to commit my first murder, but he got his shit together. He's become an incredible source of happiness for her. Watching them as a family has been a beautiful thing to witness. What is going on in that head of hers?

"Vi—" I start but don't get to finish.

"Don't tell me I'm being overly sentimental, all right?" she argues, her posture stiff and defensive. "I love being a Harris. I love having our mother's name. It used to give me anxiety, but I feel differently about it now that I'm a mum myself. Proud even."

My throat tightens at the mention of our mum. She was such a source of light, even in the end. I hate that our father tainted her absence with a wake of darkness.

Sadly, I'm really the only one who knows much about her. Vi was only four when she died. All she really knows of Mum is that they share a name and happened to be born on the same day. We've always struggled to celebrate Vi's birthday as a result. But when Vi gave Rocky the middle name Vilma, I could see that Vi found peace with her name somehow. Mum would have been so proud.

"I don't think you're being overly sentimental," I reply, my voice thick with emotion. "But I'm wondering why you don't just tell Hayden that you want to keep your name when you get married."

"I can't," she moans.

"Why not?"

"Because I feel awful about it. Hayden is proud of his family name, too. And the Clarkes are wonderful. What if they take it personally? What am I saying by telling Hayden that his name is good enough for our daughter but not good enough for me?"

I exhale heavily. "I think you're underestimating your fiancé, Vi."

"Am I? I know it's old-fashioned, but isn't this completely emasculating for a man?" She pauses, squeezing her fingers around the wheel as she searches for what she's trying to say. "I love Hayden's manliness. It's what attracted me to him…in the bedroom."

"Vi!" I groan and turn away. I can't look at her when she talks like this.

"I'm sorry, but it's true! He's an incredibly deep, soulful, sensitive man, but all that goes away in the bedroom."

"I'm not joking. You have to stop," I croak.

"He has this animalistic side to him—"

"I will jump out of this moving car!" I roar and she flinches at the sudden change in volume. "That would ruin your chance at seeing your brothers play together in the World Cup."

"For a moody sod, you sure can turn on the drama when you want to." She exhales. "Fine, fine. No more of that. I'm just worried that not taking his name will hurt a side of him that I love."

I do my best not to throw up in my mouth over the images that her words evoked in my head and pray that I get a concussion at the next match to erase those horrid thoughts. Putting aside my immature feelings, I help my sister as best I can.

"A secure man—a man who knows what he has and is confident that it isn't going anywhere—will not be emasculated by this."

"How do you know that? Truly."

I exhale slowly and shake my head. "Vi, were you never curious why I let Hayden speak to you the night of his brother's wedding after he had broken your heart? I mean, history shows that I could have just kicked his arse."

She looks over at me with a frown, passing traffic lights sliding across her curious face. "I guess that was a bit odd. Certainly out of character for you now that I think about it."

"Exactly," I reply with a deep chuckle. "It was because what Hayden said eliminated all the doubts I had about him."

"What did he say?" she asks, her voice quiet with anxiety.

"He called you his forever, Vi." My jaw clenches as I recall the stricken look on his face that night. He looked like a man who had left his heart on a battlefield and my sister was the only person who could revive him.

His devotion was impressive because the entire week leading up to that night, Camden, Tanner, Booker, and I had been threatening him. We patrolled his home around the clock to show him we weren't fucking pleased with what he did to our sister. It was a Harris Shakedown that sent all of Vi's previous boyfriends running for the hills. The four of us always said that if a bloke was good enough for Vi, he'd be willing to stand up against all of us. Well, Hayden didn't run. He walked right up to me at the wedding and told me Vi belonged to him whether I accepted it or not.

I look at my sister, who I sometimes forget is still young and figuring life out. "Hayden was going to do anything to get you back. It was then that I knew he was someone I could trust with your heart."

"You never told me any of that before." Vi sniffles and swipes an errant tear off her cheek. "You stupid prats scared away every bloody man in my life. I just thought Hayden snuck past you."

"He earned the right to you," I correct and reach over to clasp her fist in my hand. "Hayden is not the kind of man who has to be all of one thing. He can both dominate and surrender. In fact, it makes him more of a man if he can do both. Respect him enough to let him tell you that himself."

Thankful for Wine

12

Sloan

"**S**OPHIA! HURRY UP, HONEY. WE NEED TO HEAD OUT TO YOUR grandmother's now, or we won't hear the end of it!" I shout up the stairs from where I've been waiting in my foyer for over five minutes while my daughter does what she calls "primping."

"Just one more minute, Mummy Gumdrops!" she bellows from her bedroom.

I shake my head with a smile. All of a sudden, she's seven years old going on thirteen. When did that happen? She's always enjoyed dressing up and playing make-believe. Primping is completely new, though, along with a few other things I've noticed about her since I divorced Callum. Like how she doesn't want me to read to her at bedtime anymore. Or how she refuses to eat Greek yogurt and is too cool to give me a kiss when I drop her off at school.

This is exactly what I was afraid of when I agreed to shared custody. I can only control her and see what she's doing fifty percent of the time. I'm not there every day to see those moments she gets away without hugging her dad goodbye for school. Or when she looks in the mirror and asks why her belly is bigger than her friend Ainsley's. I'm not there to hear Callum tell her not to have any more sweets because those are what make her tummy big.

153

Being a divorced mother means I have lost some of my original Sopapilla. Now she's morphing into this new hybrid that I have to reacquaint myself with every other week. I know this is a lifestyle that many families endure and they survive. Some are even better for it. Deep down, I also know that staying with Callum wouldn't have been the example of family I want to impart on Sophia.

I think the divorce was hard for me to accept because I wasn't ready for it. It came sooner than I anticipated. I still had cancer tunnel vision. I was still picturing my sweet Sopapilla looking so tiny in those big hospital beds, so I was prepared to live the way we were living until I knew Sophia was truly healed and out of the scary cancer woods. I would have walked through fire to heal her, so staying married to Callum seemed a lot less painful in comparison.

But this life is my new normal. We are co-parenting and I have to accept it. I also have to accept the fact that if I'm late dropping Sophia off at Margaret's house, she will make damn sure I know about it. And I'm not sure I have the mental fortitude to bite my tongue with her anymore.

I'm blaming that part entirely on Gareth. Prior to meeting him and engaging in our crazy friends with benefits situation last week, I would have bitten my tongue when Margaret scolded me in front of my daughter. I would have held my breath when she commented about my trousers being much too tight, or my hair being far too long, or my makeup being too pale for my complexion.

I'm not one who enjoys conflict. In fact, most times, I shut down and walk away. When I became a mother, I really had to push myself to not give Sophia whatever she wanted when she cried, especially because she was a sick toddler. Keeping the peace has always felt like the easier road to travel. Who wants the anxiety of an argument with someone?

But after spending several days with Gareth last week and commanding control over our sex life, I have a newfound respect for people who assert themselves in situations. It's been empowering to have such a strong, virile, beast of a man put so much faith in me. He puts my needs and my desires first all the time. And the way his attention stays so laser focused on me when I show up at his house…I can't help but rise to the occasion. He's pushing me to be this way because it's a turn-on for him, too!

What life is this?

This kind of devotion from a powerful man is something all women should experience at least once in their lives. It would give them the strength to shoot for whatever goals they want to accomplish. Anything is possible when you can take control of your sex life.

Sophia flounces down the stairs, snapping me out of my musings of Gareth. My eyes fly wide and I bite back a laugh as I take in my daughter's appearance.

She looks like Courtney Love after a bender in London. For bottoms, she's wearing metallic silver leggings with a pair of purple Wellies. For a top, I think I see a pink tank top with silver studs around the neckline, but it's difficult to get a good look at beneath her long, white faux fur coat. Her normally perfect skin has been massacred with eyeliner, eyeshadow, and…*Is that glitter lotion?* Her big brown eyes are lost in a sea of makeup in all the wrong places.

Trying not to laugh, I ask, "Sophia, what have you done?"

Her eyes fly wide. "I've dressed properly for Grandmama."

My brows pinch. "What do you mean?"

"Grandmama said I should dress my best when I come to her house," she replies in her British accent.

My nails dig harshly into my palms. "She did, did she?"

Sophia looks down at her Wellies. "I'm not sure she'll like my boots, but those puddles simply *must* be jumped in. The last time when I jumped in my trainers, Daddy had to buy me new ones."

Irritation presses sharply into my temples like a blunt force trauma. This is a prime example of having no control over what's being said to Sophia and how it's being interpreted by her. When

155

Margaret made comments like this to Sophia in the past, I served as a buffer to explain it away.

"Grandmama didn't mean you have to play with the neighbour boy who threw mud on you. She meant that the families are old friends, so we need to be polite."

I stride over to where Sophia is standing on the steps and grab her cute little fingers in mine. "Sophia, while I love, love, love this look you have going on here and think it is one hundred percent red carpet-worthy, I think we need to go upstairs and tone it down a little bit."

She looks back at me in horror. "But Grandmama said!"

My eyes fly wide. "I know, baby! I know. But you can't wear white fur to the country!" I laugh heartily and swat her on the shoulder. "The polar bears will think you belong to them."

Sophia's furry brows crumple. "Mum, there are no polar bears out at Grandmama's."

My jaw drops. "There aren't?"

She rolls her eyes. "No. You should be embarrassed that you thought that, Mum."

I bark out a laugh but sober immediately. "I'm humiliated."

She clutches my cheeks in her hands. "No, but really, Mum. Don't ever tell anyone you said that. It's not very bright."

This elicits a genuine smile. Through a few more giggles, I convince Sophia to let me style her like one of my clients. But being the negotiator she is, I have to promise to let her style me sometime in the near future. It's a price I'm very willing to pay.

The Lake District is a good thirty minute drive from my house. Normally, I dread the drive. It's like driving down death row and preparing to give away my child to some horrid criminal.

Today it's not as hard, though. The past week with Sophia was so different than it's been in months. Ever since the divorce, I've been constantly searching for fun things to do with Sophia so she will love me more than Callum. I was desperate to make memories and ease the burden and pain of having a broken family.

But last week wasn't a constant, "What are we going to do next," state. There was a sense of living in the moment and seeing it for its simple beauty. Watching Sophia play with her dolls on her bedroom floor was suddenly so much more emotionally rewarding than all the excursions I've taken her on around Manchester this past year. Even the makeover I gave her just moments ago involved more giggles than a full day at some museum. Maybe having a bit of balance in my life isn't so bad after all.

I drive up the long gravel lane, passing through the perfectly manicured landscaping, or *gardens* as the British call them. Shrubs trimmed perfectly, fall flowers in bloom, orange leaves falling all around us. Honestly, it is dreamy. Margaret Coleridge's estate is quite similar to the one where Callum resides but older. It's also larger in the sense that it occupies two acres and is elevated so when you drive up to it, you feel a bit like you're driving to a castle.

I'm grateful for the estate in a lot of ways because Sophia has the best experiences out here. She really embraces nature. She loves running in the woods, jumping in the puddles, and going out on the sailboat whenever Callum agrees to take her. They are the kind of memories I would have killed for as a child.

When we pull around the large fountain in the middle of the driveway, Callum and Margaret walk out, clearly watching for our arrival. Hot on their heels is the oh-so stunning, blonde, and ridiculously made-up Lady Godiva.

I've been noticing her presence at more and more of my drop-offs with Sophia. Callum formally introduced me to Callie and told me they are quite serious. She looks like everything Margaret Coleridge hates. Regardless, here Callie stands, clasping Callum's hand and waving to Sophia like she's some high school camp counsellor.

Sophia squeals from the backseat when she sees Margaret's bloodhound, Rex, trotting up to her car door. "Stop the car, Mum! Rexy neeeeeeds meee!" she sings and shakes her Welly boots anxiously.

"I'm stopping, I'm stopping," I say with a smile.

As soon as the vehicle stops, she unbuckles herself and opens the door, nearly falling on top of Rex in her excitement. The old hound sniffs and licks her face like it's been years since he's seen her instead of seven days. Sophia giggles happily and begins running toward the grass with him. He bounces alongside her, nipping at the bottom of her purple coat—a much more subdued option overtop of a practical pair of jeans and a long sleeve black shirt. Paired with her Wellies, I think Sophia is dressed perfectly for the country.

I turn my attention to Margaret, Callum, and Callie, who now stand beside me.

"You're quite late," Margaret states, tossing the tail of her beige cloak over her shoulder. "We thought you might have died. Would have been nice if you'd phoned."

My face crumples. "It would have been difficult to call if I was dead."

Callum shoots his steely blue eyes at me in silent warning. "Maybe you can start ringing me when you're on your way so Mother doesn't have to worry unnecessarily."

I roll my eyes. "Sure, Cal. I'd love to call."

"This is a court ordered agreement," Margaret states, the wrinkles around her eyes stacking on top of each other as she narrows them at me. "I'm sure I don't need to remind you."

"No, I'm fully aware," I reply with a small huff and glance annoyingly at Callie, whose big doe eyes are blinking like she doesn't speak our language. "And we were late because Sophia said you weren't happy with her appearance last time she visited."

Margaret tightens her shawl and keeps her expression flat. "She wears too much pink. It's not proper."

"She's seven. How is pink not proper for a seven-year-old?"

"She can wear pink when she's with you. When she comes to the country, she should be dressed more practically."

"Well, she doesn't understand what you mean by proper. In the future, maybe you can bring it to me if you're not happy with something and not expect a seven-year-old to understand what proper attire is for the country. Styling is kind of what I do for a living, you know."

Margaret's lips thin as she drags her gaze down my body. I'm wearing a simple pair of jeans, boots, and a graphic T-shirt that says, "I'm a Mom, but a Cool Mom." I tighten my trench coat around me so she can't read the fine print below that says, "Now Pass the Wine."

"She looks fine today, so dress her more like that in the future," Callum states, smoothing a strip of his hair that breaks loose from the gel in the wind. "We'll see you next week."

I refrain from rolling my eyes at his dismissal. "Before I go, I wanted to talk to you about Thursday."

Callum frowns. "This Thursday? It's my week, Sloan."

Licking my lips, I do my best to keep my cool. "I understand, but this Thursday is Thanksgiving. I figured since you guys don't celebrate the holiday, maybe I can have Sophia over for dinner. Just for a couple of hours, then I'll bring her right back."

Callum looks at me like I'm speaking another language, but it's Callie's voice that replies, "But we're British."

I cut my eyes at her, blinking slowly. "I'm aware."

"We don't celebrate Thanksgiving." She looks to Callum for help, and he simply nods his head in agreement.

I can hardly believe the exchange. Exhaling heavily, I glance over at my ex-husband. "Callum, surely you didn't forget that I'm American."

"No," he scoffs. "You make that really difficult."

"Well, I would really love to celebrate Thanksgiving with Sophia. It's very big in America and it's one of my favourite holidays. I'm sorry I didn't think to include it in our custody agreement—"

Margaret cuts me off mid-sentence. "We'll discuss it and let you know."

My gaze turns to her. She looks like an angry headmistress who's trying to determine what sort of corporal punishment to inflict on me. She can't possibly be inserting herself into this decision. It's not even a day she would see Sophia anyway.

Callum looks timidly over at his mother, clearly unsure where her mind is at as well. I didn't think this would be an issue. I'm not asking for a whole day. Just a couple of hours. Surely they can't say no.

Margaret looks at Cal and gives him a subtle shake of the head. He nods back in response. Cal is so weak. So submissive. I could literally tie up Gareth with rope and he would never look a fraction as spineless as Callum Coleridge does underneath the withering stare of his mother.

My rage is dampened when Sophia pummels into my legs. "Mum, when can we get a dog at your house?"

My lips purse together as I try to ignore the fact that she doesn't call it "our house." I hate that she looks at my home as a place she visits and not a place that's hers.

I squat down to eye level. "Maybe someday, Soap, but I think we have too much going on right now."

She sighs dramatically. "We don't have anything going on. I don't even play football like all the other girls."

I pin her with a warning look. "Sophia. Mommy is the boss, so be a good girl and maybe we'll discuss it again next year."

She wraps her arms around my neck and squeezes, her voice muffled in my shoulder as she says, "Fine…It's probably good. Rex would be sad if I had another friend."

"That's a good girl," I reply, beaming with pride. I press my lips to her hair. "I have to be going now, baby. You be good for your Grandma and Daddy."

She pulls back to look at me, keeping her cosy arms wrapped tightly around my neck. "I'm going to miss you so much."

Heart crushing aches. Knee-trembling pain. Burning desolation all through my body. "I'm going to miss you, too. But I'll see you in—"

"Seven days!" she sings, smiling brightly.

Hopefully sooner, I think to myself. "Give me a kiss."

She plops a wet one right on my lips and squeezes me one last time. As I drive away, I try really hard to remember what it was that made me agree to marry Cal. Then I get a glimpse of Sophia waving goodbye to me in the rearview mirror and it all comes back to me.

Touch has a Memory

Gareth

SUNDAY NIGHT DINNER AT DAD'S IS MADNESS, AS USUAL. TANNER and Camden try to fight me for Rocky most of the evening, but I refuse them because I've decided my niece is my date for the night. Everyone is busy playing happy family around the table, but I'm not paying attention because I have the sweetest girl in the whole world right in front of me.

Rocky's blue eyes are big and glossy as she faces me on my lap and runs her chubby fingers over the whiskers on my chin. The touch is a little nerve-rattling, but I focus my thoughts on her fluffy blonde hair that's tied up into a spiky ponytail atop her head. She's jabbering away, not making very much sense, but telling me a story that I think has something to do with an elephant, a man, and maybe her mummy. I'm not quite sure. It's fucking adorable, though.

I can feel my dad's eyes on me the entire time. I look over and see him watching Rocky with so much affection, it overwhelms me. The way he acts with her is so night and day different from what we experienced growing up. It's like a puzzle I can't quite figure out. Does he dote over Rocky because she's Vi's child? Would he be like this with my kid if I had one?

I roll my eyes at the thought. He won't come to Manchester to

162

watch me play a football game. He certainly wouldn't coo over a fictitious child I will never even have.

My phone vibrates on the table, and I look around Rocky to read the text that says the cab I ordered is here. "Bye, Rock Star," I murmur and kiss her on the cheek before handing her over to Tanner.

"Where are you going?" Tanner asks, looking up at me as I stand.

I push my chair in. "Back to Manchester."

"You're going back tonight?" Camden probes, walking over with a confused look on his face.

"Yep," I reply simply and move to grab my bag. "I'll see you guys next week."

Dad pins me with a stare from the head of the table. "Must you go tonight?"

"Yes," I state through clenched teeth while kissing Vi on the cheek and ignoring everyone's concerned looks.

I've just opened the front door to leave when I hear my dad's deep voice echo through the dark foyer. "Gareth, wait."

I turn to see his large frame as he strides toward me and steps into the light streaming through the entryway. If I ever wanted an idea of what I'll look like in twenty-odd years, I just need to look at my dad. Aside from his blue eyes and grey hair, we are identical.

His salt and pepper hair glows in the light, the shadows severe as he stands before me. "Why are you leaving tonight? It's late."

I shake my head at him. "Because I have things going on tomorrow." More like I have someone coming over, so I'm actually excited to go home for once.

"Well, I wanted to talk to you about something quite serious."

"Can it wait?"

Dad frowns and ignores my request. "I want you to move back to London, Gareth."

"What?" I ask, certain I heard him wrong.

"I want you back in London," he says, his jaw tight, eyes serious. "I know there's no chance you'll play for me again, so I've been talking to the manager at Arsenal. The midseason transfer window opens up soon, and they're looking to sell their current defender. You could play with Camden, Gareth."

"For Arsenal?" His words nearly knock the wind out of me. I choke out a laugh. "You have got to be joking."

"I don't joke," he replies firmly.

I pinch the bridge of my nose and ignore the honk of the taxi's horn going off behind me. "Dad, why would I transfer to Arsenal? My home is in Manchester. I'm the bloody captain."

He sighs heavily, his eyes wrinkling with clear anxiety. "Gareth, I know why you went off to Man U, but things are different now. The twins are married and there are grandbabies coming. I think it's time you come home."

"Manchester is my home!" I exclaim, shaking my head to ensure that I'm actually conscious. "What the fuck is this?"

"I want everyone back in London," he nearly growls. "There are a lot of changes going on. Our family is growing. Rocky is getting bigger. Booker is going to be a father soon. I think that you should be here for the family. This is our chance to…do better."

"Better than what?" I ask, gripping the strap of my bag on my shoulder so hard I can feel the fabric indenting in my skin.

"Better than the past, of course!" He exclaims and turns away from me to gesture up the stairs.

A chill runs up my spine as the memories of our mum's final days flood back with a vengeance. This is a place in my mind that I don't often tap into, and I can't believe he's going there with me now.

My tone is firm when I reply through clenched teeth, "I don't need to do better, Dad. I was there." I thrust my finger toward the stairs like I'm pointing to a crime scene. "You were gone, but I was there. Vi was there. We held everyone together while you disappeared into seven fucking years of mourning."

"And you've never let me atone for it!" Dad nearly shouts, his voice breaking at the end. He steps closer to me and whispers, "You've punished me by moving away to the one place I can't return to, and I'm tired of it."

"Why can't you return there?"

"Because it hurts too much!" He all but howls and his eyes glaze over. "I want a second chance with you, Gareth. Having Rocky around…Seeing your brothers settled and happy…It's all making me realise how much I missed. You went to Manchester to get back at me, and I want that time to be over."

Seeing his pain only stokes my own. I was a child, yet his pain mattered more than mine. That isn't right. My fists clench at my sides when I reply, "You don't call the shots in my life, Dad. You haven't since the second Mum got sick and you turned your back on her."

My words are a kick to the gut that he's not prepared for and his face crumples with emotion. Emotion he never shows.

But I'm not done. "You want me to come back to London because of shit in the past that you still can't own up to, and that is not my problem."

"Gareth, I'm owning it! And I'm telling you, there's a lot going on in the family and I…I can't handle it all on my own. I need help around here!" He stumbles over his words and moves to touch me.

I inhale sharply and step back onto the front step, far away from his embrace. He doesn't get to touch me. He doesn't get to take anything more from me. Nothing's changed. He just wants me to take over again like I did when I was a kid.

Not. Happening.

"I am only a train ride away. I'm in London weekly and I take phone calls from everyone daily. What more could you possibly need from me?"

Dad exhales heavily and lowers his shaking hands. "I don't know."

I nod knowingly. "Then just keep answering to *Father* and we can continue to play happy family on Sunday nights like we've been doing for years, all right?"

He swallows slowly, the familiar shield of armour coming down over his face. His emotions drift away as he steps back out of the light. "Very well," he mumbles and turns to walk down the hall.

I see the disappointment my words have caused him, but it does nothing to top the lifetime of disappointment I've felt as a result of his actions.

He knows bloody well that me signing with Man U was all spurred on by him. When I was younger, I had very little control over my career as a football player. Dad was my manager and made all my contract decisions. The truth is, I didn't know how good I was until I found out about my first Premiership offer from Man City Football Club. It was my twenty-first birthday, and I was at a night club with some mates when a veteran striker for Man City happened to be there. He approached me and called me a fool for not accepting a multimillion-pound contract. I asked him what bloody contract he was talking about because I certainly wasn't making that kind of money with Bethnal. It was then he told me about the offer his team made me the year prior.

I was stunned. I had never heard of such money because my father—my manager—apparently took it upon himself to reject the offer.

I. Was. Livid.

But I wasn't about to confront him. I wanted a harsher punishment for someone who had the nerve to pretend he had my best interests at heart. I wanted to kick him where it counted.

So I reached out to Man U. At first, they wouldn't take my calls. They held a grudge against my father for breaking away from them so poorly when Mum got sick. But they must have done some digging on my stats because I eventually got an invitation to train with them. Not long after, I got an offer. An offer to laugh at all other offers.

It was a life-changing amount of money.

I thought about how wonderful that kind of money would be for my family. For my sister and my brothers. I could give them anything they ever wanted. Mostly, they wouldn't need our dad anymore. They wouldn't need to rely on him for anything. They could count on me.

With a heavy sigh, I turn to walk down the front steps and climb into the cab. As the driver pulls away, my clothes begin to stiffen on my body. A cold sweat breaks out, so I pull at the neckline of my shirt. When I get a whiff of something sweet that the driver is eating, I'm overcome by a memory I'd rather forget.

Gareth

8 Years Old

Mum's hands are clammy as I watch her chest rise and fall with short, shaky breaths. Her entire body feels cold. I squeeze my hot palms around her hands with an apologetic half-smile because they are sticky from the cream and jam I spread on scones for Vi and my brothers a little bit ago. The kids are always asking for something. A snack, a drink, help with the telly, someone to play with. It never stops. Four kids is too many. I can't wait for Vi to turn five in a couple of months. Maybe she can start helping in the kitchen and keep the twins out of my way.

At least she knows how to change Booker's nappies, though. That's one job I will never do.

On top of the kids, there's the doorbell. The neighbour lady keeps ringing our gate, dropping off big pans of food because she thinks that's what we need. She needs to come by with what we really need. Help.

But stupid Dad won't let anyone in the door. The old woman has to leave the food at the gate. Then he barks at me to go get it. It makes me so mad because I need to be with Mummy. I've spent every single day with her since she stopped getting out of bed a few weeks ago. If I didn't have to go to school, I would never leave her. She needs me.

I probably wouldn't have to do so much if Dad wasn't such an awful meanie. He won't let anyone in. Friends, the neighbour, not even our uncle who lives in America and flew all the way here to help.

And he hardly ever lets us out. The only places we can go is the back garden, the woods behind our house, and school. That's it.

I hate him.

But I love Mummy.

She's my best friend.

My breath is still heavy from my sprint up the stairs to hurry back to her. I didn't want to leave her, but I could hear Dad crying in the other room. I knew if he heard the doorbell ring again, he'd shout. He always shouts. Sometimes he even growls.

But crying…He doesn't usually do that.

Crying makes my stomach hurt.

Crying makes me think bad things are coming.

Mum and Dad think I don't know what's going on. They think I don't know Mummy is dying. But I'm eight. I'm not a baby anymore. I can understand what the doctor says around Mum even though he acts like she's not here. Dad and the doctor always talk about her. Nobody talks to her.

Only me.

That's my job. That's why I spend every day with her.

I could talk to her forever.

But I know forever isn't going to happen. Last time the doctor was here, he said one word that made everything go from bad to really bad.

"Days."

Stupid, awful, bloody cancer.

I hate it. Mummy tried to fight it. She had the surgeries she didn't want to have because Dad made her, but nothing worked. Now my mummy is leaving me.

The sound of a sniffle makes me look from Mum's hands to her eyes. They flutter open and reveal the brightest blue I've ever seen. Maybe it's because her skin is so white, but it looks like the blue food colouring we dye Easter eggs with. They almost hurt to look at because they are so pretty.

"How's my best boy?" Mum's voice croaks in the pretty Swedish accent she has that I love so much. She closes her eyes and winces beneath her smile.

"Just fine, Mummy. Do you need something? Do you want me to get out the cards?" I look over at the table where I've stashed a few things to pass the time. Dice, cards, and a notepad for her to write her poetry on. Sometimes I write it for her when she's feeling poorly.

She shakes her head. "No cards today, love. I just need you." Her chin wobbles. "We have to talk about something, Gareth. I need to ask you something."

"Anything, Mummy." I would do absolutely anything she asked me. I'd climb mountains. I'd fight dragons. I'd blast out a fire if it made her feel even a tiny bit better.

She clears her throat and touches my cheek. "I might be going to Heaven soon, and I need to know if you're strong enough to stay with me until I go."

Her words take a minute to climb into my brain. Did she say Heaven? Like, the real Heaven? Or is she talking about a poem of hers?

"What, Mummy?" I ask like a stupid idiot.

"I feel myself dying, Gareth. If you're not strong enough to stay, I need you to go now." Her voice breaks and she sucks in a big breath, like she's trying too hard to be brave. "Because as scared as I am, nothing scares me more than hurting you, my sweet, lovely, wonderful boy."

I blink and my cheeks are instantly dripping with some sort of liquid. "So you're going to go to Heaven now?"

She nods.

My head begins to shake. "I don't want you to go to Heaven!"

Stupid idiot! Don't cry! *Mum's face looks sadder than I've ever seen. I hate when Mum's face gets sad!* Stop it, Gareth. Stop being a baby! She can't take it!

I squeeze my eyes shut real tight, then open them, trying hard to be a brave man and not a scared little boy. "Do you really have to go?"

"Yes, my boy. I'm tired of not feeling well. In Heaven, I will feel so much better." *Mum sniffles and wipes a dribble of snot from her nose.* "Then you won't have to take care of me anymore."

"But I like taking care of you!" *I cry, losing the fight I have between being a boy and being a man. It's a line I've been tightrope walking since they said she was sick.* "I would do anything for you, Mummy. So whatever you need. I'm here. I'm not going anywhere."

She nods with a tightness to her jaw. "That's good. Then please just hold my hand."

"Are you sure I shouldn't get Dad?" *I look nervously at the door. Getting Dad sounds scary, but I'm scared. I'm so, so scared. What if I'm not good enough for this? What if I'm bad at helping her?*

"Dad can't be here right now." *Mum's eyes look sad. So, so sad.*

My eyes narrow, anger replacing tears. "Because he's mean." *It's the truth. I hate him.*

Her dry lips purse together. "He's mean because he loves me too much and he's afraid. Fear does strange things to people, Gareth. You see, Daddy has been my bestest friend in the whole world. We created a life together that most people only dream about and he's losing that dream. That's hard for him to accept without me there to help him. Please try not to be too cross at him."

"That's stupid. If he is your best friend, he should be here for you. You're the one who's…sick." *I hate saying the last word, but there's no other way to say it.*

She smiles sadly. "Sometimes when you love someone too much, *your heart is louder than your head."*

I think about that for a minute, still angry at Dad for doing this to her. *"That's why I'm your best friend now, Mum."* Her eyes sparkle and it makes me feel like I'm ten feet tall. *"I'll be your best friend forever. And I won't let my heart be louder than my head. Ever. I'm here for you, Mummy."*

"I'm happy to hear that, Gareth, because I need a best friend right now." She smiles and, even with the wrinkles around her eyes, she's the prettiest woman I've ever seen. *"But someday, my boy...Someday your heart will overrule your head, and it will bring me great joy up in Heaven."*

She pulls me by the hand to come closer, her other hand reaching up to the back of my neck and hugging me so my cheek presses against her chest. I can hear her heartbeat, but it sounds far away. And even her chest feels cold. If it wasn't for the soft, smooth fabric of her pyjama top, I'd forget all about how nice my mum feels. It's funny that a silly shirt can remind me of the way Mummy used to be before she was sick. When she was warm and cosy.

Her breath is cool as she drops kisses in my hair and murmurs, *"And let me feel that warm breath here."* Kiss. *"And there."* Kiss. She lets out a soft cry as she slides her fingers through my short strands. *"To spread a rapture in my very hair, O, the sweetness of the pain."* She shakes and squeezes me to her really hard.

I sniffle and look up into her wet eyes. *"Is that one of your poems, Mum?"*

She shakes her head. *"That is Keats, my love. Moments like this belong to the professionals."* She adjusts me so we're holding hands against her chest bone and adds through strangled croaks, *"Touch has a memory. O say, love, say, What can I do to kill it and be free."*

"I don't want to be free!" I gasp and a cry breaks loose from my chest that I didn't feel coming. I squeeze her hand as hard as I can, no longer caring about how breakable she is. I'm terrified, and I wish a million wishes that my hold could keep her here with me forever. I

reach down and touch the fabric of her soft shirt. "I don't want to kill this memory. I want you to stay, Mummy. I hate Heaven!"

I sob and her hand cups my damp cheek. "Hush now, my bestest friend. My bestest friend in the whole wide world."

She takes a fast breath and her eyes close tightly, wrinkles forming on the lids…

And then…

They soften.

They stop wiggling.

They stop flinching.

They turn still.

"Mummy?" My voice sounds gross. I shake her once. "Mum?"

I squeeze her hands and feel no pressure back.

Nothing.

"Mummy," I cry one more time, but I know what's come.

Death.

It came so fast, I didn't say everything I needed to say. All the things I should have said. I should have brought the kids in to see her one more time. I should have told her about how good Vi is at changing Booker's nappies. I should have told her about how the twins are starting to write their alphabet letters already. I should have told her about the nice neighbour lady's pies. I should have told her so many things.

But it came too fast.

Death.

It took her from me.

My best friend is gone.

The feeling of her long, pale fingers soft in my short, sticky ones feels like tons and tons of weight pressing down on my chest. Yucky, gross weight. Why didn't I wash my hands before I came back in here? Why couldn't Dad get the kids their snack just once? Why couldn't he answer the door? Do something!

My mum's last touch was my jammy, filthy hands because I had *too much to do!*

And now there's just a deadness to her that makes me sick. This isn't my mum anymore. This is Death.

I let go of her and slide off the bed, backing up until my back hits the wall by the far window. She doesn't look like Mum anymore. She looks all wrong. Nothing like the woman who loved to make her kids pancakes with special Swedish syrup.

She looks like something that should be in a scary movie.

This isn't how I want to remember my best friend. I close my eyes and say the words of Keats she just said to me. "Touch has a memory. O say, love, say. What can I do to kill it and be free."

Keats is right.

I have to kill it.

Technical Difficulties

Gareth

TRAVELLING IS THE ONE THING ABOUT FOOTBALL THAT I'VE grown to truly loathe. Living out of a suitcase. Constantly having a changing room smell to my clothes no matter what kind of fabric cleaner I use. Commercial airlines or team buses filled to the brim with blokes. It's a nightmare and a lot less glamorous than the papers would lead you to believe.

And after the mindfuck from my father last night, a quiet Monday at home has never felt so good. Plus, I get to see Sloan tonight, so I know I get to lose my fucking mind for the rest of the evening.

She's due to arrive after dinner, so I stride into the kitchen to make myself something to eat. I'm not much of a cook, but the team diet is normally pretty foolproof. Carbs, protein, vegetables. Mondays are always my pasta night.

I fill a pan with water to set on the stove when my security gate buzzes. Excitement washes over me when I see Sloan's vehicle enter after using the code I gave her. She's nearly two hours early, and my dick is already pulsing at the thought. I leave the pan by the stove and head to the foyer to let her in.

When I open the front door, I'm pummelled by Sloan's tall,

slender frame. Her handbag drops on the tile floor as she shoves her hands on my chest, turning me at a sharp, right angle to slam me against the wall. She lifts my shirt over my face and devours my chest with her mouth, running her tongue around my pec and biting down hard on my nipple.

"Jesus fuck, Sloan!" I exclaim, my body roaring to life from the sudden invasion.

"Call me Treacle," she growls, releasing my shirt so I can watch her yank her own up over her head and kick off her flats. "From now on, Treacle or Tre. I'm not Sloan when I'm here."

My brow furrows at the strained look in her eyes. "Are you okay?"

"I will be as soon as you take your shirt off."

My instinct is to press her about what's going on that has her so crazed, but my mind is too cluttered to worry. Besides, letting her have control will soothe whatever is troubling her the same way giving it up will soothe what's troubling me. So I do as I'm told, eager to erase all the bullshit that rests behind both of our eyes.

She stands before me in a grey bra and jeans—a much more casual look than I've ever seen her wear. Her chestnut hair is soft and wild around her shoulders as her chest rises and falls with deep breaths. The look she gives my entire body is a claiming, like she's reminding herself of the property she owns. Technically, she really fucking does. It's been far too long since I've seen her, and I'd do just about anything she demands of me right now.

She steps forward and presses her hands to my bare abs. "I want you to fuck me against this wall. Hard, fast, and dirty. Understand?"

"Yes," I pant, my dick already hard in my jeans.

She looks down. "Get that dick out of those jeans. Now."

I do as I'm told. Jesus fuck, I love doing as I'm told.

She ditches her own, along with her bra and knickers. Fuck me, she's stunning. Wild and angry about something, like a beast that can't be tamed.

She steps forward and fists me in her hand, squeezing so hard I'm wincing in pleasured pain. "God, you have a sexy cock," she husks, letting her hard nipples brush against my chest when she adds, "Do you have a condom down here?"

My face falls. "Fuck. No. I can run upstairs." I move for the stairs, but I freeze because she's holding my cock hostage.

"When was the last time you were checked?" she asks with a serious look on her face.

I swallow slowly, my body jerking as she strokes the tip of my bare dick along the top of her smooth pussy. Some pre-come seeps out of me and coats her skin. "The team gets physicals at the beginning of every season."

"What does that mean? When's the beginning of the season?"

"Two months ago," I bark out quickly as she presses the head of my dick between her folds. "Jesus Christ, you're already wet."

"Damn right," she replies, clearing her throat and clearly struggling as hard as I am to stay in control. "Have you slept with anyone since then?"

I look away and reply, "No."

"Gareth." She says my name like a warning. "I have an IUD in and was tested at an appointment this past week, so I know I'm clean. But if you're lying to me—"

"I'm not lying," I snap, my eyes fierce on hers now that she's questioning my honesty.

"Then why wouldn't you make eye contact with me? I'm just asking when the last time you had sex with someone else was. I'm considering something very serious here."

"I haven't shagged anyone since you last year," I growl, annoyance ticking my jaw from that admission. It says a lot about me that I'm not interested in sharing, so I really don't want to be given the third-degree about this.

"Okay," she replies softly and looks down with a frown as that fact sinks in. She looks up again. "Wait…No one? Are you serious?"

I exhale heavily, rueful resignation overtaking my earlier annoyance. "No one, Tre. I'm telling you the truth."

Her eyes light up with renewed excitement from this admission. "Okay, then. Are you all right with not using condoms? Because I trust you if you trust me."

"I trust you," I reply seriously and hope the twinkle in my eyes isn't visible to her. Fuck me, just the idea of pushing into her bare is going to have me coming so damn fast.

"Then pick me up and slam that big cock into me until I'm screaming for mercy."

"Yes, Treacle," I growl and follow orders like it's my fucking job.

By the time we stride into my kitchen, we're both cleaned up, halfway dressed, and feeling a hell of a lot calmer than we were twenty minutes ago.

Sloan glances over at the mess around my stove. "Oh, I interrupted your dinner," she states, clearly not sorry as she eyes me in my jeans and nothing else.

"It's fine." I shake my head and fuss with the pasta as I try to remember where I left off. "I wasn't expecting you for a couple of hours."

I put the pan of water on the burner and click the flame to high. Then I turn on the back burner where I left the pasta sauce sitting earlier.

Sloan is watching me curiously. "You look so domestic. I never would have imagined you cook for yourself."

I shoot her a half-smile. "If you call boiling linguini and heating up premade Bolognese sauce cooking, then yes, I'm a grade-A chef."

She giggles and strides around the island to peer over the stove. She's only wearing her jeans and bra, so I have a nice view as she lifts the lid off the saucepan. "Who makes your sauce?"

"Dorinda's son, Robert," I reply, staring down at her cleavage as she dips her pinkie in to sample. "He's saving up for culinary school, so I hired him to help me maintain my diet for extra cash."

She smiles a pleased sort of smile and turns to face me, her finger still in her mouth, her golden eyes fixating on mine with heated warning. I immediately imagine her lips wrapped around something else. As if she reads my mind, she smirks and her finger plops out of her mouth. "It's good."

"Well, there's plenty, so I hope you're hungry." I reach out and place my hand on her hip to pull her in close to me.

She looks down at my embrace with accusatory eyes. I quickly lift my hand away, holding it back in silent apology. *That's right, Sloan's in charge. She says when, where, and how.* With a naughty grin, I grab the linguini off the counter and drop them into the boiling water.

"How was your week?" she asks, hoisting herself up onto the counter next to the stove.

Her question is refreshing. She has no clue I played a game this weekend, let alone won or lost. The entire town of Manchester knows the score, so I'm congratulated everywhere I go. But Sloan somehow manages to continue living under a rock.

Choosing to ignore the horrid conversation I had with my dad, I reply, "It was good. How was yours?"

She sighs. "Pretty shitty."

"Is that the cause of the early arrival and assault?" I waggle my brows at her. Her cheeks flame red, so I add, "Trust me, I'm not complaining."

She issues a small smile, my comment soothing her anxiety. "I just had a bad phone call earlier."

I frown. "Some rich prat you style giving you a hard time?"

She lets out a polite laugh and shakes her head with a curious expression. "Didn't you say your dad is a famous soccer legend?"

"You mean a famous football legend?" I correct and narrow my eyes at her. She gives an eye-roll and I answer her question with a curt, "Yes."

"So, aren't you used to this kind of life?" She gestures around like my house is a direct reflection of how I grew up. "Didn't you come from money?"

"I didn't grow up like this," I reply, tensing at the mention of my upbringing. My jaw tightens as I think back to the home in Chigwell where we lived when Mum died and how vastly different it was to the small Manchester flat. The truth is, that's why it's difficult for me to imagine leaving Manchester. This is where my only positive childhood memories live on. "We lived in a big house east of London, but it wasn't a home. It was nothing like this."

Sloan glances around the kitchen casually, her bare feet swinging side-to-side. "You told me before that you hired a decorator because you wanted it to be different from where you grew up. What did you mean by that?"

Anxiety begins simmering inside of me as I shove the rest of the pasta down into the water. It's impressive that Sloan was really listening back then. I find the majority of people who meet me only listen when I say something they want to hear, which is why I am so reserved with most outsiders.

But I remember when I said that to Sloan in the early days of her styling me. It was because it bothered me that she looked at me like a typical footballer. I didn't want to be lumped into the same category as everyone else, spending loads of money on styling just because I could. I wanted her to see me differently.

I'm regretting that moment of weakness because it opened doors between us that are better left closed. "I thought we weren't supposed to get this personal," I deflect, my tone flat because I don't want to explore my past with her. Especially when my memories are currently extra raw.

"Touchy much?" she asks, her brows lifting into her hairline.

"It just seems like you're a guy who's used to getting everything he wants. I'm guessing your dad spoiled you growing up, didn't he? Fancy cars, best sports camps, best clothes."

She eyes me brazenly, and my blood pressure spikes from the mere mention of him again. "I didn't get a thing from my father. And, believe me, there are a lot of things I want and don't get."

"Like what?" she asks, crossing her arms over her chest.

"What is this, Twenty Questions?" I drop the spoon on the counter, my hand fisting in frustration.

"Hardly!" she retorts. "I'm simply trying to get to know the man who has all of this but submits to a woman so easily."

"I don't hear you complaining," I snap.

"I'm just trying to get a read on you." She leans forward, not the least bit intimidated by me, which happens to be one of the things that turns me on most about her. But that's beside the point.

"This is just fucking," I growl, pressing my fisted hand against the counter. My anger surprises me. I know it has more to do with my dad than Sloan, but I can't seem to stop it now. "This isn't personal, Sloan. This is fucking, so stop trying to get into my head."

I glance up to see her body has gone completely rigid. Her eyes narrow as she replies, "Excuse me for thinking we're friends."

She slides off the counter and moves past me to walk out of the kitchen back toward the front door. A deep growl vibrates in my chest as I splay my hands out on the island. This is all my fucking father's fault. He has me on edge. No, I'm not much of a sharer, which has been a reoccurring problem I've had with other women. But Sloan is right. We're friends.

And I'm a prat.

With a heavy sigh, I double-check the linguini is at a good temperature, then stride out to where I assume Sloan's getting dressed and preparing to leave. She's not in the foyer like I expected, though, and her shirt and shoes are still where she left them on the floor. I see a glowing light down the hall past the sitting room and make my way toward it.

I find Sloan in the media room, sitting in one of the black the-atre chairs. She's fiddling with the remote and attempting to put something on the projection screen. "I don't know how to use this. Can you show me?"

Her calm voice surprises me, so I enter the room and grab the remote from her hand. Our fingers brush and the electric current we always have is as strong as ever, even when she's pissed me off. "You're on the wrong input."

I push a button and hand it back to her as a sports channel illu-minates the screen.

"Thanks," she replies and attempts to flick the channel around my frame standing right in front of her. She still hasn't made eye contact with me.

"You're not leaving?" I ask, half expecting to get hit in the nuts at any second.

"Do you want me to?" She finally looks up, her eyes starry in the darkness. Her skin green from the glare of whatever is on the projector behind me.

I give her a simple shoulder shrug, tired of my emotions al-ready. This is why I wanted to try this control thing. It gives me the freedom of not having to think. I get exhausted when I have to think about my family. My upbringing. *My dad.*

"I want whatever you want," I reply because that's the truth. If she doesn't want to be here, I would never force her.

"Well, I don't like confrontation," she replies, her eyes narrow-ing up at me against the light. "So if you could refrain from being a dick when I'm just making small talk, it would make things a lot more pleasant."

I pull my lips into my mouth and bite back my knee-jerk argu-ment. There is no way she would know that the topic of my father is not small talk. Sharing about family is small talk to most. "My dad was a tremendous arsehole when my mum died. Mean, angry. He didn't mourn well, and we suffered for it as children. I get touchy when I have to talk about him."

Sloan's chin drops as she mindlessly fingers the remote in her lap. "That sucks."

I shrug once again. "And I didn't get a thing from my father. None of my brothers did either. Our sister was the only one whom he ever gave anything to. And if you think I'm saying that out of spite, I'm not. Vi is a saint and deserved everything he gave her."

Sloan pauses, eyeing me speculatively. "What did you deserve?"

Her question stings, but I know that's not how she means it. She's pushing for information. She's trying to get to the bottom of whatever this is all about. What she doesn't realise is it's an endless pit that I have never fully dug into myself.

My reply is firm. "I deserved a better father. But I don't want you thinking I'm some rich prick who was raised around other rich pricks. That couldn't be farther from the truth."

"I'm sorry, Gareth." Her face softens as she absorbs what I've shared. "I'm projecting my issues onto you. It's horribly unfair. It's just, in my life, I see a lot of arrogant privilege, and it makes me crazy to see that sense of entitlement sometimes. You've never shown me that, so it was unfair of me to assume you're part of that world."

I nod thoughtfully, knowing exactly what she's going on about. My teammates' kids are prime examples of arrogant privilege, all a bunch of sods. They speak to their foreign nannies like slaves because that's what they think is appropriate. And the nannies tolerate it because the parents make so much money and they need the job. It's an ugly sight.

We had no help in our childhood, foreign or otherwise. As kids, we learned quickly how to become self-sufficient because it was clear that our dad wasn't going to do a thing for us. I remember stealing his credit cards to pay bills when he forgot.

"I've worked for everything I have, Sloan. Even though my dad played for Manchester United, he did not part on good terms with them. They weren't pulling any favours by signing me. I wanted to play for them because I have this irrational need to be better than him. A better player. A better contract. Better endorsements. House. More money. Whatever it takes. I even have retirement plans set up for all of my siblings and a savings account for my niece that none of them know about. I'm consumed by taking care of everyone enough to make his existence irrelevant."

"Are you succeeding?" Her question is seemingly innocent but loaded with more than she could fathom.

I huff out a laugh. "What's success? He's still around, and it seems like every time I reach some line I've drawn for myself that will make me better than him, the line gets pushed back even farther. It's a sick cycle that I'm stuck in, and I don't talk about it to anyone really."

She nods thoughtfully. "I think that happens to kids who lose their mothers when they're young. They are driven to succeed because they have something to prove, whether it's to the deceased or themselves, or maybe it's just to society. You want to accomplish all of this because you were shorted a mother."

This brings me up short. "I don't do everything because of her."

"You don't?"

"Don't get me wrong. My mum was incredible. She was my best mate. When I lost her, it killed me. But to say I was shorted would sully the eight years I had with her. I was with her when she died and, as hard as it was, that memory is precious to me." I swallow the knot forming in my throat and push myself to continue, trying to ignore the painful memory. "I do all of this because control is something I can't seem to let go of, except with you."

She watches me for a minute, staring up at me with a million thoughts and feelings. It's an intense admission I just dropped on her. They're words I never envisioned telling her, but it feels good to actually understand why I'm craving this arrangement with her so much.

As if sensing that I've reached my maximum for the sharing I can do in one night, Sloan replies lightly, "Should we have sex now?" Her giggle that follows is like a beam of light brightening my dark soul.

"How about we eat first?" I hold my hand out to help her stand. "I have a feeling I'm going to need my strength."

Sloan

I'm overly curious about Gareth. This is just sex, but he has a heavy presence about him that makes me want to know all his deep, dark thoughts. Even when he smiles, he has sad eyes with an almost haunted look that screams mystery.

When he told me last year that his mother died, I was surprised I hadn't guessed that sooner. I dated a guy in high school who lost his mom while we were together. Both he and Gareth have that same look in their eyes. I was with him during the funeral, and it was hell. Torturous hell. About a month later, we broke up. He was a different person than when we started our relationship. Losing a parent does that to you. It changes your personality. Not negatively. Just differently. I imagine if I would have met him after his mother died instead of before, our relationship would have been totally different.

Hearing Gareth speak about his father, I know there are so many more layers to him than I ever gave him credit for. But he was right to have his guard up. What we're doing isn't personal. It's sex. That is why I'm not kissing him.

But after the phone conversation I had with Callum about Sophia not being able to come to my house for Thanksgiving, I didn't give a shit if Gareth was uncomfortable. I wanted to pick a fight with someone, and he was the unlucky person closest to me at the time.

It's making me crazy that I have no control over where Sophia spends her Thanksgiving holiday and that Callum can shut me down for no apparent reason. Just because he can. That is my life right now and it's maddening.

So to Astbury I drove, like a bandit. I went to the one place where I am not shut down. The one place where I have nothing but control over my own life, my own choices, my own decisions. The one place that lets me forget. Gareth and I have only been at this for a couple of weeks, but his house is the one place that allows me to escape all the shit I have to put up with in my personal life.

Originally, I had planned to finish my day helping Freya with alterations, shower, shave, and primp myself properly for the night. But I was so worked up after Callum called, I drove straight out to his house in my damn mom jeans! My need for Gareth's presence—his manliness, his warmth—was like I was dying of thirst and only he could quench it.

That's why I need to turn this night around. Stat.

We put our clothes back on to eat because, well, it's hot food and it seems dangerous to eat without shirts on. Gareth makes both of our plates up with the best linguini and Bolognese sauce I've ever tasted. I nearly ask for the recipe before covering my mouth and mumbling something about how it would pair nicely with a red wine. Asking for a recipe is a mom move. Super mom move. You don't ask for recipes from the guy you're fucking.

We end up hand-washing the dishes because his dishwasher is still drying a load. Brushing shoulders as we stand next to each other by the sink is some kind of kinky foreplay that probably only a mom would get turned on by. There's something about his wet, veiny hands plunging in and out of the bubbly water. And maybe the fact that Gareth actually does his own damn dishes.

I dry off my hands and open the refrigerator to see what's inside.

It's so empty, I would normally question whether anyone actually lived here. There are only a couple of Tupperware containers full of prepared foods—probably from the magical chef, Robert—some sports drinks, and a lime.

Rolling my eyes, I wrench open the freezer. The disappointment continues when all that lays inside are some gross looking protein balls. Athletes are weird.

Inspiration strikes as I close the freezer. "Can I get a glass?"

Gareth eyes me curiously and reaches up into the cupboard to grab a glass down for me. The skin that peeks out from beneath the bottom of his shirt when his arm stretches up is oh-so sexy, I can't wait to try what I have planned.

He hands the glass over to me and watches me expectantly as I fill the cup with ice cubes all the way to the top. "I think we should have sex again soon."

His concealed chuckle is appreciated. "Why not now?"

I shrug. "You got lucky with a quickie before because I was having a moment. Now I'm more in control. And because I have to torture you first, of course."

This causes him to full-on belly laugh. "Well, I'm at your service, Treacle." He winks at me, and I swear the look alone could get me off if I concentrated on it hard enough.

"Are you the type to get squeamish over unsanitary kitchens?" I ask, eyeing the large granite kitchen island that's grey with sparkles.

"Not if you're not," he replies, his forearms flexing as he stuffs his hands into his pockets.

"Good because I want you naked and lying on the counter."

His smile is sinful. "Whatever you say, Tre."

I hurry out to the foyer to get my handbag with the items I grabbed for tonight while Gareth undresses in the kitchen. When I return, he's standing by the island, shirtless with his jeans unbuttoned. My eyes instantly go to the trimmed trail of hair that leads to his groin.

When he grabs the band of his jeans, I stop him. "Hang on."

He pauses, leaving his jeans hanging on the edge of his hip bones. The deep *V* that angles toward his package is so sexy, I have to close my eyes and regain some composure.

"Hold your hands out together," I state, setting my bag on the counter and rooting around for a moment.

When I pull out a yellow rope from inside my purse, his eyes fly wide. "Are you serious?"

"Yes. Is this not okay?" I frown. "I bought it online. It's like sex rope or something. They cut to your order. It's less harsh on your wrists than regular rope from what I understand."

His tongue darts out to lick his lips and a heated look billows in his eyes. "It's okay."

With trembling hands, I instruct him to hop up onto the counter. He does as he's told and holds his two fists out to me. I begin wrapping the rope around his wrists, cinching them together and nervously looking up into his eyes. "Why are you looking at me like that?"

"Because whatever you're doing, it's working," he husks.

My eyes dart down to take in the straining erection under his jeans. "Just this does it for you?"

He shrugs. "You do it for me, Tre." He swallows slowly and pins me with a serious look. "You should see yourself right now. What are you thinking about?"

I pause to take in the full effect of his wrists bound together. His muscles and broad shoulders tight and flexed. The soft jeans. Bare feet. It's all...really, really hot.

"I think this is really freaking exciting," I croak, totally unsexy. His pleased laugh has me rolling my eyes. "Try to contain your amusement and lie down, please."

He smirks and shifts back on the counter. The movement has his abs bunching and showcasing the rivets of his perfect six-pack beneath his fisted, trussed-up hands. When he lies down on his back, he winces at the cool granite and the rivets become softer and more spread out.

I slide my hands on his forearms and pull them up to rest above his head. The effect of seeing him laid out like this at my mercy is incredible. "God, you are sexy."

He chuckles. "So are you."

I narrow my eyes. "I'm in a T-shirt and jeans."

He shakes his head and looks up at the lights. "Still sexy."

I try to hide my pleased smile as I pull my shirt up over my head and slide my jeans down my hips. It's amazing how we've only had sex a handful of times and I'm already so comfortable being naked in front of him. At first, I thought I'd want the blindfold again tonight, but feeling his heated gaze on me is part of where I draw my bravery from. Gareth has a way of making me feel like a million bucks just by looking at me. He did it that night I caught Cal cheating on me, and he's doing it tonight. He makes me feel impossibly strong.

Wearing nothing but my grey bra and black thong, I stand beside a half-naked Tarzan who's tied up on a kitchen counter like my own personal buffet. I drag my nails down his furry chest, raking over the springy muscles appreciatively. He is such a glorious specimen of a man. So masculine and powerful, like he was fathered by the legendary Atlas himself.

Gareth's eyes are on me as I crawl up onto the counter and position myself astride his groin, a leg curled up snugly next to his hips. "Keep your hands above your head," I state, dipping my fingers inside the glass and grasping a large, dripping ice cube.

Air hisses between his teeth as a few drops of freezing water drizzle onto his chest. I press the cube between his pecs and drag a moist path of water all the way down to his navel. My hair tickles his sides as I bend down and drop a soft kiss on his hard, tiny nipples. I've noticed Gareth's nipples are extremely sensitive, and I've been daydreaming all week about how he reacts when I touch them.

I continue my path downward along the ridges of his abs, my own nipples hardening inside my bra as he writhes beneath me. He twines his fingers together above his head, and his arm muscles flex with every squeeze he makes as he fights the urge to lower them and touch me.

Suddenly, my bra feels heavy on my skin. "Close your eyes," I state, dropping the ice in the glass and reaching back for the clasp.

He narrows his gaze but obeys. I slip out of my bra, then grab a piece of ice and put it into my mouth. I lie down overtop of him, the ice peeking out between my lips as I slide it down the thick column of his throat.

His low groan vibrates against my chest as my hard nipples brush against his damp skin. The skin-on-skin contact is intoxicating as the ice melts to nothing in my mouth. "Does this feel good?" I ask, dragging my tongue along a thick tendon in his throat.

He thrusts his hips up into me, his erection pressing the needy part of my centre. "That should tell you your answer."

With a little growl, I sit up and eye him in silent warning. "I want to hear you say it, Gareth."

His lazy smile is adorable. "Yes, Treacle. It feels good. You feel good."

I reach down to the firmness beneath me. "Should we get these tight jeans off?"

"Yes," he pants, his eyes hooded as he watches me stroke him firmly over the fabric.

He brings his arms down as I reposition myself beside him. As he lifts his hips, I shimmy his jeans down his ass and off his legs, smiling proudly when I see he's not wearing underwear, as usual.

I ditch my panties as well and take a moment to realise that I'm completely naked on the kitchen counter of Gareth Harris' home. What a wild turn my life has taken. I'm not sure I could be any luckier as I stare at his hard cock bobbing up toward his chiselled stomach, the vein underneath looking angry and promising all at once.

I dig in the glass for more ice. Most of it has melted, so I bring it to my lips for a cool drink and grab the small chunks at the bottom. Without a word, I dip my head and slip the tip of his bare cock into my mouth.

"Oh fuck," Gareth groans, the coldness of the ice and the hotness of my mouth tipping him into sensory overload. "Jesus, Sloan."

His fingers find my hair as he rides my movement. A few pieces of ice slip out of my mouth and fall on the counter below him. I release him and chomp down on the remaining ice while fisting him in my hand. "Treacle or Tre, Gareth. I've told you this."

"Sorry, Tre. Treacle. Got it," he states, his eyes landing on me with a worshipful, apologetic look.

Feeling brave and curious, I ask, "Did you like the ice?"

He nods and waggles his brows. "I'd like to use it on you."

I smile and shake my head. "That's not what happened in the porno I watched."

He chuckles, his tone disbelieving when he asks, "You watch porn?"

"Once," I lie. There's no way in hell I'm telling him that I've been looking up ideas for what we can do on *Porn Hub* all week. He'll think I'm a total perv. "It really helped me get you under control I think."

His abs tighten with a soft chuckle, but his amusement fades when I climb on top of him again and place his hands so they rest on his chest. "I'm going to ride you, but your hands need to stay right where they are, on your chest. Got it?"

He nods eagerly, so I position my pelvis over his tip, leaning forward a little so that my breasts are in his face. I feel his trussed fingers reach out to touch me, so I scold him with a giggle. "No touching or I'll strap your hands above your head."

I press my palms on his forearms for stability. The pressure pulls on his wrist restraints as I position the head of his penis between my folds.

SURRENDER

"Christ," he growls, watching the action between our bodies and fighting against the rope around his hands.

"Problems?" I ask, looking up at him with concern.

His jaw ticks. "I *really* want to touch you."

My brows lift. "How bad?" I sink down on him just an inch and hold myself there, his arms the perfect balancing point for control.

His low groan is wonderful. "Really fucking bad, Treacle."

I plunge down the rest of the way. "How about now?"

The veins in his arms thicken as he pulls hard against the rope. "Let's take this off."

"I'm in charge," I reply, watching his eyes on me as I sit back and completely open myself to him. Grinding back and forth over him, I work myself against the incredible friction.

"You are but…" he growls, his eyes flashing all over my chest as I squeeze my breasts and roll my nipples between my fingers. He begins fidgeting to try and find a position that gives him some leverage. His tone is frustrated when he says, "This could be so much better if you let my hands free."

"Why, Gareth?" I ask, making confident eye contact with him and arching a brow. I slowly trail one of my hands down to my centre and make a few slow, lazy circles around the bundle of nerves. "Would you touch me here?" I moan and have to force my pleasure-filled eyes to stay open.

The crazed look in Gareth's eyes is almost frightening. "Fuck, Sloan…Let me loose."

He's full-on growling now, but I'm not listening. I'm too focused on what I'm doing. I'm getting off on torturing him. This position gives me so much control as I bounce on him, making big, grinding sweeps. The pained look in his eyes has my head lolling back as I let out a low moan and relish in the feeling of him thick and hard inside of me.

I continue riding him slowly, and Gareth's growls of anger grow more and more frenzied. He manages to find some purchase with his

191

feet and begins thrusting up into me. Deep, punishing strokes that bring me to the precipice of release far quicker than I anticipated.

"Let me loose, Sloan." His voice is quieter now, more controlled as he stops his delicious thrusts. "Let me touch you. You feel so good. Let me make you come."

The need to orgasm is so strong, I hear myself croak, "Okay."

I sit forward, his dick still rock-hard inside of me as I pull my feet out from under his arms and tuck them underneath me. I ride him for a moment longer, then grab hold of his wrists and begin fumbling with the rope. It's distracting to have him inside of me while I try to release him, but he feels so damn good.

When I make no headway, I snap myself out of my sexual daze and crawl off of him. He lets out a pained groan as I kneel beside him and continue my efforts. Whatever I've just done to the knot has only tightened the tension. *That can't be good.*

"What's the matter?" Gareth asks, half sitting up. His hard, wet cock looks horribly angry. "Why is the rope so tight now?"

My hands begin to tremble as I stare down at the mess I've created. "I can't get the knot loose," I mumble, out of breath and trying not to panic.

"What?" he asks, his face leaning in close to mine to inspect what I'm doing.

My gaze snaps up to his wide hazel eyes. "I don't know how I did this!"

"You didn't know what you were doing?"

"No!" I exclaim and look down again, jerking and tugging, trying to find any loose areas to begin untethering something.

"You bloody well acted like you knew," Gareth retorts, accusation lacing his tone.

"I was pretending!" I peal, lifting his hands up to see if I can find somewhere underneath to start. *Good God, it looks even worse there.* "Gareth! I can't get this!"

The emotion in my voice is intense as angry red marks begin

forming around his wrists. Suddenly, a shaking starts happening all over Gareth's body. I assume he's having some sort of a panic attack because I'm nearly crashing into one myself. But when I look up, I don't see panic in his eyes.

He's *laughing*.

He's laughing like crazy.

He has tears running down his face because he's laughing so hard. I've never seen him like this. It's really disarming.

"This isn't funny!" I scream, releasing his hands with a hard thrust and shoving my fists against his chest so he falls back on the counter.

"I beg to differ," he replies, but it's barely audible through his deep, booming laugh.

"This isn't funny! It's mortifying!" I run a hand through my hair, doing my best to calm my nerves so I can figure out what to do next. It's difficult because Gareth's abs are tight and defined as he continues roaring. Occasionally he looks at my crestfallen face and that sets him off further. I'm only halfway serious when I punch him in the gut and add, "We're going to have to amputate."

Gareth roars once again. Finally, I can't contain it any longer. I crack a smile. Before I know it, I fall onto him in a fit of giggles. I end up losing it so much, I get a cramp in my calf muscle and have to roll off of his chest to clutch my leg.

He seems to find that even funnier.

"Fuck you," I groan, wiping tears from my eyes. "This is such a mess. I was trying so hard to be sexy."

"Mission accomplished, Treacle," he retorts, his amusement dying down so that only the delicious crinkles on the edge of his eyes remain. He is quite a sight right now. Belly-flipping sight, and it has nothing to do with the fact that he's naked.

"Don't call me that," I groan, sitting up and ignoring the tender look on his face. I slip off the countertop and place my hands on my hips. "I'm an imposter. I don't deserve the name."

With affectionate, smiling eyes, Gareth guides me to a pair of kitchen scissors in a drawer. As soon as I cut and all the rope twists loose, he's off the counter and all over me. His heat warms my trembling body as his hands fork through my hair and he twirls us so my back presses against the kitchen island. His hot breath is licking tantalising kisses up my neck as he husks, "Perhaps we need a safe word after all."

I burst out with a giggle and cover my hands over my eyes. "Yes. I think a safe word is wise considering I totally screwed tonight up."

Gareth pulls away from my neck, looking down at me with a fiery smile in his eyes. God, he's sexy in this moment. I make a mental note to make him laugh more during sex because it is the best form of foreplay I never ever had with Cal.

With a teasing waggle of his eyebrows, Gareth grabs my hand and places it on his dick. "Does that feel like you screwed anything up?"

I can't help but giggle. "What does that say about you?"

His body vibrates with a silent chuckle. "That I'm a bloody freak for you."

With the echo of my giggles, Gareth grips me by the waist and lifts me up onto the counter. He spreads my legs out wide and hooks his hands under my knees to pull me to the edge.

Our smiles both fall as he positions his tip between my folds and thrusts into me, unapologetic, hard, and bare. My earlier excitement is still present between my legs. Honestly, seeing him so relaxed and carefree has only further stoked my desire for him.

He grinds deep inside of me, swirling his hips and hitting that G-spot he seems to have a direct map to. It's unimaginably perfect as my nails score over his shoulders. The growl that rumbles up his throat in response is so damned hot, I feel close to coming already.

"Make this slow, Gareth. Make it count," I state, then lick my lips and look down to where our bodies connect.

He slams into me one more time. "Oh, I plan on it."

194

Gareth

"You know you can stay here if you ever want to," I say as Sloan gets dressed.

"What?" She gazes up at me, pushing a strand of chestnut hair out of her eyes.

I try to come off casual even though I feel anything but. "I'm just saying it's been kind of late the times you've left, and if you ever want to crash here so you don't have to drive home in the dark, you can."

"How would that work?" she asks, furrowing her brow at me like I asked her a complicated math question.

"What do you mean?" I slide my hands into my pockets and follow her into the foyer.

She pauses in front of the door and turns on her heel to eye me. "Would we cuddle?"

A smile spreads slowly across my face over how serious she looks. "I'm not a huge cuddler." I reach out and smooth a strand of hair that's sticking up above her ear. "But I could be convinced if you wanted to. You're in charge after all." I wink.

"No." She shakes my touch away, but the heated look in her eyes tells me she likes it.

My hand moves to her wrist, and I trace small circles on the inside. She watches my finger as I lean in and whisper in her ear, "If you slept in my bed, you could assault me any time you wanted."

"Oh, is that right?"

Her tone is teasing, but I'm not losing my edge. "I would be at your complete mercy."

"Such a giver," she cajoles, pulling back and smiling up at me.

She sucks her lower lip into her mouth, and my body roars back to life.

I lift my brows. "It would be a tough job, but I'm pretty strong. You can feel my muscles if you want."

She whacks me on the chest, then chews her lip more thoughtfully. "You know, Thursday would be good."

Her reply puzzles me. Our first week together, we saw each other every night. Is she trying to see me less? "So you won't be coming out here tomorrow?"

"God no!" she barks.

I deflate.

"I mean, yes!"

"Wait, what?"

"I mean, of course I'll be coming out tomorrow and the next day. I'm free all week!" She gestures between us and her face falls. "Unless you don't want me here that much?"

"No, I do!" I reply quickly, then bite the inside of my cheek. *Get control of yourself, Gareth. You don't want to look like a completely sex-starved wanker.* Tanner has that look on lockdown. "I just don't understand why you want to spend the night on Thursday in particular."

She relaxes instantly, tucking a piece of hair behind her ear as she replies, "Oh, well, it's Thanksgiving on Thursday?" She says it like a question.

I tilt my head curiously. This is not anywhere near where my head was going. "I'm somewhat familiar with that American tradition."

She purses her lips nervously. "I could like cook for us, maybe?"

My brows lift. "You cook?"

"Sometimes." She shrugs. "I mean, I've never cooked Thanksgiving dinner completely by myself, but I think I can handle it. But I know you're an athlete, so maybe you can't eat certain stuff."

My reply is instant. "I can eat stuff."

She smiles with an adorably hopeful twinkle in her eyes. "It's just, it's kind of a special holiday to me. I think it would be fun to actually make a meal and, I don't know…Celebrate. Last year, I travelled home to my mom's. Every year before that I was busy with work, so I've never actually celebrated it here in England. I'd really like to, though." She looks awkward and quickly adds, "But after we eat, we can totally fuuuck."

I fight back a laugh at her horrid attempt at sounding cool. "Is that part of the Thanksgiving tradition as well?"

She barks out a laugh. "It's not, but we can definitely make it an annual thing." When she realises what she just said, her face falls and she claps her hands over her mouth. "Not that we'll be doing this every year. I just mean…Freaking hell. I'm not saying that. Of course this isn't going to be a yearly thing. Good God, I should leave right this second."

Desperate for an escape, she turns on her heel and swings the door open. In a quick move, I step forward and wrap my hand around her stomach, stopping her momentum and pulling her back against my body. She's practically heaving with embarrassment as my other hand pushes the door closed.

"I'm such a puke," she groans and covers her face.

"You're not a puke," I chuckle, pressing my lips to her hair. "Turkey and sex sounds perfect."

She relaxes into my embrace and tilts her head back, revealing her bare neck. Her sweet scent rolls over my body. I have to fight the urge to turn her around, strip her naked, and fuck her against the door right this second.

Instead, I slip one hand into my pocket, grab my keys, and hold them in front of her. "I have practice until five and I assume turkey takes a while to cook." I slide the key off the ring and hold it out. I say against her hair, "Front door key…for your convenience."

"Thanks," she husks like we just had thirty minutes of foreplay and she's ready to come. She wraps her fingers around the key and nearly moans her next words. "I'd really love for you to kiss my neck, Gareth."

My body roars to life from the gentle command. I push her hair back with my nose and lightly brush my lips beneath her ear. My tongue slips out and draws a line up to her earlobe. When I pull the tender flesh between my lips, she sags against me, rolling her body in my arms and grinding her supple arse on my groin.

Just when I think she's going to give me round three, she pulls away and opens the door, leaving on wobbly feet. I watch her, regret and yearning stronger than I've ever felt coursing through my veins.

I watch her car drive away, then close the door, realising with a nervous thud of my heart that I can't wipe the smile off my face.

Turkey and Sex

Sloan

"YOU ARE WHAT?" FREYA PEALS AS SHE FOLLOWS ME TO THE foyer.

I bend down to grab my brown ankle boots up off the floor. "I said I'm going to be spending the night at Gareth Harris' house tonight, so I won't be home until tomorrow."

"I need to sit down." Freya drops down on the staircase and cradles her head in her hands. "You haven't told me a word since we made that suit for him, and I've been cheated some very delicious details."

"Freya, you knew something was happening between us." I slip my feet into my shoes and slide the inside zippers up, my eyes narrowing on her. "You even encouraged it!"

"I know! But to be spending the night with him must mean it is getting serious!" She looks up at me with wide, hopeful eyes.

"It's not getting serious," I correct.

"You've been out every night this week," she states like it's a confirmation that what I'm saying isn't true.

"That doesn't mean it's getting serious," I scoff. Yes, I've been back out to Gareth's. Yes, I rode him reverse cowgirl when we fucked in his media room last night during reruns of *Shameless*. That doesn't mean anything has changed. I'm just insatiable. I'm in the middle of a sexual awakening I didn't even know I needed, and I can't seem to stay away. And I'll be blowing him off for another week straight when Sophia comes home, so I'm trying to get it while I can.

"So, why are you spending the night?"

"Because we're having sex."

It's as if I electrocuted her. "You're finally shagging him?"

I want to laugh at her innocence. If she knew the full truth, she'd probably pass out from shock. "Yes, Frey. You didn't assume?"

"Well, I don't know. You said he held out on you that one time you wore the skimpy knickers, so I thought maybe he was impotent or something."

"No," I groan. "We're sleeping together, but it's just a friends with benefits thing." I shrug. The description doesn't do it justice, but it's the best I can do.

Her face crumples. "Friends with benefits is something kids in Uni do. Not nearly thirty-something-year-olds with children."

"Gareth doesn't have children."

"You do!"

"Only for fifty percent of my life!" I exclaim, my hands fisting at my sides. The notion of missing part of Sophia's life every other week still makes me crazy. I don't need it shoved in my face. "You are the one who wanted me to do something with my time when Sophia is with Callum."

"Yes, but I didn't think it meant friends with benefits and putting yourself at risk of having your heart broken. Sloan, Gareth Harris is like a steel vault. Even the media can't get a personal detail out of him."

"What do you mean? I thought he is only private about the women he dates?"

She shakes her head. "It's so much more than that. His dad used to play for Man U, and if the media ask a question about him, Gareth shuts down the interview straight away. On top of that, he's never seen with mates. Only his family. Now you're telling me that you've been sleeping with him on a regular basis. I just think that has to mean something." Her green eyes are intense on me.

"It doesn't," I reply sharply and ignore the pit in my belly that forms over the fact that Gareth has opened up to me about his dad. Feeling anxious, I move to sit beside Freya on the steps and try to explain this in a way that won't freak either of us out completely. "What Gareth and I are doing is so different from traditional. He even held off in the beginning to ensure that our lines didn't get blurred. I'm totally detached and living in the moment."

"In the moment," Freya tuts, clearly disbelieving.

"It's just sex."

"It's just sex."

I pull one leg up to my chest and turn to face her. "Stop repeating what I'm saying and trust me when I tell you that this is the perfect arrangement. More importantly, it's the best sex I've ever had."

Her eyes fly wide with excitement. "Well, it's no wonder. You're shagging England's sexiest footballer, Sloan. Do you have any idea how many women would kill to take your place?"

This makes me frown. "I try not to think about the fact that Gareth is an athlete. He always just felt like more of a client to me. Now he's just…Gareth."

Freya erupts into laughter, holding her belly as the fit overtakes her body. "And Tom Hardy is just Tom Hardy!"

I sigh heavily and roll my eyes at her hysterics. "I know he's famous, but we're different people when we're together."

She wipes an errant tear from her eye and asks, "How do you mean?"

My lips thin as I ponder her question. I know why I love our arrangement, but I'm not one hundred percent sure why Gareth loves to give up the control. He's given me some ideas, but it seems deeper than his daddy issues. "I don't know exactly, but it's like we're both working through a problem and what we do with each other helps us deal."

Freya leans in and cups her mouth to whisper, "Is it kinky? Does he have a sex dungeon?"

"No," I groan and pick at my black tights, my mind drifting off to the sense of empowerment I get when I'm with him. "It's above all that. It's like Gareth's home has become my refuge from life. When I go there, it's like shutting off the WiFi and not allowing myself to scroll Instagram. I don't worry about what Sophia is doing or how much she's changing. And Gareth doesn't know me or my life, so I get to be a different person when I'm with him. Someone who is strong, and brave, and sexy, and desired."

Freya's eyes are fierce on mine. "So he doesn't know about Sophia?"

"No," I answer, swallowing slowly. After he opened up about his father the other night, I started feeling guilty about this significant part of my life that I've yet to mention. "He knows I'm divorced, but that's pretty much it. I feel like I need to keep it that way. So much of my identity the past few years has revolved around Sophia. The weeks I spend with Gareth are a chance for me to reclaim the person I lost when I stayed married to Cal for so long. I need this fourth wall to feel like I can keep doing this arrangement we have."

"Wow." Freya looks forward, her head shaking back and forth in amazement. "I'm here binge-watching Netflix, and you're out there having mind-blowing sex and really living life."

"I'm trying." I shrug because that's all I can do at this point.

"What does he think you're doing when you have Sophia?"

"Well, it's new, so I'm just going to keep telling him I'm travelling for work or too busy to drive out there. So far he hasn't noticed because I more than make up for it when I'm free." I shoot her a lascivious smile and she covers her mouth with a snicker.

"This is properly more exciting than Zumba!" She giggles.

I give her a huge grin and reply, "That is an understatement."

"Well, you're a tart! And I'm positively green with jealousy, so don't take it personal when I hate you for the rest of our lives."

I smile broadly. "I love you."

She nudges me with her shoulder. "Mean it."

My drive out to Astbury has become one of my favourite pasttimes. It's the one hour I need every day to meditate, self-reflect, and prepare myself to let go of my stress and embrace this new, stronger version of myself. It's also a great time to fantasise about all the things I want to do with Gareth.

Like experimenting with hot wax!

Along with all the groceries I bought for Thanksgiving, I included a couple of candles to help set the mood for our meal and my plans for after dinner. I am practically panting from the anticipation of drizzling hot wax over Gareth's ridiculously amazing body. I tested it out on myself last night, and the heat it stirred inside of me made it nearly impossible to stay away for twenty-four hours.

My how far I've come.

When Gareth first proposed this control idea, I took to the internet for information and was really intimidated by what I found. True BDSM is intense and a big commitment. I knew I couldn't do the majority of what I saw. But when we spent the night texting back and forth, he assured me that it wasn't whips and chains he was looking for. He didn't want me to turn him into a sex slave or have us join some underground club where people in this lifestyle go for pleasure. It was a simple power exchange that he sought. He didn't want to be in charge of my pleasure. He wanted to be the answer for it.

Most of our nights together thus far have simply been me directing the scene. Telling him I need to sit on his face. Or telling him he can't touch me with his hands, only his lips. Sometimes it's me shoving him down on the bed and climbing on top of him just to see his eyes flash wide with lust and awe. When I'm confident, he looks at me with complete reverence. It's a glorious stamp of approval I didn't even know I was missing in my life.

Callum was always one to thrive on his control. On his power. His wealth. He prided himself on all the things Gareth seems to ignore in his life.

I mean, I'm not blind. I know Gareth hasn't surrendered *all* of his power. He manages to find a way to top from the bottom quite often, but it always starts with my control. My planning. My set-up. My terms. And our time together is completely at my discretion.

There's a whole new level of anxiety over actually spending a full night with him, though. At first, I regretted agreeing to it. What if Sophia got sick in the middle of the night and Cal called me to come? How awful would it be if I couldn't get to her in an instant?

Logically, I know that's my anxiety talking. She's not a sick baby anymore. She's become a healthy little human before my very eyes. Just last week when I took her to the dentist, I couldn't believe how big she looked in the exam chair. At some point, when I wasn't noticing, she stopped being a toddler. And every time she comes back to me after a week of being with Cal, I swear she's grown taller and more mature.

I need to recognise that, and spending time with Gareth has helped me find some new perspective. I'm a divorced woman who is co-parenting with her ex. It isn't a death sentence. It's actually quite liberating. I get to live a double life, and I get to reclaim the sense of individuality that Callum siphoned from me during our marriage.

Now I find myself in a place with Gareth where I want to be bold. I want to be surprising. Hell, I want to bring a little kink into our lives! Candle wax and all.

I pull into Gareth's driveway and type in the code to his gate. He's still at practice, but he said I could come over whenever I needed to today since the turkey will take a few hours to cook.

When I finish hauling the groceries inside, I marvel over how only a year ago I was lusting after this house and imagining what it would be like to live in it. Now I'm cooking a freaking Thanksgiving dinner in the kitchen and I've been naked in nearly every room. Life can really be surprising sometimes.

Gareth

When I step through the front door of my house eager to lay eyes on Sloan, my nose is instantly assaulted with the pungent scent of burnt flesh. I drop my football kit on the floor as a foggy cloud of smoke billows out the door behind me, surprised my smoke alarm isn't going off yet. Waving my hand in front of my face, I quickly make my way to the kitchen where the source of the smoke seems to be coming from.

My eyes instantly land on Sloan's backside. She's hunched over the kitchen island wearing nothing but a tiny string bikini. I have to fight the urge to ogle her body because, from the looks of her, she's not in a good state. Her head is bowed, hands covering her face, shoulders shaking. I look to the left and see a charred turkey in a large roasting pan sitting on the counter. It's black. Really black. The legs have fallen off the sides and the heat wafting from it looks practically toxic.

"Hiya?" I state like a question because I'm terrified of the emotional scene I've just walked in to.

Sloan's head snaps up. She sniffs in a deep breath and wipes away tears as she turns to face me. "Oh my God, you're home already?" she groans and awkwardly crosses her arms over her stomach.

"Yes…Sorry," I reply slowly, then tilt my head. "Are you crying?"

"No!" she bellows defensively. "Yes!"

"Tre," I coo and move straight to her, my arms reaching out and pulling her against my body. "What's the matter?"

"Are you joking?" she mumbles with a garbled hiccup as she hides her face in my chest. She pulls back and gestures to the turkey. "I freaking ruined it."

I pull my lips into my mouth to conceal my smile. "What happened?"

She looks up at me with wide, watery eyes. "I thought I could go for a swim while the turkey cooked because the package said it would take two hours. But I must have screwed up the temperature on the oven because as soon as I finished my swim and stepped out of the pool room, I could smell something burning."

"Bugger," I murmur and hold her head against my chest. "It sucks, but it's not a big deal."

"It is too!" she snaps, pulling out of my arms and swiping at her cheeks. "I had plans, Gareth! I worked so hard on a fancy herb rub I found on Pinterest. It took me an hour to dress that damn bird. Now the one thing I was most excited about for today is ruined."

"So we'll go out to eat," I reply, shrugging my shoulders.

She blinks a few times, her pouty lip so damn sexy, I'm finding it really hard to be sympathetic. "But…I mean, is that okay? We don't do dinner dates. And, I mean, can you just go out in public like that? Aren't you famous or something?"

I brush the comment off. "There's a pub that does a great fish and chips, and it's local so no one ever bothers me."

She nods and swallows. "I suppose that works. God, I'm such an idiot."

"No you're not." I reach out and grab her hand. "Now, command me to take these tears away." The playful waggle of my brows brings a small smile to her face.

She looks through the doorway and replies, "Come swim with me. It's the only room in the house that doesn't stink."

The corners of my mouth pull back into a smile. "With pleasure, Treacle."

Sloan leads me into the pool room and tells me to strip down to nothing for our swim. Watching her loosen the strings of her bikini and drop the tiny slips of fabric on the concrete flooring enables me to finally learn how to enjoy my pool.

It has been mesmerising to watch Sloan embrace this control the past couple of weeks. She's not the most composed, but there's always a moment when that spark ignites in her eyes. The one when I know she's finally letting go of all the baggage and stress in her life and living in the present with me. It's fucking captivating because I feel the same. When she tells me to shag her from behind on the pool steps and begs me to pull her hair, it's like I'm finally fucking free. She frees me of my complicated, stressful thoughts and gives me a sense of lightness I've never experienced in my life.

Sloan

It's dark out by the time we hop in my car and Gareth directs me to the Horseshoe Inn in the nearby village of Congleton. We're both ravenous and grateful to get away from the stench of burnt turkey still wafting through the house.

When we pull up to an extremely old looking pub nestled in the English countryside, I can't hide the smile on my face. "This place is so British, I could die."

It's an adorable white, stucco building that looks more like a house than a restaurant. It has a welcoming red front door and hanging baskets and window boxes overflowing with fall flowers. It's exactly what any English country pub should be.

Gareth smiles back at me and hops out of the car, quickly jogging over to my door and opening it for me. "I've known the owners, Charles and Mary, for years. They were some of the first friends I made when I moved out here."

He ushers me into the dimly lit pub, and an elderly hostess doesn't even smile at us when we come in. She grabs a couple of menus and walks us over to a dark corner booth near an open log fire. The place is mostly empty, and no one gives us a second look as we take our seats.

"Drinks?" the woman asks.

Gareth orders a water and I ask for a wine. She returns a few minutes later with our drinks, then puts in our food orders.

"This feels different," I say, sipping my white wine thoughtfully and eyeing Gareth from across the table. "Being out of your house and around society together. I'm not sure how to act."

He gives me a confused look. "What do you mean?"

I shrug. "Well, like, did you want me to order for you just now? Am I still in control?"

My question has his brow furrowing. Before he has a chance to reply, light from the entrance blasts in and Hobo's loud voice booms into our quiet sanctuary.

"Hullo, neighbour! Fancy seeing you here!" I turn to see Hobo stepping back and gesturing for Brandi to walk inside ahead of him. The two make their way over to our table.

My cheeks feel flaming hot as Gareth gives Hobo a forced sort of smile. "Hiya, Hobo. Brandi."

"Gareth." Brandi smiles and flicks her curious eyes to me, her blonde ponytail swinging as she adds, "Hi, Sloan."

"How are you guys?" I ask, tucking a strand of hair behind my ear and attempting to appear casual.

"We're super!" Hobo looks straight at me with a beaming smile. "Thought we'd nip in for a bite since neither of us could cook if our lives depended on it. This is great, though! Now we can have a

SRRENDER

double date!"

"Oh, this isn't a date." I look nervously at Brandi, who feels like she's inspecting me. I glance at Gareth for some help, but he remains silent, waiting for what I'm about to say next. "Gareth and I are just having a work-related dinner."

"A work-related dinner?" Hobo repeats, clearly not convinced. "That's interesting. What are you discussing?"

"Oh, erm…" I wrack my brain for an excuse, but I'm seriously blanking. My job is not the kind that requires me to wine and dine my current customers. I wine and dine prospective clients occasionally, but not people like Gareth.

"We're just friends having dinner." Gareth's deep voice saves me from my misery. His eyes are trained on mine in such a serious manner that I struggle to know what he's thinking. "Sloan was delivering some clothes and mentioned she was hungry. I told her this place has the best fish and chips around, so I brought her here."

Brandi doesn't look at all convinced, but Hobo smiles brightly and says, "Super! You won't mind if we join you then."

Hobo shoves into the booth, forcing Gareth around the corner next to me so that our knees are touching. Brandi slides in next to Hobo, and the four of us begin what I can only describe as the most awkward non-double date I've ever experienced.

They all instantly begin talking soccer. Brandi chimes in like one of the guys, equally as passionate about the sport as the men. I listen intently, actually really intrigued because I've never taken an interest in Gareth's career up until this point. The majority of my clients are wealthy athletes or business moguls, and I find the less I know, the better. And I never want to come off like a fan. My clients get that enough. They don't need it from me, too.

I also think I was resistant to the sport of soccer when I came to England because Callum loved it so much. It represented one of the British customs I was resentful of at a time when I missed our life in Chicago. But hearing these guys speak so passionately has me kind of warming up to the sport.

"So, Sloan, when did you say those dresses of mine are coming in again?" Brandi's blue eyes are wide and friendly.

"They are in already!" I waggle my eyebrows in excitement. "And they are so fierce. There's one that I think is going to look fantastic on you, but I'm not saying a word until you try them all on. I think I have you scheduled for Monday, right?"

She nods with a secret twinkle in her eyes. "Yes, that's what I remember. The event feels like it will be a bit of a Cinderella moment. I'm not really a girly girl, but the idea of getting dressed up for a proper night out is hard not to get butterflies over."

"I don't know much about the event, except that I think almost every single one of my clients is attending," I state with a huff. "Any time there's a black tie and red carpet event, it's like my company's Super Bowl. My business partner and I have been swamped getting everyone's samples in and final decisions altered."

"So, is that why you're wining and dining our honouree here?" Hobo teases, clapping Gareth on the shoulder.

I look over at Gareth in confusion. "Honouree? What do you mean?"

Gareth's jaw tightens as he narrows a steely look at Hobo. "Nothing."

"It's not nothing," Hobo jeers, not the least bit intimidated by Gareth's glower. "Our captain here is receiving the big award that night. He's been named Player of the Year on behalf of the Football Press Association."

My jaw drops. "Seriously?"

Gareth shrugs like he's in pain as Hobo answers for him. "Seriously. He's a super stud. I can't believe he hasn't been bragging to you about it. Our coach is over the moon."

"W—wow," I stammer, then my face falls as realisation hits. Gareth hasn't requested styling for this event. I didn't even know he is attending. Did he hire someone else because we're sleeping together? "Gareth, why haven't you requested styling from me?"

He finally makes eye contact with me, and I can see that he's registering the hurt look on my face. His hand reaches under the table and squeezes my knee. "Because I already have a suit."

"Which one?" I ask, nervous that he's going to wear something he's worn before. I know it's crazy, but he should not be re-wearing a suit for a red carpet event. The press will notice and call him out on it. He pays me to prevent that from happening.

It has to be what we're doing together that's making him feel like he can't ask me for anything. This is deeply upsetting because he swore our working relationship would remain the same.

His hand moves up to my inner thigh as he states firmly, "I'm wearing the one you made."

"Made?" Brandi and Hobo echo each other.

I can feel their surprised eyes on me, but I can't look at them. Instead, my eyes are locked on Gareth's, who's looking annoyingly indifferent. "What do you mean?" I ask, my voice sounding far away for some reason.

"The suit you made me a couple weeks ago. I haven't worn it anywhere yet. I figured it'd be perfect for the event."

"I didn't know you are a designer, too," Brandi states, clearly impressed.

I continue to ignore her. "Gareth, you should wear designer. Not mine."

"I don't need designer," he scoffs, tightening his grip on my leg. "I love the suit you made. I tried it on and it fits perfectly. I want to wear it. End of."

"Not end of," I bark and shove his hand off my leg. "This is a big deal. There will be press, a red carpet, media asking who you're wearing."

"Just tell me what to say then." He flinches as a thought pops in his head. "In fact, you can go with me and tell them yourself."

"Go with you as what?" I am so shocked, I don't know what

end is up. I just found out a famous athlete is going to wear my suit on a red carpet. This is the kind of thing that aspiring designers only dream of, but it's a dream that I've locked away inside a vault of pre-Sophia life goals. Not to mention Gareth Harris is never seen with women!

"My date, of course." Gareth turns his eyes from me and faces Hobo and Brandi while taking a sip of water.

"I'm not sure that would be appropriate," I grind out through clenched teeth. What's he trying to do here?

I swear I see Hobo and Brandi eating popcorn from the other side of the table as Gareth and I have this non-fight right in front of them.

"Fuck what's appropriate," Gareth scoffs. "If I don't take you, I'll have to take someone else. I'd rather have a friendly face as my date."

Anger simmers in my veins. Anger spliced with a dash of jealousy. Would I be okay with Gareth taking someone else? It would bother me for sure. Especially after Freya said every woman in England wants to have sex with him. But what is he trying to do? Our arrangement doesn't include dating. It's fucking. And him putting me on the spot in front of his friends is really maddening.

Gareth's eyes are firm on mine, flaming with a look of determination that I've never seen on him. "It's a great opportunity for you to get your name out there as both a designer and a stylist. You can network. It would be excellent publicity."

"Gareth," I state in a warning tone, my hands itching to strangle the smug look off his face.

"Sloan." He says my name so deliberately, I know this is about a hell of a lot more than networking and publicity.

Hobo interjects. "It's going to be a fun party at the very least. Come have a laugh with us. Brandi will be there with me and could use the support. She always hates the women my teammates bring to these events."

SURRENDER

Brandi groans her approval. "Oh my God, yes. You'd be a welcome breath of fresh air for all of us."

I force a smile and silently agree to their insane request. I'm not about to fight with Gareth in front of his friends, but we're certainly having words when we're done here.

We finish our dinner with much more comfortable small talk. Then Gareth and I trail behind Hobo and Brandi as we all make our way out of the pub. We wave our goodbyes and part ways.

When we get to my car, Gareth snatches the keys from my hand.

"Um, excuse you, those are my keys." I begin to argue and reach for the keys in his hand.

"You had wine, Sloan. I had water. I'm driving."

With a frown, I slowly cross my arms over my chest and hold my place in front of the driver's side door. "I had two small glasses of wine in two hours. I'm fine."

Gareth's gaze is serious as he looms over me, forcing me back against the door. "I'm not letting you put either of us in unnecessary danger. I'll drive."

I grind my teeth together with annoyance. I know he's right. Him driving makes the most sense, but I don't like that he didn't ask. He's just telling me. He's commanding me. He's kind of been commanding me all night, and it's really getting on my nerves.

Not wanting to cause a scene, I bite my tongue and walk over to the other side of the car. Gareth tries to open the door for me, but I push him away and do it myself.

As soon as both our doors are closed and we're concealed in the silence of the dark vehicle, I turn on him. "What the hell do you think you're doing?"

"What do you mean?" he asks, adjusting the driver's seat and putting the key in the ignition.

"In there...In front of Hobo and Brandi. Were you trying to show off?"

213

"Show off?" he barks, one hand resting on the wheel even though he hasn't started the car yet.

I turn in my seat to face him more fully. "Yeah, you manipulated the whole scene to get me to go to the awards gala with you."

"I wasn't being manipulative. I just think it'll be a great opportunity for you."

"But it's my decision. Not yours!" I exclaim, leaning in closer to him. Even in my state of frustration, I can't help but want to be close to him. He smells too damn good. "What is this, Gareth? You want me to be in control, but the minute we're caught in public together, you fucking flip on me like a switch."

His eyes are severe on mine. "I didn't flip on you."

"The hell you didn't!" I peal. "What's going on? Am I still in control here or not?"

"In the bedroom, yes," he grinds through clenched teeth and reaches down to turn over the key.

"But not in front of your friends," I bark unattractively and face forward with a laugh. "I can't believe I didn't see this coming. You're not surrendering your control. You're topping from the bottom. You've been topping me this whole time!"

"That's utter bollocks!" he roars and hits the heel of his hand on the wheel. "When we get back to my place, I'll let you do whatever the bloody hell you want to me. You can fucking whip me if you think that's what I deserve, and it will turn you on because that's what turns me on. But when we are out in public, I absolutely refuse to let you miss opportunities because we agreed to fuck each other a certain way."

"Well, it would have been nice if you had warned me."

"Why?" he asks. "Because then you wouldn't go out in public with me? That's bullshit, Sloan, and you know it."

"I don't know what I know," I growl. I feel like a petulant child, but I also feel a bit out of whack because of what's happening between us.

Gareth's warm hand grips my arm. When I refuse to look at him, he reaches over the centre console and clasps my face in his hands, forcing me to do so. "Sloan, in case you need reminding, I get off on surrendering to you." He pauses and stares down at my lips, his nostrils flaring as he husks out, "I even get off on pissing you off because I know it's only going to add to what you do to me later. Fuck me, I'm getting hard just thinking about it."

I have to fight back a moan that's traitorously clawing its way up my throat over the heated, turned-on look in his eyes. God, I want him underneath me so badly, but he's not done.

"But you need to know that there's a whole other side to me. A side that doesn't submit. I'm not just one thing."

My eyes flick back and forth between his, curiously trying to decipher him like a complicated puzzle. "So, what else are you?"

He licks his lips. "I'm my own fucking man out on the streets. That means I get pushy and assertive and I claim what I want, when I want. But behind closed doors with you in front of me, I fucking give myself to you because, bloody hell, it feels right. I can be two things. Understood?"

I fight back a gasp just as he releases me and puts the car in gear. He looks over his shoulder to back out of the parking stall as confusion envelops my entire body. Why is this so hot? Him all angry and demanding. This isn't what I want from Gareth. I want control. I want power. I want to say when and where. I've been thriving on it! Finding myself with it! It has changed my life in such an elemental way. But right now, the steely firmness in his gaze is making my body hum to life.

Instead of admitting all of that—instead of apologising for yelling at him and making a scene—I purse my lips and reply, "That's fine, but you're going to pay for it when we get back to your place."

The corners of his eyes crinkle with a frown, anger still ticking in his jaw muscle as he says, "I'm rock fucking hard just thinking about it."

Gareth is spread out naked on his bed. The blue lighting from his closet casts sexy shadows on his erection, which is already at full salute from the slow strip-tease I just tortured him with.

An orange flame glows brightly against my bare breasts as I hold a pillar candle inside a clear jar. "Are you scared?" I ask, my voice revealing how turned on I am by the anticipation on his face.

His eyes rake over my naked body. "Completely."

"Do you want me to stop?" I ask, cautiously staring back at him.

His face is resolute. "Never."

I kneel down next to him on the bed, tucking my feet underneath me. I considered wearing sexy lingerie again, but this is something quite different for us, so I thought it would help him feel comfortable if I am naked, too. Plus, the way he looks at me when I'm naked makes me feel like I can conquer the damn world.

I look up at him, brandishing the white candle in my hand. "The wax is vanilla scented because you said before you like how I smell so sweet all the time."

The corner of his mouth lifts up. "I love how you smell."

"Well, it's vanilla," I say, swirling the wax building up inside the jar. "I use vanilla essential oil as a perfume. I make it myself with almond oil and water because it has lots of health benefits. I read somewhere once that it has an aphrodisiac quality to it as well."

Gareth's abs flex with a low chuckle. "I was doomed from the beginning." He looks up at me fondly, our earlier argument forgotten.

"Completely," I reply with a smirk and hold the candle over his stomach. "I want you to lay your hands out flat beside you and try not to move too much." His muscles tighten and outline his beautiful six-pack as he braces himself for what's about to come. "I want you to really feel this. Not only on the surface, but inside yourself. Absorb it, then tell me what goes through your mind as you do."

He nods, looking equally nervous and excited.

I tilt the jar and drip a few dots of wax on his broad furry pecs. He hisses a sharp intake of air from the initial shock of the heat, but he relaxes and closes his eyes as soon as the wax dries.

My fingers move to touch the pools of dried wax, relishing in the smooth texture over the coarseness of his hairy chest. "How does it feel?"

"Hot," he states with a half-smile.

"Anything else?" I drizzle a little more. This time it runs down the valley between his pecs and over the ridges of his abs.

"It's creating a burning inside of me."

"Like what?"

"Like I was already hard when we started, and now I feel like I'm going to explode."

"What would ease the pain?"

"You." His answer is instant as he opens his eyes, his expression deathly serious.

I run my hands over the drops again, digging my nails into the design of the wax I've created. "Are you having any texture issues with this?"

He shakes his head. "Not with you."

"What do you mean?"

He swallows and watches the jar tilt as I drip more wax on him. With a groan, he answers, "I trust you I guess. I don't have any texture issues with you anymore because I always want what's coming."

"Even hot wax?" I tease, gazing down at my masterpiece.

When he doesn't respond, I look up to see his eyes completely hooded. "If you could see what I'm seeing, you would understand."

With a pleased smile, I throw one leg over his groin and position his tip between my folds. In one swift move, I pour more wax on his chest and sink down onto him, pulling him inside me completely.

"Jesus Christ, Tre," Gareth moans, clearly on sensory overload.

His eyes are pinched together in pain as I sit completely still on his cock, allowing my body to stretch and adjust to his girth.

"How do you feel now?" I ask, switching hands with the candle.

"Like I want to fuck you until you scream." His stern eyes open to me.

"But I'm in charge," I warn.

He swallows slowly and looks almost forlorn as he nods. "You're in charge."

"And tonight you tried to take that from me," I state, making slow, small circles with my hips and trying not to get too carried away yet.

"It was for your own good," he husks, fisting the sheets in his hands.

"I decide what's good for me, Gareth," I reply, then drip more wax on him.

He groans in pain and pleasure—a heady mix of confusing emotions.

"I make my own life decisions," I add firmly.

He sighs heavily. "I'm sorry."

His apology is surprising. I thought he'd fight me on this more. I thought I'd get to continue torturing him, and punishing him, and making him remember what we're about. Instead, he's submitting. He's apologising, and it is really freaking sexy.

I blow out the candle and stretch over Gareth's body to set it on the nightstand. My hair and breasts brush against his face, and his hands reach up and caress my back.

I pull back and smack his chest. "I didn't say you can touch me."

His lips form a thin line. "I'm sorry, Treacle."

"Good," I reply and sit upright on his cock. I press my hands to his chest and rake my nails through the wax coating on his trimmed chest hair. It's messy, and flaky, and animalistic, and I find myself grinding down on him even harder. "Now, let me remind you why we do this."

It took nearly an hour to scrape all the dried wax off of Gareth's body, and it's almost ten o'clock before we're showered and back in his bed. Both still naked per my command, and both still gloriously satisfied. I watch Gareth's muscled back as he stretches to flick off the bedside light.

He lies on his back next to me as I turn on my side to face him. "Did you like the wax?"

I can see his profile nodding in the darkness. "I like pretty much everything you do. Especially if you're really into it."

"Yeah?" I purse my lips to prevent the excited butterflies from escaping.

He nods and props a hand behind his head so his face is tilting down toward mine. "Although, I have the most *fun* when you mess up, which means that sex with you is always bloody fantastic."

I can't help the Cheshire Cat grin that spreads across my face. "That is so crazy to hear."

"Why?" he asks, eyeing me with a frown. "Didn't you have great sex with your ex? I mean, you married him. It couldn't have been that bad, right?"

I'm grateful for the darkness because he can't see the guilty look flashing over my face. "It was never like this," I reply, giving only a smidge away. "It was pretty basic. Traditional. Maybe if I had tried something different, it would have saved our marriage."

Silence stretches between us. I think Gareth is looking at me, but it's too dark to know for sure. His voice is soft when he asks, "Do you wish you would have saved your marriage?"

I frown at the thought. A few months ago, I might have said yes because not having Sophia every other week was killing me slowly. The dark days weren't worth leaving a loveless marriage. My response is different now, though. I have found a life outside of

Sophia and I'm learning to appreciate it.

"No, I think divorce was meant to be for us. I married him for all the wrong reasons."

"What do you mean?"

I exhale at his heavy question. I can't exactly tell him I got pregnant. And even though that was a large part of why we got married, it wasn't the only reason. "I was young when I met Callum. Fresh out of college and a bit of a dreamer. My friends and I were talking about opening up our own boutique, but it seemed impossible to actually accomplish. I didn't really grow up watching dreams come true."

Gareth turns on his side to face me, his twinkling eyes smouldering on me when he asks, "How did you grow up?"

"We were broke," I reply with a simple shrug of the shoulders. "Our dad took off when my sisters and I were little, so our mom raised us on her own. She worked two jobs only to still be a month behind on the bills. Even groceries were hard to afford. I remember she brought home chicken strips that were left in the fryer at the restaurant where she worked nights. She only got a couple at a time, so she froze them until we had enough for a meal. It wasn't awful, but it wasn't easy. Then I met Callum, and he was the opposite of poor. He was the epitome of wealth and responsibility. He was older than me, really established, really stable. I remember he always wore custom tailored suits. He had a good business, a good family. I met him at a bar, and he looked like he had it all together. I was still trying to figure out how I was going to pay my student loans once I got out of the grace period."

I pause my retelling and think back to the child I was when I met Cal. I was a baby having a baby. Marrying him seemed like the only responsible decision.

Gareth continues watching me quietly, not feeling the need to fill the silence. Just instinctively knowing I need a moment.

Sighing heavily, I continue, "When he asked me to marry him,

I saw myself being more responsible with someone like him. Less of a dreamer and more of a provider. I wanted stability. But we never really had that lustful attraction. We sort of skipped the fun stuff and went right to the grown-up stuff. Everything else was sort of forgotten about."

"So you were attracted to his stability?" Gareth's voice sounds disappointed, and I know what he's thinking.

"I wasn't a gold digger if that's what you're thinking—"

"That's not what I'm thinking," Gareth cuts me off, grabbing my arm urgently. "I'm just trying to figure out how a beautiful, strong woman like you could think she needed a man to make her feel stable."

"I wasn't strong back then," I defend. "I was young, and weak, and scared. I wasn't who I am when I'm with you. You bring it out in me." I sit up on my elbows, propping my head in my hands and looking down at him. "Being with you like this is really helping me find a strength that I never gave myself the chance to find before. That's why I got so mad earlier tonight when you were trying to interfere with my business. I should be able to figure those things out for myself."

"I really was just trying to help," he replies, his other hand coming out and playing with a damp strand of hair draped over my shoulder.

"I know, Gareth. I really do understand. And I'm not mad. I'm...grateful." The word is hard to find, but it's the right one for the moment. "You were just being a friend. I should have accepted that and not put you in the ex category."

His eyes widen. "I don't want to be anywhere near that wanker."

This makes me giggle. "How do you know he's a wanker?"

Gareth runs his thumb across my lower lip. "Because he didn't see you the way I see you."

My mouth falls open as tears prick the backs of my eyes. "How do you see me?" I ask, my voice thick with fear.

He sighs heavily like he's been sitting on his answer for ages. "Like a fucking lioness. And any rightful king would be a fool not to bow to his queen."

No Seconds for Me

16

Gareth

"**O**I! GARETH! I ASKED IF YOU WANT SECONDS?" BOOKER shouts, waving a plate of Vi's famous Swedish pancakes in front of me expectantly. "This is your last chance, or Tanner says he's eating the rest."

I shake him off, then scowl at Tanner as he forks all three and plops them onto his plate. When he reaches for the syrup, I can no longer bite my tongue. "Tanner, how can you eat like that right now?"

Tanner looks at me with wide, curious eyes. "What do you mean?"

"You're in the middle of the season. Eating like that will have fans yelling, 'who ate all the pies,' at you, bro." I glance around the table at Camden and Booker. They both nod knowingly.

It's midseason. This is the point where we all usually hit our stride in the game. While we use Sundays as our cheat days because Vi's cooking can't be missed, Tanner is going above and beyond the small cheat.

Tanner rolls his eyes and stuffs a bite into his mouth while mumbling, "My game has never been better. I'm celebrating."

I look over at Dad, who's sitting at the head of the table with

Rocky on his lap, cooing at her like she's better than football.

Don't get me wrong. Rocky is a million times better than football. She's pretty much everything in life. We're all happily wrapped around her little finger. Regardless, Dad has spent most of our lives controlling our diets and fitness routines because of his obsession with football. He even pushed all of us to live with him well into our twenties because he said it was best for our careers.

Now, his star striker is stuffing his face with pancakes and syrup, and the man can't look away from his granddaughter to interject. What is happening?

Vi leans over me to grab my plate off the table. "Are you all right, Gareth?"

"Of course I am. Why do you ask?" I stand up and take the dishes from her hand, noticing that Dad chooses now to look away from Rocky to pay attention to the outside world.

We haven't spoken again about him asking me to move back to London. It was a ridiculous request. But the truth is, watching him on Sundays lately, I can see that something is definitely changing in him.

Vi follows me to the sink in the kitchen. "You seem like you're in a mood again."

"What do you mean *again*?" I frown at her.

"Well, a couple of months ago you were like this. Then you got better. Now you—"

"Kind of suck again," Camden finishes, setting some plates on the counter next to Vi.

"I'm not in a mood," I defend but know deep down that I'm completely in a mood.

Sloan is making me tense. Once again, she has pushed me off for another week. I get the occasional texts and phone calls, but I don't understand her. She wants to see me every bloody night one week, then cuts me off dead for several days in a row the next week. It's making me bloody mad.

I know this is casual, but it feels like she's playing fucking games or something. It's making me realise how very little I know about her. I don't know where she lives or if she has flatmates. If she's in a house or a flat. I know things about her upbringing, but nothing about her real life other than how she likes me to fuck her.

The first couple of weeks I loved the release sex with her gave me. Now that she's spending the night more and more, I guess I feel entitled to a bit more.

"Here, your dad had to take a call," Hayden says, handing Rocky off to me. I shift my grip to hold her against my chest as he adds, "Rocky brightens all my dark days."

Vi smiles at Hayden affectionately, but Rocky diverts my attention back to her as she clasps her tiny fingers on my cheeks. "Garee," she coos.

I swear to fucking Christ my heart stops.

"Did she just…" Tanner barks from the table, his chair scraping loudly against the marble floor as he shoots to a standing position.

"Was that?" Vi's voice is high-pitched as she rushes over to where I stand stock-still, staring into Rocky's beautiful blue eyes. "Did she just say your name?"

"I don't know," I reply, then look back at my perfect niece. "What did you say, Rocky?" I ask softly, not wanting to frighten her.

With a wide, toothless smile, she says it again. "Garee." Then she slaps my cheeks happily.

I burst out laughing. "She's saying my name!"

"This is utter bollocks!" Tanner bellows, stuffing the last bite of pancakes into his mouth. "I see her more than him by miles!"

"Garee," Rocky coos again, then nearly kills me as she rests her head on my shoulder and gives me the most heart-melting hug I could ever imagine. She tucks into me like my shoulder was created just for this moment.

"Give her to me," Tanner says, his arms outstretched as he walks toward me.

"Piss off," I state, turning my back on him. "My niece and I are having a moment."

Vi wraps her arms around the two of us and whispers, "Even Rocky knew you needed cheering up."

A Switch

Sloan

Draped naked over Gareth isn't a bad way to fall asleep every night. We've spent another full week screwing like wild animals. I even got to try my hand at spanking him earlier tonight. I can't believe the rush I got when I had him push me against a wall and fuck me.

Good God, how am I ever going to quit this arrangement when it only gets better and better? And it's not about having control over him that gets me off. It's the strength he displays in his submission. Anyone can yield from a position of weakness, but to truly surrender entirely of his own free will simply because he wants to…That is what's so freaking sexy. He's so unexpected but wonderfully perfect for where I'm at in my life. I can't believe he's mine.

I sigh contentedly and lift my head to look up at him, the blue light from his closet pouring in, illuminating his smouldering features. We're in bed early because Gareth has a game tomorrow. I learned quickly that he needs his sleep on Friday nights, but I can't stop myself from asking a simple question.

"How did you get this?" I ask, propping myself up on his chest and running my finger down the ridge of his imperfect nose.

Before he answers, I stick my finger in his mouth and wordlessly will him to suck.

He sucks.

I smile.

"Football accident," he replies after my finger retreats.

He watches me hungrily as I bring the digit to my mouth and suck off his spit. There's not a thing I'm uncomfortable with around Gareth anymore. He's turned me from an insecure, emotional wreck of a divorcée into a sex goddess who's currently in love with life. "What happened?"

His Adam's apple slides up and down his throat as he adds, "I took a boot to the face during my first season with Man U."

"Ouch. Did it hurt?" I ask, propping my chin on my hands.

He shrugs. "Might have hurt if I hadn't liked it so much."

My brows lift. "You enjoy pain outside of the bedroom?"

He runs his hand slowly up my spine, his thick, rough fingers causing a riot of goosebumps to erupt all over my body.

"No," he replies and splays his hand flat on my arm. "But I do enjoy hurting my dad."

"How did your injury hurt your dad?"

"Because he couldn't get to me. He couldn't fuss over me, or help me, or be any part of the doctor appointments."

"Why not?" I ask, frowning curiously.

"He refuses to return to Manchester."

"Do you know why?"

Gareth shakes his head. "I'm sure it has something to do with my mum. Something he'll never share because he's a selfish sod."

I eye him dubiously. "And you're Mr. Sharer?"

His relaxed face hardens. "I've shared more with you than any-one in my life. I'm bloody well sharing right now, aren't I?"

His tone has me narrowing my eyes. "I know how you are with other people. The press. You give them nothing."

His body feels like stone beneath me. "I thought you don't re-search me."

"I don't."

"Then how do you know I don't share anything with the press?"

I pause, trying to decide if my reply will give too much away. "My…roommate tells me."

"Roommate," he repeats with a mean laugh. "That's the first I've heard of that." His tone is scathing, his relaxed mood completely vanished.

"What do you mean?" I ask, bracing myself for his response.

"I had no idea you have a fucking roommate because I know nothing about you, Sloan."

It pisses me off that he called me Sloan. He knows I prefer Treacle when I'm here. I sit up, not giving a shit that my boobs are on full display. There's nothing sexy about this moment right now. "I've shared a lot with you. I freaking shared my entire upbringing with you a couple weeks ago!"

He sits up with me, his eyes dark and angry. Scary even. "But what about your real life?"

"What do you mean?"

"What do you do when you disappear on me for a week?"

"I'm working!"

"Bullshit. You worked today. You're working tomorrow. I know what your work looks like."

"What are you insinuating?"

"That I know nothing about you, except for how you like to be fucked! Are you out fucking other guys like this? Asking them to bend over so you can whip them like a sadistic whore?"

I slap him. It wasn't a conscious decision. It certainly wasn't something I did to bring him pleasure. It was something I did to make him hurt as much as his words hurt me.

My palm tingles as his cheek erupts with the outline of my hand. "You think I'm a sadist?" I hate the trembling in my voice. I hate that I care what he thinks of me. This isn't how we are supposed to be.

"I think there's a reason we fuck the way we do and neither of us are truly owning up to it."

"I don't want to own up to it," I reply, turning and throwing my feet off the side of the bed. "That isn't what our arrangement is about. We have boundaries for a reason!"

"I get it, Sloan. We have a deal. You're in control and I'm not."

"Exactly!" I roar and stand up, turning my angry eyes on him. "I'm in control and you get the freedom to not think. It was a win-win here, Gareth. I thought we were both enjoying this."

"We were!" he exclaims, thrusting a hand through his hair and making no fucking sense.

"Then what the hell is the problem?" I cry.

"Maybe it has something to do with the fact that I don't even know how your lips taste!"

His response knocks the wind out of me. He's deathly serious from his spot on the bed, his bare chest heaving with anger. His muscles tensed in frustration. Veins protruding down his arms like angry lines on a map.

This is not what I expected from him. In fact, it's the complete opposite of what I expected. A terrified part of my mind thought he found out about Sophia, but all he wants are my lips? He wants to kiss me?

"What the hell does that mean?" I ask.

He exhales like it hurts. "You hold this enormous part of your-self away from me and it drives me mad."

I huff out an incredulous laugh. "If that's what you want, then maybe you should be a man and ask for it instead of picking a damn fight!"

His eyes fly wide. "I can't ask for it because those aren't our rules! You decide everything. I just…submit."

The word coming out of his mouth looks painful for him to say. Honestly, I don't like hearing him say it. I know that we're in some version of a dominant and submissive situation, but it doesn't feel like that to me. It feels like a luxury. Like an arrangement we were both enjoying. But if he's not enjoying it because he can't kiss me, it's not okay. Part of my job is to make sure he's okay. I'm also nowhere near ready for our arrangement to be over. The thought of Gareth pulling away because of this hard-line has anxiety climbing in my chest.

"Well, you can kiss me," I utter, my voice soft in the quiet room.

"Is that an order?" Gareth asks, his shoulders tense and full of brooding. Full of…Gareth.

"No," I reply quickly. That's not how this should happen. I can't command him to kiss me. If it's important enough for him to pick a fight with me about, it needs to be on his terms. "In fact, I don't want you to do it now. I want you to do it when *you* want to do it. When it feels right for you."

"That's not part of our deal," he states, clearly confused.

"I know. If you don't like the idea, tell me and we can forget the whole thing."

"I like it." His voice is soft, his eyes downcast, like he's ashamed to be saying these words.

I nod slowly. "Then a kiss is yours. Whenever you want it, I'll accept it."

He nods and stares down at the empty side of the bed.

"Do you really think I'm sadistic?"

"No," he croaks painfully and slides off the edge of the bed. "I just said that to hurt you. I think you're incredible."

I cross my arms over my chest, still upset over the tone he took with me. Maybe I'm not giving him enough attention after we do what we do. Aftercare is an important factor in unconventional relationships.

"I don't want anything to change between us, Treacle," he says, staring back at me like I'm a wild animal that's going to bolt.

"Are you sure?" I ask, needing the confirmation again.

He nods, his eyes full of sadness and shame and a whole mess of emotions I'm too exhausted to dissect. "I'm sorry I said all of that. I didn't mean it. You have to know that."

I stare back at him. I do know because I know Gareth, sexually and emotionally. I might not know some basic things about his life, but I know who he is. I know he's not Cal. He's not manipulating me or trying to control me. He just has feelings.

My voice is soft when I whisper, "I need you to hold me."

"Anything," he answers on a breath. In two enormous strides, he pulls me into his arms, his lips raining kisses in my hair. "I'm sorry, Treacle. I'm so sorry."

I nod against his chest. "I believe you," I soothe.

I soothe him because we do know each other despite what he says. We know each other better than I'm prepared to admit.

Gareth

I wake in the middle of the night and find myself completely wrapped around Sloan's naked body. I thought she was going to go home after our fight, but she didn't. And even though she offered me something I didn't realise I was longing for, there was still a sense of uneasiness between us as we went to sleep. Perhaps makeup sex would have helped with the unsettled feeling. Instead, she climbed into bed, turned away from me, and fell asleep without another word.

Now she's woken me up because she's moving beneath the blankets. At first, I think she's awake and interested in that makeup sex after all. But as I unfold myself from her body and sit up to look down at her, it's clear she's completely asleep.

Her hips mindlessly swirl in slow, tiny motions. A soft moan escapes her lips. I swear I've died and gone to Heaven because it dawns on me that she's having a sex dream.

Her hand slips under the covers. When she begins touching herself, I think I might fucking lose my bloody mind. She better be thinking about me and not that wanker ex of hers. Our fight tonight probably brought back some old memories, but I hate the idea that she could be thinking of him again. How many years did he not see how incredible she is? How many times did he overlook how much she holds back?

Rather than lie here and let her subconscious decide who's bringing her pleasure, I take action into my own hands.

Gently, I pull her shoulder so she's flat against the bed on her back—a position I rarely see from her. Sloan likes to ride on top most of the time. I think it helps her stay in control, but I don't want to see that hard strength right now. I want to see this vulnerable softness she's giving me.

I press my hand on top of hers where she's mindlessly rubbing her mound. As soon as my rough palm joins the pressured movement, she stops.

Her lids flutter open and she looks up at me. Starry pupils dilated. Lips parted. Chestnut hair splayed wildly all around the pillow. "Gareth?" she croaks through her much too large lips.

"Yes," I murmur and drop a tantalising soft kiss on each swell of her breasts.

"What's going on?"

"I think you were dreaming," I reply, kissing the dip between her breasts. "Want to tell me what about?" I pull back and stare down at her. She shakes her head, so I press further. "Can I give you a happy ending?"

She looks hesitant but nods her acceptance.

I move overtop of her, her soft legs wrapping around me and gripping my sides. She looks like she doesn't know what to do with her hands, so without asking, I grasp her wrists and hold them above her head.

"Oh my God," she moans loudly, her back arching off the bed as I press my tip between her folds. I haven't even pushed into her yet and she's dying for it. She raises her hips up toward me with needful wanting. Her brown eyes wide and blinking, staring up at me with a silent request to take her.

Jesus fuck, she wants me to take her. Her guard is completely down, and it's fucking magic.

This is the moment I could take. I could kiss her. I could accept the gift she offered me earlier this evening, but there's a part of me that feels like it would be wrong. We've been sleeping, and we're not fully cognizant of our surroundings. When I take Sloan's lips with mine, I want to remember everything about it. I want to see her face in the light when I do. I need it to matter. I don't know what's happening right now, and kissing her would further complicate the situation.

I sink inside of her with a smooth, deep thrust. A low groan escapes my lips as our foreheads press together and I fill her to the brim. God, she feels good. She's fucking soaked, and soft, and tight, and ready. Like she's clay under my hands, ready for me to do with as I wish.

I bury my face in her neck and murmur, "You're fucking soaked. It's going to take all I have not to come inside of you immediately."

"Gareth!" Her breath trembles with a sharp intake of air as I thrust in again, gradual and deep.

"And you're not in charge this time, Treacle." I nip softly on her neck and suck. "I am."

"Yes," she cries, her body rolling under me.

"I'm going to fuck you hard now," I husk, pulling back and gauging her reaction. "Because I can tell that's what you want."

Her eyes are wide as she groans out, "Yes, yes, yes."

"You want that, Tre?"

"Yes!" she exclaims in clear frustration. "God, Gareth. Just fuck me."

My fingers squeeze tightly around her wrists, an animalistic urge overtaking me from her husky command, moaning my name in the quiet dark of night. Even when I'm in charge, she has all the power.

I continue holding her hostage as I ram myself in and out of her in needful thrusts. Hard in, slow out. Grinding in deeper and deeper with each stroke. I move one hand down to squeeze her leg in a bruising, punishing grasp. I want to feel every inch of her skin touch mine. I want to be inside of her deeper than any man has ever been.

Her thick lush lips reflect in the faint light of the room. Moist and plump and begging to be fucked by my tongue. I want them for myself. I want to bite and lick them until I taste the moans of her voice. They belong to me after all. But not tonight.

If I take more in this moment, she'll crumble. I'm also not sure exactly why I want more all of a sudden. In the beginning, I just wanted the freedom her control gave me. When we fucked and she was in charge, I didn't have to think about my family, my past, my future. I just had to listen to her commands and appreciate everything she was giving me.

But somewhere in the last couple of weeks, things have shifted. For once, my mind isn't getting in the way. My mind and my dick are in sync, and they want to fuck her. Own her. Make her mine in this single moment in time.

So I do exactly that. I fuck her brains out until the most powerful climax I've ever had tears through both of us…

…destroying everything I thought we were.

Jitter Ghost

Sloan

MY PHONE RINGS FROM THE CUPHOLDER IN MY CAR, AND I SEE Gareth's name pop up for the third time today.

Freya eyes the screen from her spot beside me. "Please tell me you're going to answer that."

"I'm not," I reply and shoot her a scathing look.

"You can't possibly be ghosting him again. You already tried that once and it didn't take."

"I'm not ghosting him. I have Sophia this week. He knows I'm busy."

"Why are you still hiding her from him? It's obvious you two are a semi-regular thing now."

My hands wrap tighter around the wheel. There is no way in hell I'm telling Gareth about Sophia. We're already blurring so many lines because I can't seem to quit digging into his personal life.

I cut a look at Freya. "Telling him I'm a mother will personalise things even more than we already have, and I can't handle that right now. We're just having sex. He's okay with that."

"Then why aren't you taking his calls?"

"Because I don't know what I want to say!"

She sighs heavily. "You snuck out of his house before he woke

236

up Saturday. He's been calling you all weekend, even when he's been busy with a home football game. It's Monday now. You've had some time to breathe. Just talk to him and stop being a bitch."

"I am not being a bitch!" I argue, my hands clenching the wheel in a death grip. "I'm trying to figure out how to handle this. We had an agreement and he broke it. Now I'm trying to decide what it all means before I talk to him."

"Well, considering we're going right by his house in a few minutes, I hope you're going to talk to him today. He lost his game Saturday. He's probably feeling awful."

"We have a fitting with Brandi."

"I can take care of the fitting. You should take the car and go over to his house. Fix this so you stop obsessing over your mobile."

I frown as I turn down the private drive toward Hobo's home. "Gareth might not even be home and I'm supposed to be out of town." I glance at his gate with a forlorn sort of pit in my belly. I hate that he lost his game on top of what's going on between us.

"You are impossible!" Freya tuts with a growl. "If I had a man like Gareth Harris phoning me nonstop, I'd never let it go to voicemail. You have issues, love."

"Don't I know it," I murmur.

When we pull onto Hobo and Brandi's property, I learn that my issues can no longer be ignored. Gareth is sitting on the front step of Hobo's house and he does not look happy.

Freya's green eyes fly wide. "He looks pissed. Christ, he's sexy."

I shut the car off and swallow slowly. "I don't care."

She shakes her head and slides out of the car. "I'm just going to nip in with these gowns and get started with Brandi. You, erm…take care of business." Freya shuffles awkwardly with the garment bags in the backseat and turns to see Gareth pass by her in his pursuit to me.

My heart lurches when I realise Sophia's booster seat is still in the back, so I hurry away from my vehicle toward two quaint little outbuildings.

I shoot an angry look at Gareth. "Over here," I snap, pointing to the alleyway between two dilapidated barns that look to be at least a hundred years old.

I make my way down the narrow alley between the two moss-covered brick structures and can feel Gareth's eyes burning holes into my back. When I turn to face him, the expression on his face is similar to that of a cornered bear.

"We need to talk," he growls, the vein on his neck looking like it could burst at any moment.

"This is not okay!" I exclaim, stepping into his space and poking his chest with my finger. I'm taking control of this conversation. Not him. He's one-upped me enough this week.

He wraps his hand around my finger. "What you're doing is not okay!"

"Gareth, I am working right now!" I seethe, yanking my finger away and balling my hands into fists at my sides. "You can't just show up at an appointment of mine and demand to speak to me."

Gareth gestures angrily toward the house. "You told me you were travelling! So imagine my surprise when Hobo said you were coming over today."

"I am travelling. I leave…later," I lie, unable to look him in the eyes as I do so. "This is the second time you've made me look ridiculous in front of Hobo and Brandi!"

"Bollocks," he growls. "Stop fucking ghosting me and I won't have to show up like this!"

"I'm not ghosting you!" I retort, running a frustrated hand through my hair. "I'm travelling and…processing."

"Processing what? The fact that I fucked you and not the other way around for once?"

"Exactly!" I respond, my voice rising in pitch as I lean into him, desperate to drive my point across. "That wasn't part of our arrangement. I need boundaries for this to work, Gareth."

"Why?" he bites back, his eyes dropping to my lips.

I fumble with my thoughts for a moment, terrified he might kiss me. I gave him that gift, but I'm not sure I'll be able to handle it if he takes it now. I shake my head and muster up all my strength. "I don't want to turn back into the person I once was, Gareth. The reason this arrangement was working is because we had clear expectations of each other. If we're going to keep doing this, that cannot happen again."

"I don't want you to change, Sloan!" he exclaims, his gaze raking slowly over my body. His hazel eyes turn to fire as he blatantly undresses me in his mind. His voice is softer when he adds, "I was just doing my due diligence. You seemed to be getting awfully worked up in your sleep, and I didn't want you to feel uncomfortable down there."

The wicked gleam in his eyes sends a traitorous jolt of need right between my legs and my knees wobble. I inhale a big gulp of air, feeling my cheeks heat so much I have to look away from him when I reply, "I need to know that nothing's changed, Gareth."

"Nothing's changed," he states and moves in closer to me, backing me up against the cool bricks. "You're still in charge, and I still want to lose myself when I'm with you. But I need you to not run every time you get scared."

He cages me, his heat enveloping all around me. It would be so easy to turn into a puddle of goo right in front of him. He has a strong presence that I could lose myself in completely. But if I want to continue this arrangement, I need to hold my feelings and personal life at bay and correct him. The way he's approaching me right now is like a dog with no discipline.

I'm not going to let him alpha me anymore.

Narrowing my eyes, I shove both hands against his hard chest and push him backwards against the other building. Shock registers on his face first, then excitement. Fiery, passionate, lusty excitement.

My voice is firm when I reply, "I'm not scared. And fine, no more ghosting. Just remember who's in charge and we'll be able to continue this." I stare down at his lips and lean in. "Now go home before I decide you need something more painful than hot wax or my hand next time I see you."

His nostrils flare with a possessive thrill. "When will I see you again?"

Sophia instantly comes to mind. "I get back next Monday."

His brow furrows. "You sure travel a lot."

"Gareth!" I scold, stifling my anxiety over how I'm going to keep this up much longer if he's already pushing back like this. "This isn't a relationship. This is an arrangement you are breaking right now. If you want this to continue, why are you questioning me?"

He lifts his hands up in surrender. "All right, Monday."

"Monday."

Without another word, I turn sharply on my heel. My hair flicks in his face before I stride away with my back straight and shoulders high. The weight of his heated stare on me is enough to make my steps falter.

My greatest challenge isn't controlling Gareth.

It's controlling myself.

Lioness and Her Cub

Gareth

STANDING IN THE MIDDLE OF THE PITCH AT THE CLIFF, I AM pummelled by a memory of when I was about six years old and Mum had brought me out here to watch Dad practice. We were allowed on the pitch, and I remember picking several blades of grass and putting them in my pocket with big dreams of becoming a footy player just like my dad. He looked so massive out here with all the other players. I remember thinking how cool it was that they got to play football every day for their job.

And Mum looked so happy watching Dad play. Her eyes were so big and excited, like she was watching her own personal superhero save the world. I remember thinking I couldn't wait for her to see me play someday so she would look at me the same way.

My memory fades as soon as I see my three brothers striding toward me. Tanner and Camden are mirror images of each other with their blonde hair and large frames. They aren't identical twins, but they were difficult to tell apart until Tanner grew out his hair and beard. Booker looks a lot more like me. The two of us take after our dad's darker features while the twins and Vi look more like our mum's Swedish heritage.

The three of them are kitted out in warm, footy active wear. I smile and wave them over to where I'm standing with several bags of kid-sized footballs. This is a big day for Kid Kickers. I've been wanting to extend this program outside of Manchester for some time now, and we open our facility to potential sponsors today. They can check out the facility, see how camps are run, and decide what level of contributor they want to be. Helping with this has been a welcome distraction from Sloan.

Since I couldn't handle today alone, I asked my brothers to join me in running a session. My agent thought it would be a good promo for the World Cup, which I could care less about. The Cup isn't about promos. It's about skill. Regardless, I knew having them here would help bring in the sponsors, and they were all too willing to jump on a train.

Tanner jogs ahead of the pack. I brace myself as he jumps up into my arms, wrapping his long legs around my waist in a ridiculous embrace.

"My broseph!" he bellows in a pitch similar to that of a whining dog.

I shove him off of me and grumble, "You are such a wanker."

Camden smiles happily and claps me on the back in a big hug. Booker comes in next, giving me that small baby brother smile of his even though the prat is taller than me.

"Thanks for coming, guys," I state with a big exhale, trying to expel my nerves.

"Anytime I can get out of training and see you, I'm all over it," Camden says with a playful punch on the shoulder. "And it's for a great cause, which is really cool."

Tanner elbows me. "He's trying to sound so mature and noble, but the creep was sexting his wife the entire time on the train. So embarrassing." Tanner rolls his eyes dramatically like he didn't just jump into my arms in the middle of a football pitch a minute ago.

Booker shakes his head at the two of them. "I was more mature than both of them as an infant."

I clap Booker on the back and tease, "That's not a huge achievement."

Tanner stretches his arms out wide, clearly not the least bit put off by our jokes. "So, how is today going to go? Kids bloody love me, so all of you should prepare to be totally outshined."

I smile and shake my head. "Well, we're going to keep it nice and easy because they just got out of school, so they're probably a bit knackered. Basically, we'll each get sectioned off with a group of about ten kids. Two boys teams and two girls teams. We have five-to seven-year-olds, so just play some fun games and easy drills. No scrimmaging or anything competitive. The point of today is to have fun, and I asked you guys here because no one knows how to have a laugh better than you lot."

"Too bloody right!" Camden states, pulling a piece of paper out of the pocket of his Tiro trousers. "I have the best games in mind."

Tanner's face falls. "You prepared?"

"That's what Gareth's email said to do." Camden laughs heartily. "Plus, I've never coached kids before. I needed to read up on some ideas."

"Shit!" Tanner mumbles, turning accusatory eyes at me. "I didn't see an email!"

"I texted you to check your email, Tanner," Booker chastises with a heavy sigh.

"I only read part of your text. You're a wordy wanker. Who has time to read all of that?" Tanner grumbles and moves closer to Camden. "Share your notes with me, Cam."

"No!" Camden jerks his paper back. "You were just bragging about outshining all of us. I'm not giving away my hard work."

Tanner pins Camden with a serious look. "It's for the kids, broseph. You should share."

"You're one to talk!" Camden exclaims. "You made an art form out of the Bacon Sandwich Rule! You licked stuff you hated just because you didn't want me to have it!"

Tanner puts his hands on his hips. "This is for the kids!" he repeats, slowly moving closer to Camden's paper with his hand outstretched.

Camden rolls his eyes. "God, why are you like this?"

Camden hands over the paper and Tanner begins scrolling through the list at lightning speed. "It's a gift."

Camden and Tanner each take one of the boys teams while Booker and I take the girls teams. The four of us divide into our own sections marked off on the pitch. The plan is to start with some fun games before diving into drills.

Several suits file into the sideline accompanied by Kid Kickers staff members who are there to answer questions about the daily running of the facility. I am here to be the headliner. Same goes for my brothers. Our positions in the sport of football give us the power to really make a difference, and that's what we're all here for today.

The little girls are all giggling and messing about, so I blow my whistle. Their wide eyes snap to mine curiously. Most of them don't have a clue who I am, which makes things a lot easier. The older kids would have been too star-struck to perform appropriately for the potential sponsors, so we opted for younger groups today.

"I want everyone to take a football and form a line," I state, grabbing the bag of balls and tipping it upside down to empty.

The girls flounce over with their swishing ponytails, bright-coloured socks, and shin pads. A few showed up without guards on, but our facility has a supply on hand for them.

I direct a couple of girls where to stand. The others begin to fall in line, but one girl stands back from the pack, frowning at the others who are fighting over various balls.

I squat down next to the little brunette. "Are you okay there, kid?"

She nods, but the puzzled look to her brows goes nowhere. "These are called soccer balls, too, right?"

She blinks her big brown eyes at me. The adorably serious expression lifts the corners of my mouth. "In some parts of the world, yes."

She nods her head. "Do they play soccer in America?"

"Yes, they do," I answer with a smile. "They call it soccer and we call it football, but it's the same sport."

She chews on the tip of her thumb and mumbles, "That's what I was afraid of. I'm not sure I should be playing this."

"Why not? Don't you like football?" I ask, grabbing a ball and tossing it in my hands in front of her.

"Yes, I think so, but my mummy wouldn't like me playing."

"Did she not sign the waiver?" I ask, glancing over to the sideline for a staff member. If a parent didn't sign a waiver, this little girl can't play.

"My dad signed it," she says, redirecting my focus to her.

I stand up and hold the ball out to her. "Then we should be okay. You only need one parent's signature."

She squeezes the green neon ball in her hands and stares down at it intently as she asks, "What if I get hurt? Mummy says football can be kind of rough."

The sad slump of her shoulders nearly breaks my heart. I squat down in front of her again, and she pins me with her innocent eyes that are probably exactly what got her father to bring her today against her mother's wishes. It'd be bloody impossible to refuse this little beauty anything she wanted.

I tuck a finger under her chin and lift it to me with a soft smile. "Cheer up, kid. Injuries are part of being an athlete, but we're going to be taking it easy today. Today is just about fun. We won't get rough, I promise."

"Just fun?" She pins me with a look like she's not sure she can trust me.

I smile and make an *X* over my chest. "Cross my heart."

Her eyes alight with this new information "That is excellent news." Without warning, she drops the ball and wraps her arms around my neck in an unexpected hug, nearly knocking me backwards in the process.

She releases me, grabs her ball, and jogs over to the hoard of girls all waiting. I give Brown Eyes a thumbs up when she finds a place to stand, then instruct the girls to have a seat on their footballs.

A photographer comes over and begins snapping photos as I squat down and explain what we're going to do. "We're going to play a game called Sharks and Minnows. The minnows will each have a ball while the sharks try to steal them. Now, who wants to be a shark?"

All the girls' hands shoot up into the air, except for Brown Eyes.

"You can't all be sharks, so I'll have to count you off. Ones are sharks, twos are minnows."

I begin counting them off, and Brown Eyes ends up being a shark. "I really wanted to be a minnow," she pouts.

"Everyone will get a chance to be both."

She sighs heavily. "Okay, I'll just have to try extra hard to get a ball because I really want to kick a ball. I've never kicked a ball before."

"You'll have lots of chances to kick a ball today," I huff with a laugh.

Sharks and Minnows is a mess. None of the girls know how to properly kick a ball. When I decide to join the sharks and try to steal from the minnows, the girls swarm me, asking me to steal their balls. Regardless, the game is full of giggles. I even end up falling on the ground in an attempt to not pummel a little girl I didn't see under my feet.

When I'm down on the ground laughing and trying to figure

out how to regain control of this horrid game, my eyes fall over to the sideline. My smile dies when a familiar figure comes into view.

Sloan is over there, thrusting an angry finger into the face of a suited man who's standing amongst the other potential sponsors. At first, I think she's interested in contributing. Then I recall the fact that she told me she was travelling this week. What the fuck is going on?

The man is clearly uninterested in what she has to say, barely looking away from his phone as Sloan continues screaming at him. She pauses for a second and the man finally looks up from his mobile and points out toward me.

Sloan's eyes scan the pitch and go wide when they land on me. Taking a deep breath, she diverts her gaze to the right and marches out onto the pitch, her purse clutched tightly on her shoulder. She's on a mission.

I assume she's coming out to talk to me, but she veers right and heads toward the brown-eyed stunner who's been charming me for the past thirty minutes.

"Sophia, we have to go." Sloan's voice is shaky as she reaches out and grabs her hand.

The little girl yanks her hand away and states firmly, "I'm finally a minnow. I just got a ball! I don't want to stop playing. I like football."

"Sophia!" Sloan shrieks, turning her back on me. "Do not argue with me. We are leaving."

I stand up from the ground and make my way over to them, ready to help with whatever is going on. How does Sloan know this child?

"We're just playing. It's not a real game. I won't get hurt!" the little girl whines, then adds at the end, "Please, Mummy!"

I swear my heart leaps into my throat. "Mummy?" I don't realise I voice the word out loud, my tone sounding like it's a hundred miles away.

Sloan twirls on her heel to eye me standing behind her. Her face a hard, emotionless mask, like I'm nothing more than a stranger to her. I'm close enough to smell her familiar scent, but she still won't make eye contact with me.

"Don't say a word," she barks, lifting a finger my way to silence me. "I mean it. Nothing."

"Mummy, please let me stay. I like football—I mean, soccer." the girl quickly corrects herself. "It's soccer, Mummy. I'll call it soccer if you want. Please!"

"It's the same thing, Sophia!" Sloan's voice is shrill and panic-stricken. "And you can't play it."

"Sloan," I state, my jaw tight with anxiety as a couple of photographers begin walking toward us. I move in closer to her, desperate to hide her. Hide the scene. Desperate to figure out what the fuck is going on.

This is the woman I've been sleeping with. The woman whom I've opened up to and have been intimate with on more levels than I've ever been intimate with a person in my entire life. But everything about her is so night and day different right now. The way she stands, her tone of voice. She's not my Treacle. She's someone I've never met before.

I reach out to touch her shoulder. "Just tell me what the problem is?"

She jerks away from me, her eyes swerving to the kids and people all gawking at us. Out of the corner of my eye, I see my brothers push back a couple of photographers to give us some space. Sloan's chin trembles as she finally looks me in the eyes, dropping her shield. Her golden, watery eyes are mirror images of the little girl's eyes staring up at her. I can't believe I didn't see the resemblance.

She is Sloan's clone through and through.

"I'm so sorry, Gareth," she croaks, wiping her nose and cheek in one swoop. "I don't know what else there is to say."

I move in closer, desperate to touch her. Desperate to take the pain from her. The sensation she's putting out is like a phantom pain in my soul that I've worked my entire life to avoid, roaring back to life with a vengeance.

She inhales sharply and steps out of my reach. Jaw tight, she grabs the girl's hand and hurriedly hauls her off the pitch. She passes the man she was talking to before, and he follows in their wake, looking agitated and pompous beyond belief.

I blink rapidly and fully process what's just transpired.

Sloan has a kid.

What. The. Fuck.

My PR rep for Kid Kickers soothes the media's curiosity about an upset mother, but my brothers aren't as easily deterred.

Back in the changing room, I'm stuffing my clothes into my bag when I hear Tanner's voice behind me. "That was your stylist," he states, his tone more serious than it's been all day. "Sloan, isn't it?"

I look over my shoulder and see the three of them leaning against the lockers on the opposite wall. They all have their arms crossed over their chests like they are here for a fucking Harris Shakedown or something.

My voice is curt when I reply, "Yes."

"Was that her daughter?" Camden asks.

I turn on my heel to see his grave eyes. "How should I know?" I snap. I hate that my two worlds are colliding. I hate it even more that I have no fucking clue what's going on with Sloan.

Booker's voice is timid when he speaks up next. "Why was she looking at you like that? It's clear there was something significant happening between the two of you, even if you weren't saying it out loud."

"It's none of your business," I growl and instantly feel bad when

Booker's face falls. "I'm not discussing it with all of you."

Camden's face furrows with confusion. "You're in our business all the time!"

"Because you put me in your business!" I exclaim.

Booker steps forward with determination. "We're Harrises, Gareth. We're all in each other's business. Always. That's just how it works in our family."

"Oh sod off, Book. That may be true for you guys down in London, but the lot of you don't have a clue what I do here in Manchester. None of you do."

"That's not our bloody fault!" Tanner roars, stepping forward and shoving his hand against my chest. I shove him back, but he's undeterred as he continues, "You're the moody sod who doesn't say a word about your life here. We just assumed your life was still in London with us. Tell us what's going on!"

"I don't fucking know!" I roar, my hands thrusting through my hair in frustration. I squeeze the back of my neck and attempt to calm the fuck down. "I didn't know she had a child."

Silence envelopes the space as the unspoken words are processed. They know. They are my brothers and they've never seen me upset over a woman.

But me not knowing she has a kid makes it clear that our involvement isn't cut and dry. Here I thought I had gained some ground with her when she told me I can take a kiss from her whenever I want. I thought it meant we were evolving. Changing. Maybe even for the better. But what happened out on the pitch just goes to show how dead fucking wrong I was about everything.

"Well, how do we fix this?" Camden asks, crossing his arms over his chest.

"We won't," I nearly growl. "There's no *we* here. It's just me. I don't need you guys getting involved."

"You solve all of our problems!" Camden retorts, his jaw ticking angrily. "Let us help you, Gareth."

"I'll be fine." I slam my locker closed and turn on my heel to stare at my brothers. The three of them stand shoulder-to-shoulder. Legs wide. Chests out. Chins lifted. Like they're ready for battle. My brothers—thick as thieves and willing to bend over backwards without knowing a shred of the full story.

How do I tell them what I've been doing with Sloan all this time? How do I tell them that I was so exhausted from my family, my responsibilities, football, everything that I wanted a woman to overpower me in the bedroom just to give my mind a fucking break? How could they possibly not take that personally? I've shouldered their burdens for years, yet I wasn't willing to share mine with them.

This isn't a battle my brothers can fight with me. They can't see me like this. I can't let them find out about my arrangement with Sloan. I also can't show them how much it fucking guts me that Sloan chose to hide something—someone—so monumentally important from me. She kept a child's entire existence from me. What the fuck does that mean?

I've spent my entire life using my head to handle things and look where that's gotten me. Perhaps now it's time to say "fuck it" and use my heart for once. My heart is not submissive, though. It will not surrender.

It will fight back.

Mama Bear

Sloan

I'M SHAKING WHEN I FINALLY GET SOPHIA TO BED. POSITIVELY trembling with rage, adrenaline, fear. All of the above. Not only am I upset with Callum for putting Sophia into a soccer session without consulting me, but he actually picked her up from school on my week! He wouldn't give me two hours on Thanksgiving, but he thought it was fine to put Sophia's health at risk on a day that is mine? How dare he!

Normally, she goes to an after school club for the hour or two I need to finish my day out. I wouldn't have even known Sophia left if her teacher hadn't emailed to let me know that she forgot her art assignment on her desk that needs to be done for tomorrow. When I called Callum to find out where Sophia was, he gave me some bullshit response that he was going to drop her back before I arrived. Oh, and he said it was for a good cause, like he's ever been generous a day in his life!

When I saw my daughter on that field, I saw red. The wrench in this insanely mucked-up mix was Gareth. I didn't see him until I was already halfway out on the field, so deep in mama bear mode that there was no way to stop myself from blowing up my whole life.

I knew the moment I took hold of Sophia's hand I lost something that wasn't even completely mine to lose. Gareth will never forgive me for blatantly lying to him.

Now that the dust has settled—now that Sophia is safe and back under my roof—the realisation of everything I've lost is finally sinking in.

No more Astbury. No more escape. Empowerment. Freedom. Sexual discovery…

No more Gareth.

My dark days when Sophia is gone will return, and I must own the fact that keeping Sophia a secret was probably the biggest mistake of my life. An even bigger one than marrying Callum Coleridge.

That heavy notion hits me like a ton of bricks as I hurry down the steps and yank open my front door. Manchester winters have nothing on Chicago, but the cool December night air is exactly what I need as I come to terms with everything.

I exhale slowly and watch the cloud of air form by my lips when a set of headlights come to a stop on the side of the road in front of my house. It's an unfamiliar vehicle, so I squint to see who's in the driver's seat.

My heart completely stops when I see Gareth unfold his giant frame out of the car. He slams the door shut in a huff and looks straight at me as I stand beneath the dim yellow lighting on my porch. I pull my cardigan tightly around my body as he makes his way toward my short cast iron fence.

Instead of walking down to the gate opening near my driveway, he grips the fence and hauls himself over the railing in one swift, athletic move. He cuts through the grass in my direction. Once his dark figure is illuminated by the light, I see with great clarity that Gareth is *pissed*.

I swallow.

His nostrils flare.

I swallow again.

His jaw grinds from side-to-side.

I drag in a deep breath as he exhales a long, heavy sigh, forming his own puff of cold air.

"H—how did you find where I live?" I stammer, finally breaking the silence.

His hazel eyes narrow. "Your ex."

My hands fly up to cover my face. This day couldn't get any worse. "Where did you see my ex?" I mumble against my palms, barely able to look at Gareth knowing that he's actually spoken to Callum.

"His house."

Oh my God, he's been to Callum's house! *I think I might be sick.* I peek through the slits between my fingers. "How did you find him?"

Gareth's face relaxes slightly. "We had his information at The Cliff as a potential sponsor. He wasn't hard to find." He steps closer to me, looming his angry presence over me. "He's a real fucking dick, you know that?"

My hands fall as I stare up at him. "What did you tell him about us?"

Gareth's eyes flash with anger. "I deserve a bit more credit than that, Sloan."

A knot forms in my throat. "I didn't mean—"

"I told him I had to pick up an order and only had your old address. It took everything in me not to punch the smug fucking look off his face when he told me how embarrassed he was by your behaviour today."

"What do you mean?" I ask, trying to shake off the effect Gareth's close proximity has on me.

"How the fuck could you ever marry a pompous prick like him?"

Is Gareth *jealous*? I want to laugh at the notion. Or cry. Probably both. "Isn't it obvious?"

"Not to me," he grinds through clenched teeth.

"I got pregnant, of course!" I swirl away from him, taking a couple of necessary steps back so I can breathe again.

"Were you ever going to tell me?" His voice is clipped with an emotion I can't quite place.

"Yes…No…I don't know," I reply, feeling like a total puke. I cross my arms to brace myself for his reaction.

"Why, Sloan?" His eyes are sad on mine. He's hurt. He's hurt that I hid such a large part of my life from him.

"It wasn't what we were about," I reply with a shrug. "You said it yourself not that long ago. We were just about sex."

He rears back like I slapped him, his hands balling up into tight fists at his sides. "Got it. Message received. I didn't realise I had been demoted from friends with benefits to a casual fuck."

"Gareth!"

"Fuck this," he growls and turns to walk away.

I rush over to him and grab his tensed arm, using all my strength to haul him back toward me. "Just…listen to me!"

"You listen to me!" he exclaims, twirling on his heel and grabbing me by the arms. In one swift move, he has me pressed against the cool bricks of my house, his hands on either side of my face. "In the beginning, we were just fucking, but you know damn well that changed."

"It did?" I croak, my stomach doing flips inside itself as his familiar scent wafts over me.

"Yes!" he growls, veins protruding on his neck as he crouches to eye level with me. "We've changed. We're not just one thing anymore. We're *more*, Sloan."

"Treacle," I correct, my voice wavering.

"Sloan," he retorts. "In my mind, you are my Sloan and my Treacle. You're not just one thing to me. And the fact that you didn't tell me you're a mother fucking kills me. What are you afraid of?"

"That you'll see me differently!" I cry, my eyes watery with annoying tears. "That what we have will stop. You have been my saving grace since I got divorced, Gareth. This half custody thing with my ex was tearing me apart from the inside out. But when I'm with you, I'm in control, and I feel strong, and I remember who I am. Who I want to be! I don't want to lose that. Why do we have to change?"

"Because I can't continue as we were," he answers, glancing down at my trembling hands that ache to touch him. His voice is softer when he adds, "And it's not because you have a kid. I don't care that you're a mother, Sloan. It doesn't change things for me. Your ex was embarrassed by you on the pitch today, but I was fucking proud. Even when I was stark-raving-mad at you for hiding something so monumental from me, I couldn't help but think, 'Bloody hell, she's the most fearsome mother I've ever laid eyes on!'"

A sob erupts from my throat, and I cover my mouth to try to get hold of my senses. I don't know why his words affect me so much, but they do. I finally don't feel alone and terrified that I'm doing this motherhood thing all wrong. Someone supports me. Someone believes in me. Someone whose opinion I value more than I realised.

But Gareth says the words I'm most afraid of next. "I want more, Sloan."

My knee-jerk response isn't what he wants to hear. "I am at capacity, Gareth. I'm doing everything I can to be a strong, working mom. To be better than I've been. If I give anyone any more, I will lose myself completely, and Sophia needs me too much for that to happen. I can't give her any less of me because, if I do, she could turn into Cal, or his mother, or any of those soul-sucking vultures they associate with. I only get her fifty percent of my life. I need to be in complete control to ensure she has all of me."

"And you think I'd take that away from you," he says knowingly.

I shrug. "We have a good thing going. Why can't we stay as we are?"

He pulls back and slides his hands through his hair, gripping the back of his neck. "Because it's not enough for me anymore."

My shoulders sag in defeat as I stare down at the space between us. We're so close, yet so far away. He's asking for something I'm not sure I have inside of me to give, and I know that means he's going to walk away.

My heart begins breaking. Suddenly, his warmth is pressed against me. I look up as he roughly shoves my back against the wall. His hands reach down and are vice-grips around my wrists as he pins them above my head so high, my feet nearly lift off the ground.

I cry out in shock as his lips crash down on mine in the most feral, possessive, intensely passionate kiss of my entire life. Like a savage, he parts my lips with his tongue and sucks mine into his mouth, a deep growl vibrating from him as he devours me to his fill.

My eyes squeeze together, willing my concentration to stay deeply focused because I know I'm experiencing something I've never felt before. I have to take it all in. I can't miss a single tiny detail of what's happening between us.

He sinks his teeth onto my lower lip, sucking it between his lips so hard, it's like he's draining every last part of me. All those bits I've been holding back. All those feelings I've denied for weeks, for days, for minutes, for seconds. I've kept this part of me away from him because I knew deep down what would happen if I didn't.

This.

This would happen.

Gareth Harris would claim me.

His lips continue pillaging, sucking, tasting, grazing, teasing my entire mouth into such a frenzy, I can't help but participate. His tongue massages mine, and he kisses me like he was born to do so. Like I've never been kissed before.

My back arches into his firmness, my feet dancing on the ground as I yearn for more and less at the same time. My body and mind at war with each other as he takes the gift I gave him.

A kiss.

Just a kiss, but also so much more.

When he breaks away, I moan from the loss of his pressure on me. My hands feel pasted to the bricks above me as he steps back with a fire in his eyes, like he's ripped an organ straight from my body and is holding it hostage in front of me.

"We're not all one thing, Sloan," he repeats, his voice guttural and his face haunted as he looks me up and down in a possessive sweep.

He's proud of the work he's done.

Then he leaves.

He walks away…

…and he doesn't look back.

I watch him drive away and admit with an earth-shattering thud of my heart that we are more than one thing. But am I strong enough to not lose myself beneath him?

Flip Flop

Gareth

I SMOOTH DOWN THE LAPELS OF MY SUIT AS I SIT IN THE BACKSEAT of a stretch limo that's just pulled up to the red carpet of the National Football Museum. Photographers, fans, and fellow attendees swarm the grand entrance as celebrities and footballers make their way inside for the FPA Awards Gala. The same gala where I'll be named Player of the Year.

How crazy is that?

What's even crazier is that all I can focus on is the nauseous feeling this suit is giving me. The suit Sloan made me.

The texture of the material wasn't an issue before. Come to think of it, nothing was an issue when I was with her. As we grew closer, she became the only woman who could touch me any way she liked and not send chills down my spine. My texture sensitivity had been magically cured. She was like my own personal anxiety medication that soothed away the unusual strain that a lifetime of painful memories had inflicted on me.

Now, everything aches. It's like I can feel the stitches closing in on me with every breath, tightening around me like a noose.

My mobile vibrates in my hand. I glance down to check it, sickeningly hoping to see Sloan's name on the screen.

Dad: I'm very proud of you, Gareth. Wish I could be there.

My traitorous heart splinters down the middle from the tone of his text. Part of me wants to text back and ask him what it would take for him to put me first for once in his bloody life. Even when he asked me to move back to London, I knew he was only thinking of himself. But there's this new part of my heart—a part that never existed before—that understands a tiny fraction of the pain he feels on a daily basis.

It's been over a week and still no word from Sloan. I thought for sure she'd be in touch for tonight because this is clearly a big moment for me. But nothing. It seems that the second I stopped chasing Sloan, she stopped turning around. And every day since I left her house, the memory of her lips on mine becomes fainter and fainter, like a melting ice cube evaporating before my eyes.

If she was just some random bird, I wouldn't give a toss. I'd move on, grateful that I don't have to worry about how little she knows about me. But Sloan isn't random. She isn't casual. She knows things. And the second I saw her with her daughter, something inside of me shifted. The wall between us has been knocked down, and she has been humanised to me outside of our sexual relationship. It wasn't until I was staring down my pushy brothers that I realised what that truly meant to me.

I was seeing Sloan with my heart instead of my head.

But it was all for nothing because she's not here. Now I have to go in front of all these people tonight and pretend like the last couple of months didn't change everything I thought I knew about myself. Everything I thought I knew about Sloan.

I can do this…

…because control is something I'm far too familiar with.

Sloan

My heart leaps into my throat when Gareth's large frame climbs out of a black stretch limo. I've been standing here for ages in my enormous black ball-gown, waving at multiple clients whom I styled for the big night as they make their way inside. I was able to score a ticket to the event from one of them, and I took that as a sign that I'm exactly where I'm supposed to be this evening. However, I didn't know what time Gareth was due to arrive. Now I'm regretting this whole, grand gesture notion as I stand here like an idiot.

I positioned myself in front of the security officers that are holding fans back, and they all shoot me sympathetic smiles like I'm a girl getting stood up on prom night. But when I see Gareth's stunning frame wearing the sleek navy suit I designed for him, I realise that I'd endure a lot worse for this sight of him. This moment is why I knew I had to style myself tonight as well.

Gareth freaking Harris.

I run my hands down the fitted bodice of the Alexander McQueen, long sleeve dress that Freya and I carefully selected for me this evening. It's understated elegance—the perfect dress for a stylist to wear to an event because the very last thing one would ever want to do is outshine their clients.

It has a full sweeping skirt with pockets and an off-the-shoulder neckline that shows off my collarbone. My brunette curls are tucked back into a low, chignon hairstyle, and I chose a deep red lipstick to give me a sense of drama that I need in order to be brave enough to stand alongside the honouree tonight.

And standing beside Gareth is exactly what I intend to do.

Aside from the stress of work, he is all I've thought about for the past week. That kiss. Those hands. His words.

He said a lot, but what broke me—what changed me in my core—were his remarks about being proud of me for protecting Sophia. Gareth understood me more in the two minutes he

261

witnessed me as a mother than Callum ever did in the six years we were married. As that realisation settled in over the week, I knew it wasn't our arrangement that made me strong.

It was Gareth.

I also knew it would take a big moment for me to truly show him that I'm ready to dive in. I'm ready to change and stop running. To take charge of my life…together.

With a nod of determination, I move to head over to Gareth but pause mid-step as a stunning blonde in a gorgeous red dress climbs out behind him. He reaches down to offer his hand as she wobbles in her strappy silver sandals, and the affectionate exchange between them has my stomach dropping.

Just as Gareth's hand moves to the small of her back, his eyes pass over me but immediately snap back with a confused, shocked expression.

Completely mortified, I turn away from him and begin pushing my way past the security team that's evidently decided they aren't just keeping people out. They are holding people in, too.

"Please excuse me," I croak desperately. My need to flee is strong, but not stronger than eight grown ass men.

Why did I think showing up unexpectedly was a good idea? Why do I keep forgetting that he's Gareth Harris—a famous soccer player who can get any woman he wants with the snap of a finger? Of course he wouldn't sit idle for an entire week. I'm such an idiot!

A calloused hand wraps around my arm and slowly spins me in my black stiletto heels. "Sloan." Gareth's voice is so familiar and wonderful, I have to close my eyes to prepare myself for the sight of him up close.

My lids flutter open and I take in his masculine, strong beauty. The sexy scruff on his jaw. His smoky, hazel eyes rimmed with dark lashes. The perfect bend of his nose.

"Gareth," I reply uncomfortably.

"What are you doing here?" he asks, his eyes searching my

entire face for answers I'm embarrassed to admit.

I look over his shoulder at the blonde. "I should have called."

"Called for what?" he asks, redirecting my gaze back to him.

I shake my head. "It doesn't matter. You're...here with somebody. I should have assumed."

"With somebody?" he snaps and tightens his grip on my arm with urgency. "You mean my sister, Vi?"

My jaw drops as I look behind him again and see that the blonde is now flanked by three enormous guys whom I instantly recognise as Gareth's brothers. I met them when I styled them for a wedding last year.

"That's your sister?" I ask because I'm still forcing myself to believe it. "I've...never met her."

"Tonight's sort of a family affair." He shrugs.

"How wonderful," I reply hopefully. "Did your dad make it?"

Gareth's face darkens and the muscle in his jaw ticks. "No."

I'm instantly transported back into Gareth's house. Back into the beautiful sanctuary that his home became for me. For us. Back into the moments of tender sharing that we only scratched the surface on.

There's still so much I don't know about him, yet I know enough to know the pain behind his reply. I force a wobbly smile. "Well, it's nice your siblings could be here for you."

He nods and looks back at them. "They all head back tonight, though...Games tomorrow." He turns his eyes to me. "It's good to see you. Are you here with someone?"

I shoot him a shy smile. "Hopefully you."

The serious look on his face disappears. It's replaced by a knee-trembling intensity that I can't seem to look away from. It's like a wall has dropped and he's not holding anything back now. "What does this mean?" he asks, his voice deep and melodic.

"We're friends." I shrug and step closer to him, running my hands along the lapels of his jacket. "That's all I know for certain at this point because this is complicated. I'm a mother and I have baggage we need to discuss. But I do know that I care about you and want to be with you tonight." I tilt my head to look up at him through my long mascaraed lashes. "Is that enough?"

He stares down at me. Longing, and pain, and desire flick across his face like a slideshow just for me. "For now."

With sweet, sweet relief, I reach out and grab the pocket square out of his jacket. "You look incredible."

His chest vibrates with a silent laugh. "I know this woman who thinks she's just a stylist, but she's so much more."

With a proud smirk, I refold the fabric the way I want and tuck it back into the pocket. "Is that right?" I look up at him and feel a riot of butterflies take flight in my belly.

"I'm always right," he replies with a wink, then turns on his heel to offer me his elbow. "Are you ready for this?" he asks, staring down the red carpet like he can see the future.

"I'm ready for this and more," I state with a meaningful look that he picks up easily. Then, off we go down a path I never saw myself travelling with a damn soccer player.

It's an uncomfortable feeling to go from having a relationship with someone where you never leave the bedroom to being thrust into the limelight in front of friends, family, and, let's face it, the rest of the world.

The entire first hour, I'm on the red carpet with Gareth in a flurry of photos, handshakes, and interviews. His brothers disperse, answering their own questions to the press, but they eventually make their way inside with their sister. Gareth, on the other hand, is moving at a much slower pace through the crowd, giving generous time to all the media outlets that are in attendance for him this evening.

Despite being the man of the hour, he is determined to pull me into every conversation. I do my best to be polite, but I can't help but fidget when he continually introduces me as an up-and-coming designer. This isn't something I was prepared for this evening, and the questions directed my way are not things I've considered yet.

Gareth gracefully dodges questions about the status of our personal relationship and pretty much anything pertaining to his father. He's so damn charming, offering only a wink and a smile, they let him get away with it.

Above all, it's an enlightening hour for Gareth Harris history. With every reporter's question, it's like hitting another Google search on the man whom I know intimately but not publicly. He's being honoured tonight for his outstanding season and the work he's done with his charity, Kid Kickers. He speaks so passionately about soccer, but when he mentions the children he gets to help because of his career, I have to admit to tearing up on more than one occasion.

It's Gareth's turn to get emotional when the press discuss the World Cup team potential with him. At one point, when he talks about playing alongside all of his brothers again, he presses his fist to his mouth to fight back the reaction that caught him off guard.

This man is so much more than I ever let myself see before.

Gareth

When we finally make our way inside, the event coordinator ushers Sloan and me over to a large round table where my sister, my brothers, and Hobo and Brandi are seated. Their eyes are locked on the two of us holding hands, like we're some sort of foreign objects they've never seen before.

Let them fucking look.

I'm done with the games. I'm done with the arrangement. The bullshit. The back and forth ghosting. I know part of me could be angry at the fact that Sloan went silent on me for an entire week, but she's here now. Her hand is squeezing mine in a death grip, and a woman's touch has never felt more right to me.

"Are these two seats taken?" I ask with a teasing waggle of my brows when we reach our extravagantly decorated dining table. My family and friends groan and roll their eyes at my daft question as I hold Sloan's seat out before sitting down beside her. I unbutton my suit jacket and place my hand on the back of her chair. "Most of you know Sloan, but allow me to formally introduce you all. This is Sloan Montgomery. Sloan, this is everyone."

I gesture across the table and point out Camden, Tanner, and Booker. Then I introduce Vi, who's shamelessly shooting daggers at my Treacle. No surprise there. She's in protective, fearsome mother mode, full stop, and I know there's not a bloody thing I can do about it.

Sloan finally turns her attention to Brandi and Hobo, who are sitting on the other side of her. Her shoulders relax at the sight of a couple of familiar faces.

"Jaysus, this is a fancy soirée," Hobo states, counting the number of forks on the table as several servers begin placing starters in front of us. "All for the likes of you, Harris? Don't they know you're rubbish on the pitch without me?"

I raise my brows at Hobo. "I'm sorry, is this coming from the midfielder who's played for no less than nine teams in ten years?"

My brothers erupt with laughter and Hobo mock stabs himself through the heart. "You cut me deep, Harris."

"Just ignore our moody older brother," Camden interjects around a laugh. "He's feeling the burn in those knees, I can tell."

I pin him with a warning look. "I'm pretty sure I stopped a couple of your attempts this season already."

Cam scoffs. "I let you block my shots. I have the utmost respect for the elderly."

Sloan giggles beside me, and I turn to watch her cheeks flush with humour. I lean in close to her and slip my hand under the table to squeeze her knee. "Something funny?" She nearly chokes on her champagne when my hand moves higher.

Licking her lips, she looks at me from the corner of her eye and replies, "Just enjoying someone getting a rise out of you for a change."

I blink at her surprising response because no one has ever gotten under my skin more than the woman I'm staring at right now. Moving in to whisper in her ear, I let my lips tickle her earlobe when I reply, "I'm pretty sure you've gotten a rise out of me on several occasions."

She pulls her lower lip into her mouth and turns to face me so our eyes are inches apart. "Am I getting a rise out of you now?"

I lift a brow and purse my lips, willing myself to ignore the demanding thump of my cock in my trousers. She's giving me those eyes again. Those powerful, magnetic, knee-drop-worthy eyes that I want to worship at the altar of.

With a chuckle, I remove my hand from her thigh and back to my food. "You wind me up like no one ever has, Treacle."

She laughs happily at my familiar term of endearment, and the banter around the table continues as the main courses are served.

Over dessert, Sloan looks at my sister and says "Vi, I love your dress. Where did you get it?"

Vi's brows rise as she dabs at the corner of her mouth with her cloth napkin. "I'm a bit of a Harrods lover I'm afraid."

Sloan nods knowingly. "We do a lot of Harrods merchandising for our clients. That's a Nicholas design, right?"

Vi nods. "Yes, I love his stuff."

"It suits you beautifully," Sloan replies.

Brandi chimes in next. "Sloan styled me tonight, too. I'm certainly more comfortable in football gear, but I have to admit that I feel quite brilliant. Next time I want a Sloan original, though."

"Original?" Vi asks, turning her eyes to me and Sloan in question.

Brandi confirms that the suit I'm wearing was made by Sloan, and I can't help but smile at my family for praising her work. It's sometimes difficult for them to talk about anything other than football, but they are making a great effort with Sloan that I more than appreciate. Sloan is talented after all.

On the red carpet tonight, I looked every bit as stylish as everyone wearing well-known designers, and I'm glad she was here to see it for herself. I've always had the feeling that Sloan isn't happy in her line of work. Since the second I met her, I knew she wasn't fulfilled in her career. Tonight I can see her mood changing, though. I can see the light in her eyes as she accepts all the questions at the table and volleys back her answers. She's stunning when she's in her element and speaking passionately about something she truly loves.

It makes it bloody impossible to wipe the smile off my face.

Something important has happened to Sloan this evening. She's no longer nervous and unsure of herself. She's not twitching uncomfortably like she did on the red carpet. She's not holding back her answers. She's tucked herself under my arm and leaned on me in a way that I've never experienced from her. It's not just the physical act of her movements, but the emotional as well.

We are connected. United.

She's embracing me completely and it feels fucking fantastic. It makes me want her in ways I've never wanted a woman in my life. I feel protective of her. Possessive. Proud.

The longer the night drags on, the more I realise what exactly it is I need from her.

I need to claim her.

Sloan

I excuse myself from the table to hit the bathroom before the awards portion of the night begins. I need a minute to collect my thoughts. To breathe. To pinch myself and make sure that tonight is really happening. That Gareth Harris is real and I've not slipped into some alternate universe. It isn't until I step out of a ladies room stall that I finally get a dose of reality.

"Hello there," a voice states, zapping my pulse with just a simple greeting.

My eyes shoot up to see Vi propped against the bathroom counter, arms crossed over her chest, staring at me like some sort of Jessica Rabbit spy who's getting ready to interrogate me.

"Um…hey," I reply stupidly as I make my way over to the near-by sink.

"I just wanted to take a moment to chat privately while we have the time," she states, watching me out of the corner of her eye. She chuckles softly and adds, "Up until tonight, all I really knew about you was that you were Sloan—the stylist who's been jerking my brother around for some time now."

My blood runs cold at the tone in her voice. It's as ice cold as the water coming out of the faucet. I look at Vi's reflection in the mirror and reply, "It's more complicated than that."

She nods knowingly and eyes herself in the mirror, gently fluffing her long blonde curls. "I can respect complicated. Lord knows I've had my fair share of complications with my fiancé, Hayden." She stops primping and stares at my reflection when she adds, "What I can't respect are lies."

Instantly, my eyes drop down to focus on the soap I'm pumping into my hand, willing the act to calm my nerves. "I'm not sure I know what you're referring to."

She exhales and leans herself on the counter to face me. "I'm told you're a mother." My face falls further when she adds with a wink, "No secrets in the Harris family."

I stare into her clear blue eyes to search for what mood she's going for right now. Her eyes aren't cold, but they aren't warm either. They're…cautious. She's sending me a warning, and I'm picking it up loud and clear.

"You're a mother, too, right?" I ask, reaching for a towel and recalling how excited Gareth was when he became an uncle last year. Maybe this small commonality will help Vi understand my point of view.

"Adrienne is one year old," she replies with a serious nod.

"Then you know how important it is to protect our children from things we're unsure of," I reply, straightening my shoulders.

"Oh, I understand that completely," Vi replies, moving in closer as she points to the bathroom door. "Adrienne has four uncles out there who would literally take a bullet for her if it meant they could protect her from something that might cause her harm."

Tears prick the backs of my eyes from the conviction in her voice. She's not overstating a thing. She's speaking one hundred percent truth. This is the kind of family devotion that I've only ever dreamed of for Sophia.

"That's incredible," I state simply because it's the truth.

Vi's furrowed brow remains in place as she ignores my response. "Gareth may be my older brother, but he's protected me his whole life, so now it's my turn to protect him."

"Vi, this isn't necessary—"

"Speaking mother-to-mother here, I will kill you with my bare hands if you break his heart." Her jaw is tight, but her face is so gorgeous, it's at complete odds with her threat. Her beauty doesn't stop the nervous goosebumps from erupting on my scalp, though.

"Why do you think I'm going to break his heart?" I croak.

She shakes her head, her eyes softening only slightly. "Because Gareth doesn't smile."

"What?" I ask with a frown. What the hell does that mean? I've seen him smile loads of times.

"Not the way he's been smiling at you tonight." Her eyes are no longer scary. They're shiny and vulnerable. Afraid.

"Okay..." I reply slowly, my voice trailing off.

"Mother-to-mother, don't screw this up, Sloan." Her voice cracks as she moves back and clears her throat, clearly frustrated that her emotions are getting the best of her.

I'm reading through the lines, though. This isn't a threat. It's a plea. An intimidating plea, but one I can understand on so many levels.

She flicks her hair playfully. "I may not be as big as my brothers, but I am mighty."

I smile at that. "I think that's a Harris thing."

"Bloody well right." Her prideful smile is back as she makes her way to the door. Pausing, she looks over her shoulder and softly adds, "Thank you."

"For what?"

She takes a deep breath. "For showing me this side of Gareth. I thought it was gone forever."

With that, she strides out of the bathroom, leaving me in a wake of feelings that will take me years to fully process.

Gareth

If I could sum up what tonight felt like in two words, they would be *sexual fucking tension*.

Okay, three words.

After I accept my award, say my speech, and offer up departing hugs to my family, Sloan and I are back in the limo and ripping at each other's clothes before we're even out of the city lights of Manchester.

"Tonight was incredible," Sloan moans as she straddles me in the back of the limo. Her dress is rucked up like a sack between us, her fingers trembling on the buttons of my shirt as my hands slide up her bare thighs under her skirt.

I can hardly contain myself. It's been two weeks since I've felt the warmth of her, but there's so much we have to discuss. So much to figure out. She gave me herself tonight, but she has to know I need more.

"Do you have to go home to your daughter?" I ask. The words are unfamiliar on my tongue, but they've been on my mind since the second I saw her tonight.

She shakes her head. "No, Sophia is with Callum."

Sophia, I think to myself. It's a beautiful name, completely fitting the little girl whom I met on the football pitch last week.

I squeeze Sloan's thighs to direct her attention back to me. "I liked your daughter."

She pauses her action on my shirt and looks up to stare into my eyes. Her voice is shaky when she asks, "You did?"

"She had a spark to her. I noticed her straight away on the pitch," I add, the corner of my mouth lifting as I recall how seriously she took all the instructions. "So many of those kids that day were pissing about, not paying attention. But Sophia…She had determination all over her adorable little face. She reminded me of someone I kind of like."

Sloan inhales a deep breath, her eyes glossing over before me. "She did?"

I nod and move my hands off her legs to cup her face, my thumb grazing her lush lips that I've been longing for. I pull her to my mouth for a tender kiss. It's not sexy. It's not assertive.

It's a sign of respect.

Sloan's eyes open when she pulls back. She looks at me with

such warmth that every nerve in my body roars to life. "You are being so incredibly sweet right now, but I have to admit that my mind is getting dirty really freaking fast."

I laugh heartily as she resumes her earlier work on my shirt, the heat of her warming my groin and turning every part of my body to stone. My hands slip up her skirt again, and I nearly cry out in pain as I reach her arse and realise she's not wearing any knickers. "Sloan, where are your knickers?"

She smiles and pulls her lip into her mouth. "I Gareth Harris'd tonight."

"You what?" I ask as she grinds down onto my now rock-hard cock. Her head lolls back like I've just entered her, but we haven't even gotten my trousers off yet.

"Do you have underwear on?" she asks, splaying her hands on the roof and riding me.

"No," I reply, my hands roaming up her sides and cupping her breasts beneath the thin black fabric. She's not wearing a bra either. I can feel her hardened nipples perfectly, and it's making me lose my fucking mind.

She drops her head and squeezes my hands on her breasts, massaging herself with my embrace. Her chestnut hair falls down around her face in a sexy halo. "No underwear...I Gareth Harris'd."

"Fuck me," I growl and flip us in one quick shot so she's flat on her back on the bench of the limo. Her legs wrap around me and my hand reaches between them, shoving past the layers of fabric to cup her smooth mound. "You're fucking soaked, aren't you?"

"Yes!" she cries when I glide my palm over her slickened clit. "I can't help it. You were fucking amazing tonight. I wanted you so badly."

"I don't even know what I said," I husk, ravishing her neck and sucking so hard, I hope I leave a mark. "All I could think about was getting you back to my house and fucking you until we both die."

I plunge a finger into her hot, wet centre. She cries out, her hand fisting my hair so tightly, I roar in pain.

"I mean it. I'm so fucking proud of you," she moans loudly, riding my finger and greedily pumping her hips against my hand. "There's so much I still don't know about you, Gareth. You're…Oh my God! You're so much more."

I pause my assault and pull back from her neck to look in her eyes. "Sloan, I'm going to fuck you tonight."

"Yes," she cries, annoyed that I've stopped working her into a frenzy.

"And I'm going to kiss you tonight."

She nods, her eyes hungry for me to continue, but I want to be sure she fully understands what I mean.

"What I'm saying is that there's no more of what we were. You're not in control right now, Treacle. Tonight I'm fucking you. I'm claiming you. I'm going to come in you so hard that no man will ever have what I take from you tonight. Do you understand?"

Her breath leaves her body, her pupils dilating into saucers. She pulls herself up close to me, her body quaking with need against mine as she cradles my face in her hands. "Yes, Gareth. Yes to all of it."

It takes everything I have not to rip off all of our clothes and sink into her. To not fuck her into oblivion during the hour long drive out to Astbury. But I don't want to claim her in a limo. I want her in my home. In my bed. In the one place I've claimed her before. But this time, I'll hold nothing back.

When we arrive at my home, I can barely take my lips off of Sloan's as we slowly clamour up the steps to the front door. The limo is long gone, but I can't seem to get enough of the taste of Sloan to stop and open the door.

Finally, she pushes me away. "If I leave you in charge, we'll never get inside and it's freezing."

I pull her into my arms. "I can warm you up."

She giggles and gestures for me to unlock the door. When I fish my keys out of my pocket and begin fumbling with the lock, I realise we waited for nothing because the door is already unlocked. Did I forget to lock it earlier? It's entirely possible because my head has been fucked since the second I left Sloan's house last week.

I step back to let Sloan walk in first. Before I even have a chance to catch her, she crumples to the floor in front of me. I hear a familiar voice from inside, but my instinct is to crouch down and check on Sloan first.

Suddenly, a sharp force assaults my left temple, and I crash to a heap beside her motionless body. The last thing I see before my vision goes black is a pool of blood growing between us.

To Be Continued…

Part 2 of Gareth's Story is Coming August 2, 2018!

Check out the other Harris Brother books, available now.
Challenge: Camden & Indie
Endurance: Tanner & Belle
Keeper: Booker & Poppy
Or go back to the sister's story before the brothers became the
brothers with T*hat One Moment*: Vi & Hayden

And sign up for my newsletter to be notified of the next release
date.
www.AmyDawsAuthor.com

Read on for the full list of all my books.

More Books by Amy Daws

The London Lovers Serie:
Becoming Us: Finley's Story Part 1
A Broken Us: Finley's Story Part 2
London Bound: Leslie's Story
Not the One: Reyna's Story

A London Lovers/Harris Brothers Crossover Novel:
Strength: Vi Harris & Hayden's Story

The Harris Brothers Series:
Challenge: Camden's Story
Endurance: Tanner's Story
Keeper: Booker's Story
Surrender & Dominate: Gareth's Duet

Payback: A Harris Brother Spin-off Standalone
Blindsided: A Harris Brother Spin-off Standalone
Replay: A Harris Brother Spin-off Standalone
Sweeper: A Secret Harris Brother Standalone

The Wait With Me Series:
Wait With Me: A Tire Shop Rom-Com
Next in Line: A Bait Shop Rom-Com
One Moment Please: A Hospital Cafeteria Rom-Com
Take A Number: A Bakery Rom-Com

Pointe of Breaking: A College Dance Standalone by Amy Daws &
Sarah J. Pepper

Chasing Hope: A Mother's *True* Story of Loss, Heartbreak,
and the Miracle of Hope

For all retailer purchase links, visit:
www.amydawsauthor.com

More about the Author

Number 1 Amazon Bestselling author Amy Daws writes spicy love stories that take place in America, as well as across the pond. She's most known for her footy-playing Harris Brothers and writing in a tire shop waiting room. When Amy is not writing, she's likely making charcuterie boards from her home in South Dakota where she lives with her daughter and husband.

Follow Amy on all social media channels, including Tik Tok under @amydawsauthor

For more of Amy's work, visit: www.amydawsauthor.com